"Is that your father's writing?"

Beale suddenly grabbed a handful of Linsey's hair.

Linsey felt a wash of new fear. Her father's left-handed scrawl was unmistakable. Should she be denying everything? Would she make things worse admitting the truth?

"Your pa was quite a joker. Read it!"

She swallowed to get some moisture in her mouth. "Visit the family's Sawtooth Fox and look beyond the chimney rocks."

"Some funny man, your pa, but we ain't laughing."

Linsey read the sentence again silently, still without a dram of comprehension. None of the words triggered any memory that would give meaning to the nonsensical sentence. What did it mean? Before she could say anything, she felt the sharp prick of a knife blade at her throat.

"Now, baby, it's time to talk."

ABOUT THE AUTHOR

Leona Karr is a native of Colorado and lives in a suburb of Denver, near the front range of the Rocky Mountains. She is happiest when writing or pursuing a story idea that promises an exciting mixture of love and danger. A simple comment, "I really like your new book," can make her glow for days.

Treasure Hunt

Leona Karr

Harlequin Books

TORONTO • NEW YORK • LONDON
AMSTERDAM • PARIS • SYDNEY • HAMBURG
STOCKHOLM • ATHENS • TOKYO • MILAN

To Cassie Miles and Jasmine Cresswell,
whose friendship made collaborating on
our series such a delightful sharing

Harlequin Intrigue edition published August 1989

ISBN 0-373-22120-7

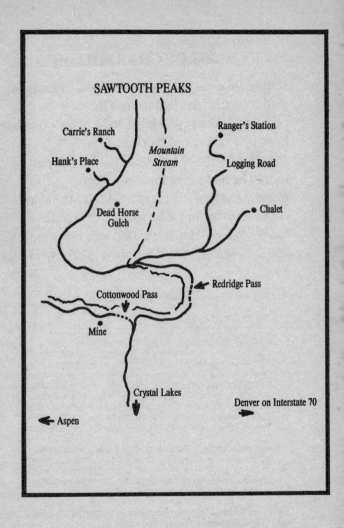

CAST OF CHARACTERS

Linsey Deane—She had inherited a treasure in gold, but first she had to find it.

Darren McNaught—He joined Linsey's treasure hunt by chance, not by choice.

Douglas Brady—He found that he was part of a family he had never known.

Ronald Deane—The legacy he left his daughters could only be found by solving the puzzle.

Carrie Bates—Her friendship was her undoing.

Hank Green—He and his army buddy went way back.

Prologue

Douglas Brady was usually a beer drinker, but tonight he ordered a double Seagrams on the rocks and downed it in short order. He was celebrating.

"Another one?"

Douglas hesitated. A beer chaser would keep the glow on nicely, but he'd better not. He didn't know these Colorado mountain roads. "No, thanks. This one'll do. Got to drive to Crystal Lakes tonight."

"Nice little resort. Going fishing?" The bald, middle-aged man behind the bar looked envious as he wiped some glasses.

"Nope. Meeting someone." Douglas reached into his pocket for money. "How much?"

A couple of guys who had been sitting in a booth stuck some money into the jukebox and punched a selection. A black record rose into position and the raucous, bawling lyrics of "Elvira" blared out into the small room with such volume that the glasses behind the bar rattled.

The bartender collected Douglas's money and said "'Night" to the two men as they sauntered past him and out the front door.

"Do your customers always play loud music and then leave?" asked Douglas, raising his voice to be heard.

"Nope. But nothing that people do surprises me anymore. Never saw them two around here." The bartender glanced at the wall clock as he rang up the amount on the register. "Eleven o'clock. A slow night. I wish I could close up and go home." He handed Douglas his change. "See you around, mister. Enjoy Crystal Lakes."

A bank of cool mountain air hit Douglas as he came out the door of the log building. He stood there for a moment, buttoning his coat. The tavern was set back from the highway against a backdrop of mountains, dark with thickly forested slopes of aspen, pine and spruce. Out on the narrow highway, a pair of headlights cut the shadowed darkness as a tanker truck, like a night animal, rumbled its way higher into the Colorado Rockies. Its laboring engine faded away and only the bellowing of the Oak Ridge Boys song broke the silence of this isolated spot.

Douglas fished for his keys and headed for his car which he'd parked around the corner of the building. The stiff whiskey sat warmly within him, and a glow of well-being sluiced through his body as he put his key into the car door. The sudden movement from behind caught him completely unaware.

"Wh—?" Douglas swung around, but it was too late. He couldn't dodge the blow. A fiery skyrocket of pain penetrated the right side of his skull, and his body felt as if it had disintegrated into unmanageable pieces. He opened his mouth, but no sound came out. For one blurred moment he saw the two men, two figures that wavered like cardboard under water and then faded away as he crumpled to the ground and was enveloped in a swirling mass of nothingness.

At first Douglas's attackers ignored his wallet and expensive gold watch, preferring to search his clothing until they found an envelope in the inside pocket of his jacket.

"Here it is," said the pock-marked youth, giving it to the older man.

"Better take the wallet and watch, too. Jake, make sure you don't leave any identification. Mr. Linquist won't like it if we foul up."

"Can I have the money, Beale?" Jake asked, peering into the wallet. "The boss don't need to know how much was in it. Look, nearly a hundred dollars."

"Give me that!" The squarely built man stuffed the money into his own pocket. "Let's get the hell out of here."

The blond youth glared at his partner but didn't say anything. Ten minutes later they were closeted in a nearby motel room with a smartly dressed man, whose diamond ring flashed gaudily on one finger.

"We got the envelope, Mr. Linquist," said Beale.

"It was in his pocket, just like you said," added Jake.

The man impatiently smashed out his cigarette. "All right. All right. Give it to me!"

Linquist drew out the contents, a letter and two colored photos. One was a typical mountain landscape; the other was a photograph of an old metal identification tag, bent and stamped with lettering that was too blurred to read. He turned over the photograph of the mountain scene and read aloud. "'Visit the family's Sawtooth Fox and look beyond the chimney rocks.'"

Jake scratched his head of straggly blond hair. "Don't make no sense."

"It has to make sense," snapped Linquist. The smooth-shaven, dark-haired man read the words aloud for the second time. "'Visit the family's Sawtooth Fox and look beyond the chimney rocks.'"

Beale shrugged and young Jake looked worried, as if expecting some kind of explosion.

"Sounds like gibberish to me," said Beale boldly, yet with deference. He scratched his square head; it seemed to sit right on his thick shoulders. "Whatcha think?"

Linquist swore. "I think old man Deane revealed the location in some kind of code, that's what I think." Hard cheek muscles flickered in his lean face. "This letter of intent says that old man Deane wants Douglas Brady to share in the loot along with his daughters, but these pictures don't tell us anything."

"Maybe we shouldn't have clobbered the guy," whimpered Jake. "Now who'll figure it out for us?"

"One of the family, of course," snapped Linquist. "Shut up, you goons, and let me think. Ronald Deane had three daughters. He mentions their names in this letter. Linsey, Abigail and Kate. They'd know all about a family fox and the rest of it. The clue probably makes good sense to any one of them." His eyes narrowed, as they always did when he was planning something.

Beale sat down on the edge of the bed and waited. Jake leaned against the bathroom door, his eyes darting to Beale for reassurance that he wasn't going to get blamed for something.

Linquist drew out a fresh cigarette. "We'll just have to get one of Ronald Deane's daughters to decipher the damn thing for us."

"How we gonna do that?" Jake's eyes widened.

Linquist straightened his shoulders, lighted the cigarette, drew deeply on it and pitched away the match with two fingers. His eyes narrowed as the smoke curled up in front of his face. "This guy Brady was blowing off one night in a bar about an aunt who owns a place near Crystal Lakes. Said he was going there to meet the Deane family. Since he ain't gonna get there, I guess we'd better go in his place. We'll arrange to have a nice, private little chat with one of them Deane gals.''

"Good idea, boss." Jake sniggered, nodding his head in approval.

"What if she won't tell us nothing?" Beale cracked the knuckles in his thick hands as if he were anticipating the answer to his question.

"We'll ask her real nice, of course, but if necessary we'll use a little persuasion."

"How much persuasion, boss?" Jake's pale blue eyes glinted with anticipation.

"As much as we need to find out what we want to know."

"Right on," said Jake with a smirk, all signs of nervousness gone as he confidently hooked a thumb into the pocket of his tight jeans.

Linquist ignored Jake's enthusiasm and addressed the bulldog of a man sitting on the bed. "Beale, you know what to do. Keep her alive until she talks. Got it?"

"Sure thing, Mr. Linquist." Smiling, he drew out his knife and gave it an arrogant swish on his pant leg. "We'll get the information you want from the little lady."

Chapter One

Late afternoon shadows stretched across the mountain valley as Linsey shifted her backpack and eyed the familiar Victorian-style house that stood poised on the side of the hill. She always enjoyed the two-mile hike up from Crystal Lakes. The isolated valley was lovely, but lonely, Linsey thought as she quickened her steps. Her aunt's house somehow looked displaced in its setting of green conifers and red rocks, as if a wind had swept it up from some Eastern residential street and set it down here in the midst of the Rocky Mountains.

Calico, an old Appaloosa mare, was grazing in the corral. She raised her head in welcome as Linsey mounted the flight of wooden steps leading to the wide porch that skirted the front of the house.

"Kate, I'm here. Surprise!" Linsey called as she opened the door and went in. Her youngest sister had called yesterday to say that their Aunt Etta had left on a Golden Girls cruise, and that she was watching the place for her. Linsey had decided to come to Crystal Lakes and spend some time with Kate. There was a family problem they needed to talk over. Somehow, Linsey thought, when Kate's around there's always a problem.

The foyer was dark. Narrow stairs mounted against one wall and disappeared into more darkness. Linsey dumped her pack at the foot of the stairs, and the sound made an echoing thump in the silent house. "Kate? Are you there?"

The silence was oppressive. Some intuitive awareness made her stiffen and then spin around. An apelike man with thick, bulging muscles and a square head came at her from the sitting room. Linsey saw the knife in his hand and her gaze froze. The blade was slightly curved, as if it could slash open her stomach with one quick swipe.

She screamed. All rational thought flew away, swamped by raw terror. A second intruder, a pock-marked youth with straggly blond hair, lunged at her from the hall. Aunt Etta's favorite antler coatrack clattered to the floor.

Linsey only had a split second to circle the newel post and bound up the stairs.

"Get her!" shouted the man with the knife.

The blond youth leaped over the scattered coats and fallen coatrack and grabbed the ankle of one leg as Linsey scrambled upward, two steps at a time.

"No, you don't." His faded blue eyes sparkled as he pulled her down; one hand glided up the inside of her leg.

His impertinent touch incensed her, and anger overrode her fear. With her free foot she kicked him in the face.

He cried out in pain and tried to grab the banister, but missed and fell back against the heavier man who was right behind him. Linsey bounded upward to the second-floor hall.

For another split second, the shock of what had happened immobilized her when she reached the top of the stairs. Which way should she run? She wanted to shout at them to leave her alone, but the words caught in her throat.

With a frantic thrust, she tipped over one of Aunt Etta's tiered flower stands and sent it tumbling down the stairs.

African violets flew through the air, their fragile blossoms making a shower of color as clay pots shattered into a million jagged shards. She gained a few seconds while the men climbed over the stand, flowers and shattered pots.

She heard them swearing at each other as she leaped down the hallway, sobbing as she ran. The wild beating of her heart was as loud as the banging of cymbals in her ears. What did the men want? Had she interrupted a burglary? No, they wanted her—not Aunt Etta's possessions. And where was Kate? Had they already attacked her? Linsey wouldn't let herself think the word, "murdered."

Dear God, the men were coming up the stairs. Where to hide? She slipped on one of Aunt Etta's hooked rugs and went nearly to her knees before she caught her balance. With a cry, she bolted to the end of the hall. The bathroom! She slammed the door and turned the old lock. The minute she shoved home the bolt, she knew it wouldn't hold. The simple lock was never intended to keep out vicious attackers. The hardware was old and weak. What stupidity! She'd put herself in a trap. Desperate now, she surveyed the bathroom. Kate's toiletries were collected in a casual grouping on shelves above the marble sink. Mussed towels hung on a rack near the claw-footed tub.

The knob on the bathroom door turned. "Come out!" a man shouted. "We'll break the damn door down if you don't."

Linsey cowered back into the room.

"You're just making it harder on yourself," the same voice warned.

"We ain't gonna hurt ya," promised the other one with a smirk in his tone.

"Open this door! Now!"

"All right. I'll open it," she lied, playing for time. She couldn't see anything with which she could protect herself.

"Come out, you stupid woman!" The door shuddered as someone kicked it.

Linsey backed up and jerked open the door of a walk-in linen closet. Shelves ran the length of the small enclosure. Towels, sheets, pillow cases and blankets lined the shelves. Familiar scents of rosemary and tansy teased her nostrils, but fear dominated her senses.

The loud sound of battering made her quiver in terror. The bathroom door began to splinter away from the molding. One hinge dropped loose. Repeated kicks caused the workings in the lock to loosen. In another minute they would be in the room.

Sobbing almost hysterically, Linsey backed into the closet and slammed the door. No lock. Nothing to brace against the door. No place to hide. She backed up to the far end against a pile of blankets and comforters. Muted light came through a small dormer window above her. A window! She'd forgotten the window, but it looked too small for the passage of a human body. Desperation made her grasp at it as the only possible exit.

Using the shelves as a ladder, she climbed up to the window. A pane of glass was set in a wooden frame. It looked painted shut, but terror sent adrenaline racing through her. She shoved at the window until it finally moved upward; then, to her horror, it stuck. She couldn't budge it any farther.

The bathroom door gave way with a sickening clatter, and a mocking voice told her to give up. The window was not open more than a foot. It was no use. She was trapped. Yet a primitive urge for self-preservation denied the hopelessness of her situation. She would get through that win-

dow! Turning her head to one side, she thrust it through
the small opening. She bent and twisted like a contortionist until her shoulders were halfway out. They stuck. She
flattened her torso as much as possible and sucked in her
breath. With the help of a strong thrust from her legs, her
shoulders scraped through. "Thank God for narrow
hips," she breathed, as the rest of her body followed.

She grabbed a gingerbread overhang and swung herself
to one side of the dormer that projected from the steep
mansard roof. She was two stories above the ground, but
she wouldn't think about that. The branches of a cottonwood tree brushed the roofline at one side of the house.
She crawled toward it, praying she wouldn't slip on the
asbestos shingles and tumble off.

"There she is!" The man she had kicked in the face
stuck his head out of the window.

"Get her!" snarled the other one.

"I can't get out. The damn window won't move."

"Don't let her get away!"

"She's heading for the tree." The man's head disappeared.

Linsey pitched herself into the center of the old cottonwood tree she had climbed since childhood. Her father had
even built a tree house in it one summer, and the family
had had many picnics underneath its branches. As she
scrambled downward, she was thankful that her jeans and
denim jacket were thick enough to protect her arms and
legs. When one of the branches swayed under her weight,
bending low enough to bring her close to the ground, she
let go and fell the rest of the way. She landed with a thud.
The jolt knocked the wind out of her, but terror kept her
moving in a staggering half run, heading for the corral.

The back door slammed. Her attackers were outside!
She knew they would see her the minute they came around

the corner of the house. The mare, Calico, nickered softly as Linsey bounded into the corral and ducked behind a shed where oats, straw, saddles and bridles were kept. Crouching low, she pressed her fists against her mouth, trying to still her breathing. She knew that if she fled from the shed in any direction she'd be seen.

"Where'd she go?"

"Don't know."

"Check around the front."

"She's a fighter, ain't she, Beale?"

A grunt. "We'll tame her soon enough."

Retreating footsteps. Linsey's ears strained to hear any movement in her direction. One man had gone to the front.... The other one must be standing still looking around, she reasoned.

The old mare ambled over to the corner of the shed, looking down at Linsey and curling back her mouth the way she did when she wanted to be fed an apple or carrot.

Linsey tried silently to wave Calico away but the Appaloosa just stood there, marking Linsey's hiding place as plainly as a spotted flag stuck in the middle of a bull's-eye. Linsey had always loved the old mare, but at that moment she would have gladly sent her to a packing plant without a second thought.

Who were the men? Why did they want her? Where was Kate? She had walked into a nightmare. Linsey stiffened. The noise she heard was the creaking of the garage door being opened.

Linsey didn't hesitate. While one man looked in the garage for her and the other man was around front, she might get away. Not on foot. She'd never be able to run fast enough. Without weighing her chances, she grabbed a bridle from a nail inside the shed and slipped it over Calico's head. No time for a saddle, but she and her sisters had ridden the mare bareback many times. She eased open the corral gate.

"There she is!" A man came running around the front of the house. "She's taken the damn horse."

Linsey grabbed Calico's mane and sprang onto her back. With a fistful of horsehair in one hand and the reins in the other, Linsey gave the mare a hard kick. Surprised, Calico jerked forward into a fast run, almost jolting Linsey from her back.

The men shouted and ran to the corral. Linsey bent low on the mare's neck and urged her across a clearing and into a band of trees that thickly covered the mountainside. The terrain was rugged, but Linsey knew it well and deftly reined Calico around rocks and trees and forest deadfall until they reached a bridle path that led up to a promontory overlooking the valley.

The hillside was already in shadow, and shades of silver-gray twilight warned that night was coming, yet a sense of exhilaration spurred through her. She had gotten away! She knew that the men couldn't follow fast enough on foot to overtake her. Linsey's relief grew as the valley below fell away and the crest of the hill came closer.

"Good girl," she said, patting Calico's neck as they clambered upward and the mare's hooves clattered on the rocky path.

The praise was a few seconds premature. Just as they reached the top, her mount gave a startled lunge to one side.

"Whoa!" Linsey gasped, losing her balance as Calico reared. She clamped her legs around the mare's belly, but they wouldn't hold on the slick hide. As she pitched off Calico's back, she caught sight of a scowling face, framed by shocks of sandy-red hair.

She lashed out at the firm hands that pulled her from the ground. Another man! *There are three of them!* "Let me go, you punk!"

"Hold on! It was your horse that dumped you, not me."

She wrenched free of his grasp. "How did you get up here so fast?"

"So fast? It took me all morning to climb this high."

"All morning? How did you know I would run this way?"

"Lady, I think that fall gave you a bump on the head. Sit down a minute and draw in your claws. I'm sorry I startled your horse. I'm afraid he's taken off again down the hill."

"Calico!" Linsey screamed, but there was no spotted mare in sight. Then she sat down, simply because she had no energy left. Tears came to her eyes. She couldn't fight anymore.

"Don't need to cry. He'll find his way back home," he said impatiently. "Horse sense, you know."

She resented his patronizing tone. Fear and anger mingled as she glared at him. Shocks of sandy-red hair harmonized with a lightly freckled nose. His features were too craggy to be handsome, but he didn't have the vicious look of the other two men. Maybe she could reason with this one. "I don't know what you want with me. Please, let me go," she began. "Please."

He held out his hands in a surrendering gesture. "Go. Be my guest, lady. I wasn't looking for company when I decided to camp out on this ridge. In fact, I thought I'd hiked far enough to get away from crowds and hysterical women. Sorry I startled your horse. I didn't know who might be crashing through the trees like that and I didn't want to get trampled." He had light brown eyes that were returning her appraisal. "Goodbye. Enjoy your hike back down the mountain."

"You're not one of them!" She almost choked with sudden relief. She could see him mentally labeling her as a female hysteric. "Two men jumped me," she said with a rush. "They were waiting for me inside my aunt's house."

"That Victorian clapboard below? I saw it on my way up. Nice house," he said with conversational superficiality.

"Don't you understand what I'm saying?" She lurched to her feet. "I'm being chased. They may be coming after me right now." Her frantic gaze swept the hillside below. No sign of any men. But she couldn't be sure. "You have to help me!"

"Sure," he said in a placating tone. "Tell me who's after you and why."

"I don't know! I tell you, they jumped me when I came into the house. I climbed through a window to get out onto the roof. Then I got away on Calico. But I'm afraid they may come after me."

His auburn eyebrows knit as if he were trying to believe her. "Sounds like they were robbing the house and you surprised them."

"I don't think so. They weren't burglars." She shook her head emphatically. "I heard one of them say they'd tame me soon enough. They were after me or my sister. I'm sure of it." Linsey bit her lip.

"Where's your sister?"

"I don't know. I tried to call her from the train station, but no one answered. She didn't know I was coming. I'm afraid they got to her first. Oh Lord, what's happened to Kate? If only my other sister, Abigail, had come with me. She'd know what to do. She's the best one in a crisis."

Linsey could see that the man was skeptical. He was eyeing her as if she'd escaped from a funny farm. She knew she looked a mess; light brown hair in a tangle on her shoulders, her clothes dirty, sweat and grime on her face. Her incoherent talk only added to the wildness of her appearance. He had chalked her up as a loony. Well, she couldn't waste any more time on him.

"Where are you going?" he asked as she started walking along the rim of the promontory.

"There's a place on the ledge where you can look down on my aunt's place. You can see anyone moving around." She eyed the twilight sky now deepening into shades of gray and purple. Very shortly it would be too dark to see anything clearly.

She quickened her steps and he followed her. She had eaten many a picnic lunch with her two sisters on this high rocky perch above her aunt's house. She stopped and pointed. "There."

The white two-storied house was directly below the high cliff. They could see the back door and the clearing before the outbuildings. Linsey's heart threatened to stop beating. Two tiny figures came around the house and crossed the clearing. They climbed into a pickup truck parked behind the garage and roared down the gravel road that led to the Crystal Lakes highway.

"Thank God. They've gone!" She spun on her heel.

"Where are you going now?"

"To see if my sister is safe. Kate may be somewhere in the house, hurt."

"You can't go down there alone."

She paused and raised a questioning eyebrow. "Are you coming with me?"

He hesitated. "Well, I—"

"That's what I thought," she said sharply and turned away.

"Wait a minute. Maybe I ought to know your name."

"Linsey Deane. And yours?"

"Darren McNaught. I came to Crystal Lakes for a seminar on acid rain that starts in a couple of days. Thought I'd take a little camping vacation before then."

"Happy camping, Mr. McNaught."

"Wait a minute. You're an impatient little gal, aren't you?"

"My sister may be lying hurt or—worse—in that house. I'm going to find out."

"All right. I'll go with you. But it's going to be blacker than pitch before we reach the bottom."

"I could find my way in the dark."

"Good. You may have to."

He stopped at his camping site and took a flashlight out of his knapsack, leaving his pup tent where he had pitched it.

Linsey could have hugged him for coming with her, but his attitude did not invite familiarity. It was obvious he had taken a dislike to her, and she could hardly blame him.

She led the way down the forested mountainside, anxiety over Kate's welfare rising with every step. The moon had risen by the time they reached the band of trees behind the house. A wash of moonlight touched the roof and windowpanes, turning the glass into unseeing eyes.

"See anything?" she whispered as they crouched behind a mass of scrub oak and viewed the house. They had checked the garage.

"The house looks deserted to me. No sign of lights anywhere. Of course, the men could be parked somewhere, waiting."

"But we saw them drive away. You don't think they came back?" Terror climbed into her throat once more.

"I don't know what I think," he said bluntly. "But we're never going to find out anything if we stay hunched down behind these trees." With that, he left her side and strode across the clearing. As he walked, moonlight burnished his red hair with a soft glow, as if he were surrounded by fireflies. For the first time, Linsey realized how tall and muscular he was; his physical stature was most reassuring, although she knew that nobody, however large, would have much luck against the man wielding that curved knife. She shivered, just remembering the way he had flashed it.

"I'll go first," he said as he opened the back screen door.

Linsey didn't argue. The memory of the two brutes leaping out at her was enough to quell any objections she might have had.

Once inside, Darren touched the light switch and instantly the homey kitchen was bathed in bright yellow light. Dirty dishes waited in the sink. An empty, clouded milk glass sat beside a paperback novel that lay open on the table. Kate had been here, all right, thought Linsey, recognizing the telltale signs of her sister's indifferent housekeeping. But where was she now?

"Stay here and I'll look through the house."

"No, I'm coming with you."

He gave her an impatient look. "Don't you ever do anything you're told?"

"No. Should we arm ourselves?"

"With what?" Without waiting for an answer, he brushed past her into the dining room.

Stealthily they went through every room, turning on the lights throughout the house. Nothing. The overturned coatrack and everything that had hung on it still lay on the floor. Dirt, flowers, broken pots and the dumped plant stand remained on the stairs. Linsey blanched when she saw the mess, remembering the terror that had nearly paralyzed her.

"Looks like a disaster area," he commented. A puzzled expression marked his face.

"Now do you believe me? One of them knocked over the coatrack when he lunged at me. He caught me on the stairs." Her voice trembled. "I kicked him in the face, and he fell back against the brawny ape behind him. When I got to the top of the stairs, I pushed over the plant stand. Aunt Etta is going to skin me alive for what I did to her African violets."

Darren looked solemn as he surveyed the physical evidence of her story. For the first time he seemed to put some credence in her weird account of the attack.

"Come on. I'll show you how I got out." Linsey led him to the broken bathroom door and the opened closet window.

"You couldn't get out that," he declared, viewing the tiny opening.

"I did. You thought I was lying about all this, didn't you?"

"You have to admit that it's . . . it's quite a tale."

"It's the truth."

"Yes, I can see that. I'm sorry I doubted you. The whole thing seems too farfetched. Why did they go to all this trouble to break in and then not steal anything?"

"I don't know. I can hardly believe it myself." Linsey's voice trembled. The impact of everything that had happened hit her and she shuddered.

He surprised her by slipping an arm around her waist. "It's all over now. Come on. Let's call the sheriff."

They went downstairs to the kitchen wall phone. Deadly silence greeted her ears. "It's dead," Linsey said grimly. "They must have cut the wires before I got here."

"Do you have the keys to your aunt's pickup?"

Linsey's gaze flew to a key rack that Kate had given Aunt Etta one Christmas, because the dear lady was always misplacing her keys. She breathed a prayer of thanks as she recognized a pair hanging on a brass hook. "Yes, they're here."

"Good. Let's get moving," Darren said as she took them down. "You can tell your story to the sheriff and see what he thinks."

They went out the back door and Calico neighed a greeting.

"I told you she'd come back."

The mare was munching grass on the outside of the corral. She made no objections when Linsey caught her and put her back inside. Linsey stripped off the bridle and told Darren where to hang it in the shed. Then they went out to the garage.

For the first time since the nightmare began, Linsey felt a sense of relief. Kate's car wasn't there, so her sister was probably happily cruising around somewhere, perfectly oblivious to what was happening. Thank God. And the sheriff would know what to do about the intruders.

"I'll drive," she said and started around the back of Aunt Etta's pickup. She never made it to the driver's seat. The blond attacker she had kicked in the face stood there, waiting for her.

"Hello, honey."

She screamed as his arms pinned her against his greasy body. Out of the corner of her eye she saw two other men grab Darren, just as he put his hand on the car door to open it. He took a hard blow to the chin and an apparently pulverizing blow to the stomach. He crumpled.

Linsey's assailant clamped a sweet-smelling cloth over her face. The pressure of his hand cut off air from her nose and mouth. Nausea rose in her stomach. She kicked and scratched, but her struggle grew weaker and weaker; enveloped by vertigo, her arms and legs seemed to detach themselves from her body and float away.

Chapter Two

Fear lay crouched and waiting in a corner of Linsey's mind when she first awoke—but her fuzzy brain would not recognize it. She came back to consciousness in a drifting state of detachment. With great effort, she lifted heavy eyelids and squinted at solid boards just inches above her face. She was lying on her back. In a box? A coffin? No, it was a wooden ceiling of some kind. She closed her eyes again and felt a sensation of movement. Vibrations. Bumps. Jolts. Was the motion real or imagined? Unanswered questions pricked at her and then floated off like leaves on the wind. She tried to gather them up, but they whirled away in confusing and bewildering patterns.

When she awakened the second time, a deep, throaty, masculine groan penetrated her consciousness. This time her mind was clearer, the dizziness less intense. Like jagged pieces of a shattered mirror, bits of memory flashed back. Aunt Etta's house. Masked men. Assault!

Fighting a new wash of vertigo, she held on to the sides of a lower bunk bed and sat up. Her eyes slowly registered a small interior. A basement room? A motel? A flying hotel with slivers of moonlight coming through narrow, metal-slatted windows? Wheels hissed on the pavement.

Outside, the sounds of truck and automobile engines and passing traffic created a cacophony of highway noise.

She pressed her hands to her head, trying to orient herself in the weird, constantly moving room. More groans drew her eyes downward. Darren McNaught lay on the floor in a narrow aisle between a kitchenette counter and a built-in table, breathing deeply, apparently in a drugged stupor.

The scene in the garage surged back; two men grabbing him by the arms, beating him until his muscular form crumpled to the floor. They must have drugged him, too, she thought, slipping down beside him. "Wake up! Wake up!"

Darren heard her pleas as if from far away, a pleasing voice, deep and rich. He opened his eyes and an anguished face wavered in front of him. He couldn't identify it. Who was this tearful woman with wide blue eyes, crying and pleading with him to wake up? His head felt as if it were swollen at least two sizes beyond normal, throbbing as if it were going to burst open at the seams. "Who are you?" he gasped.

"Linsey Deane. Don't you remember?"

Fragments of memory plagued him. Camping. He had been camping out for a couple of days, waiting for his seminar to begin. He sat up and propped his head in his hands. It was all coming back slowly, but strange images overlapped in his mind. A pretty woman thrown from a horse... a hike down to a Victorian house.

"They jumped us in the garage," she said. "We thought they'd gone." She swallowed hard. "But they came back."

He remembered it all now. Seeing anguish and fear on her ashen face sent a fierce anger raging through him. Every protective instinct in him surged to the front. "Are you all right?" he asked, wavering to his feet.

"I'm okay." She sat down on a bench that stood behind a small table.

He knew she lied. Her stomach must be just as nauseous as his and her head thumping with the same painful bongo drums. A roaring vibration accompanied the constant swaying of the floor and walls. The room was moving at great speed. An orangish night-light gave feeble illumination. None of it made sense. He must be dreaming. Even the girl who looked so much like Laura must be a figment of his imagination. Anger fused with his bewilderment. Two gorillas had barreled into him with four fists, and his jaw felt as if it had been shoved to the wrong side of his face. He wanted to strike out at somebody.

"We're in a camping trailer, I think," she said.

He sat down opposite her, reached out and took her hand. Soft. Warm. Real. His thumb stroked the back of her hand. "You must know what this is all about. Nobody goes to all this trouble to kidnap somebody without a reason," he argued, more stridently than he had intended, and felt her stiffen.

"I told you—I don't know." She pulled her hand away. Her blue eyes snapped and her jaw hardened. She had a soft, sweet mouth that trembled appealingly. He knew she was fighting for control. "I've told you everything I know."

"Everything isn't very much," he countered candidly. He hated to badger her, but he had to find some rational explanation for this apparently well-planned abduction.

He surveyed the trailer. About eighteen feet in length and seven or eight feet wide, he estimated. There were signs that the camper was not new; a trade name painted over the door was faded and chipped; floor tiles were torn, woodwork was scratched. Iron slats, like venetian blinds bolted on the outside of two narrow windows, allowed only tiny slits of light to enter. They could not see out and no one could see in.

"It wasn't robbery," she offered, as if trying to appease him. "When we went through the house, I didn't see anything missing."

Darren reached into his pant pocket. His wallet was still there. "They weren't after money." He had a considerable amount of cash in it for his vacation.

"There's no money in the house. Aunt Etta keeps everything in the bank. She's too forgetful to have anything of value lying around." Her eyes softened. "My aunt is a lovable little scatterbrain. She's in her sixties, but younger in heart than most women half her age."

It was the first time he'd seen her smile and he felt a peculiar flip-flop in the middle of his stomach. Watch it, he scolded himself. She's the kind of gal to reel in any guy, using those soft kitten-eyes and kissable lips. Yet there was something about her that definitely aroused his interest, in a way that most women didn't. It wasn't only her looks but her fiery spirit, too. He pulled his thoughts away from the impulse to tell her she shouldn't look at him like that. "What about your sister? How old is she?"

"Kate? Twenty-six. Abigail's twenty-eight, and I'm the oldest." She sighed. "Just turned thirty last month."

"My, my, you hold your age well," he teased. He saw another delicious smile at the corner of her lips. Good. She was relaxing a little. "Could they have been after something of Kate's?"

"She never has very much money on her, and her jewelry is more likely to be a string of hazelnuts than pearls."

"Could she be into something...illegal?"

"Absolutely not." She shook her head. "Not Kate. She's disgustingly honest, almost obnoxiously so, sometimes. Her only intolerance is dishonesty in others. No, Kate's not mixed up with anything," Linsey told him with conviction.

"Well, if it isn't robbery, what is it? Why are we being abducted in a camper, going God knows where? This is no spur-of-the-moment kidnapping. Look at those iron slats on the window. And those men had the chloroform ready. They were waiting—"

"But no one knew I was coming. Not even my sister. I tried to call her twice last night, but no answer." Linsey's voice quivered. "Maybe they've got Kate, too."

He moved closer to her on the bench and put an arm around her shoulders. "Stop it!" he ordered gently but firmly. "Don't invent dragons. Save your energy to fight battles that are real. Your sister's probably perfectly safe. Right now, we've got to figure out a way to get out of here."

"But the camper's going at full speed," she protested.

"It has to stop sometime."

His words only caused fear to bring a new tightening to her chest. What would happen when the camper stopped and the men came back?

He felt the tension in her shoulders. Fear was evident in the tightness of her lips. He had to do something. "Maybe there's a way out of this coop. Let's have a look."

It took only a couple of minutes to examine the inside of the camper. A minuscule kitchen counter contained a sink with running water, a two-burner stove, and a small undercounter refrigerator. Beside the table and bench there were two narrow bunks with bare mattresses and a couple of small cupboards. "Chipped mugs and plates."

Linsey wrinkled her nose. A lingering stale odor suggested that the cupboards had contained food at one time. Her already queasy stomach took another dive.

Darren opened the refrigerator and drew out a loaf of bread. "Ironic, isn't it?" He gave a short laugh. "Bread and water."

"Just like a real prison," she quipped with a wan smile, but there was no lightness in her tone. The thought of being confined in this rolling cage for any length of time was enough to demoralize anyone. She felt a guilty thankfulness that she was not alone. Thank God for Darren McNaught. A lucky break for her when she fell off Calico at his feet. She knew the men had been after her, and he had just been caught in their vicious snare. His presence was unbelievingly reassuring, and at the moment his strongly chiseled face was the most beautiful she had ever seen.

She watched him examine the windows. He couldn't open the glass to touch the iron slats, but they looked firm. The door was locked and maybe bolted on the outside. He tapped the steel-reinforced walls. No chance of breaking out through the sides of the camper. He didn't say anything out loud, but the message in his eyes was clear. *The prison is secure.*

He sat down again. "Maybe they're after ransom. Are you worth anything?"

"I like to think so."

He grinned at that. "Sorry. I meant are you wealthy? Do you have enough money to make kidnapping worthwhile?"

"Not really, but some people have been murdered for a quarter in their pockets," she reminded him. "Abigail could tell you our net worth, but I can't. Inflation has made some mountain land and mines my father bought years ago valuable, but I doubt very much that we have the kind of wealth that would cause someone to go to all this trouble to kidnap one of us."

"If not money—then what?"

"I don't know. I just don't know. It's crazy."

"But someone will be alerted to your absence, won't they?"

He watched her face. He knew before she said anything what the answer was.

"I don't think so. I closed up the house. Told my neighbor that I'd be taking a little vacation. Abigail has gone to Washington. She's an archivist for the state of Colorado. When she's traveling, a couple of weeks could go by without us calling each other."

"No boyfriends?"

"No entanglements, if that's what you mean."

"I find that hard to believe." He was strangely relieved and frankly surprised. An attractive woman like her didn't usually reach her thirties without a ring on her finger. She had style. Her shiny brown hair had been cut in layers to fall in casual waves around an oval-shaped face. Her best features were her large blue eyes, but her slim nose and kissable mouth were harmonious with high cheekbones and a lightly tanned complexion. "No one at all?"

"I assure you no man is going to be hanging on my telephone, wondering where I've gone."

"You've never been in love?"

She stiffened. "What has that to do with anything?"

"I'm just wondering if a jilted lover could have arranged all of this."

"Oh." She laughed at that, showing even, pearly teeth. "Hardly. The man I thought I was going to marry was happy to escape to New York and his own career. Gordon Van Dines. Maybe you've heard of him—a young pianist on the rise to fame and fortune? We had a thing going while we were in college. After graduation, our ways separated by mutual agreement. No, this has nothing to do with Gordon, I'm sure of that.''

"What about your sisters?''

Linsey frowned. "Kate's too busy playing the field. She's never had a serious attachment. Lots of admirers . . . but no 'significant others.' ''

"And Abigail?''

"She was married right after college, but they divorced years ago. Greg wasn't a very nice man, but I can't believe he'd organize something like this. And as far as I know, there's been nobody since Greg. I guess we're all pretty independent where men are concerned. I just wish I'd been able to tell Kate I was coming.''

"Won't she be suspicious about the mess in the house?''

"She'll probably think it was vandals. There's been some of that in the valley lately. If I hadn't put Calico back in the corral, that might have set her wondering.'' Linsey sighed. "I guess there's no one who will miss me right away. How about you?''

"Nope. Not for a month, at least, when I'm due to visit my parents in the state of Washington, on my way to Canada.''

"No romantic entanglements?'' She grinned, enjoying putting the same question to him.

"Nary a one.'' He skirted that tender subject. "And I didn't preregister for the seminar. I have a motel reservation, but if I don't show up, they'll give my room to someone else. Maybe someone will stumble on my camping site.''

"I doubt it. You were camped on private land. My aunt's.''

"Whoops. Trespassing, was I? Well, there were no signs posted,'' he countered defensively. "And it looked like a good place to get away from the world." What a misconception that had been, he thought ironically.

"What do you do when you're not camping on other people's land . . . or attending seminars?" A twinkle in her eyes made them deepen in color. "What about a job? You have one, don't you?" She was obviously enjoying needling him.

He laughed. "Well, some people might question whether or not I'm gainfully employed. I work for the EPA. That stands for—"

"I know what it stands for. Environmental Protection Agency. Are you working in Colorado?"

"No, I'm on my way to a new assignment in Canada, working on a mutual acid rain project. I heard about the seminar and decided to combine it with a little quiet fun and relaxation for a couple of weeks."

"I'm sorry. I really am. Dragging you into all of this."

"It's not your fault." He saw the struggle going on inside her. She was trying to control her fright, but her lips quivered, and her lovely eyes blinked rapidly to hold back the tears that threatened to overflow at the corners. He wanted to take her into his arms and let her cry on his shoulder. Then he remembered another woman who had plied him with tears and twisted his life into a miserable mess. No more of that kind of vulnerability. Instead he said briskly, "The only escape hatch is a ventilation duct, four inches in diameter. Think you can handle that?"

"Sorry. I left my shrinking pills behind."

"Too bad." He smiled at her. "After seeing that closet window, I thought maybe you could slip through any crack."

Her lips quivered. "What can we do?"

"Wait."

She bit her lip, started to say something, then apparently changed her mind.

"I know that's the hardest part, but I don't know what else we can do." His mind was reeling. This kidnapping had been well planned. Every indication was that their abductors were planning a long confinement. How long? And why?

"We're slowing down!" Linsey gasped.

He stiffened. She was right. The camper's speed had lessened. Scattered flashes of orange light hit the steel slats across the windows. Not enough neon lights for a town, he judged. They must be passing a filling station or mountain junction.

Linsey's eyes widened. "Listen!"

A siren! Its sharp wail suddenly overrode all other sounds, growing louder and louder. Hope surged through her. Maybe by some miracle someone knew they had been kidnapped.

Linsey leaped to her feet. She pressed herself against a window, peering through the slats. A flash of red hit them as the blinking car passed by.

"Damn," Darren swore.

Linsey jerked off one of her walking boots and pounded it against the window. "Help! Help!" The glass shattered, but the iron slats outside held firm. She pounded and pounded until the siren faded away.

The camper picked up speed again.

Darren took the boot from her hands, put an arm around her shoulders and eased her back to the table. "Good try," he said.

"It was dumb, but I feel better," she said with a wry grin. "Just sitting around, waiting like this for something to happen, can really light my fuse."

"I bet you threw tantrums when you were a kid."

"How'd you know?"

"Me, too. I guess it takes one to know one. I felt like kicking that window out myself."

Cold air rushed in through the broken window, and he tightened his grip on her shoulders as the camper began to rock and jolt from side to side.

"We've left the highway." he said, listening to the changing sound. "We're on a dirt road." *Going where?* They must still be in the Colorado Rockies. "We're gaining elevation, that's for sure."

From the angle of the camper it was obvious that they were climbing higher and higher. Night winds came in through the open window, lowering the temperature enough for them to see their breath. He saw panic in the haunted shadows that were deepening in her eyes.

"How about some bread and water?" he said brightly. "If the conversation's interesting enough, we may fool ourselves into thinking it's meat and potatoes. Used to do a lot of pretending back home when I was a kid. My father was a preacher, and a pot of beans was a feast. How do you like your steak, m'love?"

The endearment was flippant and casual, but it warmed Linsey. She'd bet he had a line a mile long when he wanted to use it. "Medium rare."

"Me, too. Nice and juicy, smothered in mushrooms." He offered her a slice of stale bread and a mug of water. She looked so darn wan and fragile that he had to keep from giving in to the desire to cradle her on his lap and forget about the pretense of making everything seem normal. "All the comforts of home," he mumbled as he chewed on the hard crust.

"Where's home?"

"Originally the Saskatchewan prairie, but my family moved to the state of Washington when I was ready for high school. Worked my way through the University of Washington. Became a naturalized citizen of the U.S. Chose a career as government ecologist. Pretty boring stuff, huh?''

"And you're interested in the acid rain problem."

"That's my new assignment. A joint Canada and U.S. effort. What about you?''

"Born and raised in Colorado. Live in Boulder. Teach piano. How's that for boring? But I like my life," she added hastily. "I do exactly what I want to. The family house is a little big for just one person, but none of us wanted to sell it after my father died unexpectedly. I have two sisters, as you know. And—'' she stopped abruptly. She'd forgotten her reason for going to Crystal Lakes.

"And what?''

"And maybe a half brother." She told him about the telephone call from Kate. Was it only yesterday? She had just come in with some groceries, when she'd heard the telephone's shrill, insistent ring. She had grabbed it and uttered a breathless, "Hello."

"Is that you, Linsey? You sound funny," Kate said, laughing.

"I'm out of breath. Is everything all right?" An automatic question when dealing with her youngest sister.

"Fine. I'm staying with Aunt Etta. The weirdest thing has happened. You're never going to believe it."

Linsey's hand had automatically tightened on the receiver. "Try me.''

"I've found our half brother."

"Our what? We don't have a half brother."

"Yes, we do. I just found out . . . from Aunt Etta. She showed me a letter from him. His name is Douglas Brady. It seems that dear Daddy was guilty of a little romantic indiscretion when he was in the army. Fathered a boy baby with an army nurse.''

''I don't believe a word of it, Kate.''

''It's true. Now the baby's all grown-up and coming to Crystal Lakes to meet us. Isn't that wonderful?''

Linsey could picture Kate's luminous blue eyes sparkling with anticipation, ready to steam ahead at full throttle with no more thought than she gave to adopting a puppy that took her fancy. ''He's a fraud,'' Linsey asserted flatly.

''Nope. He has a letter from Daddy, mailed from the hospital just before he died. Guilty conscience kind of thing, I guess.''

''The letter's a forgery. It has to be, Kate. Use your head. You know Daddy was devoted to Mother and the rest of us. It's not the first time some ambitious manipulator has tried to get their hands on the Deane investments.''

''Oh, Sis, don't be a drag. Come on up to Crystal Lakes and meet him yourself. And call Abigail to come, too.''

''She's in Washington on business.''

''Then you come.''

''I'll think about it.''

Linsey told Darren that she had thought about it; she had called Kate twice to tell her that she had decided to come, but couldn't reach her. ''My car was in the shop getting a valve job so I took the daily excursion train. I'm convinced this newly found brother is an imposter, trying to get his hands on the Deane money. You don't think he has anything to do with this, do you?''

''I don't see how he could. But then none of it makes sense, does it?'' His reddish-brown eyebrows were raised questioningly.

"I guess we'll find out soon enough," she said as evenly as the knot in her stomach would allow. She shivered as drafts of cold air surged in through the broken window.

"You might as well try to get some sleep," he said briskly, knowing she shivered from fear as much as from the cold.

"I couldn't."

"Yes, you can. Quit arguing, for heaven's sake." He pulled out a storage drawer under the bottom bunk and drew out an army blanket. "Here, wrap up in this."

Too tired and emotionally drained to argue, she took the blanket and lay down on the bed. She could hear rocks being spat out by the wheels of the camper. The roar of the laboring engine accompanied the continuous shaking of floor and walls.

Darren was acutely aware of her supple body, molded by the blanket as she stretched out on the lower bunk. When she had fallen off the horse at his feet, his chest had involuntarily constricted because she looked so much like Laura. They both had the same wide, expressive blue eyes, a sweet mouth that seemed ready to tremble with a smile, and a treacherous femininity that brought male urges to the fore. Laura. The name stabbed him. Even now he wasn't free of the woman who had put his life into a shambles for five years.

As he stared blankly at his folded hands, the past rushed back. He had accepted a confining bureaucratic job in Washington, D.C., because he thought he couldn't live without her. He hated the office job, pushing unnecessary papers when he longed to be out in the field. But he had made a career sacrifice to make Laura happy, and then she'd left him without a backward glance when a young congressman caught her fancy. Darren had been trying to get his life back on track ever since. Now he had the assignment he wanted, he thought with satisfaction. Working in Canada. He wasn't going to let anything or anyone derail him this time.

He cradled his head with one hand. It felt as heavy as a twenty-pound bowling ball. He couldn't believe that playing the good Samaritan had ended up getting him into this mess. He wished he'd never seen Linsey Deane. But his next thought mocked the wish. He was glad he was here to protect her as much as he could. Heaven knows, she was completely vulnerable in this situation. But she was a fighter. He admired the way she had outwitted the men the first time. Maybe if he had taken her more seriously, they wouldn't have been fooled by the men's return. His thoughts roved over the bewildering "ifs," then all speculation was sent out of his head.

The camper stopped.

Darren jerked to his feet, facing the door, waiting.

Linsey sat up. They must have reached their destination, she thought. Every nerve ending vibrated with expectancy. She heard movement through the broken window, felt the camper tip, and then the sounds of a vehicle going away.

Silence.

"They left us." The anticlimax brought a mixture of anger and bewilderment. "What on earth is going on?"

"I suspect we'll find out soon enough," he said dryly. "Better get some sleep while you can. They'll be back."

She lay down again, and he seated himself at the table.

Her eyes were wide open. "I never was much good at counting sheep."

"Try bald-headed men."

While Linsey slept, Darren stayed awake, waiting and watching the night fade away into morning.

Sunlight splashed through the narrow window slats when the sound of movement outside the door alerted them.

Darren was instantly on his feet. "Linsey! They're here!"

She sat up, every muscle tense. She caught her breath as they heard the sounds of someone unlocking the door.

Chapter Three

Linsey stifled a cry as the kidnappers pushed open the door. She recognized her captors all too well—they were the two men who had attacked her at Aunt Etta's house. The swarthy-faced man held his knife with frightening efficiency. He would plunge it straight into Darren's stomach if he tried to jump him. The unshaven youth with straggly blond hair stepped forward eagerly. "Shall I waste the guy, Beale?"

"Let's see how the lady cooperates first."

"What do you want?" demanded Darren, the fiery glint in his eyes as red as his hair.

"Nothing from you, buster. So keep your mouth shut! And don't try anything funny or I'll slit her throat." Beale jerked Linsey up from the bed. "Linsey Deane. Right? That's what the tag on your knapsack said. Wrong sister—but no matter." Beale smirked. "One Deane sister is as good as another."

Linsey moistened her dry lips. "Where's Kate?"

"Don't know. We intended to pick her up when she came back, but you and this guy swam right into our snare, real nice like."

"What did you want with her?" Linsey's heartbeat thudded loudly under her rib cage.

"The same thing I want from you, baby—information." Roughly he shoved her down onto the bench seat. "Now you listen—and listen good. I'm going to show you some pictures, and you're going to start talking. Got it? And if you don't, we'll try a little persuasion." He laid a photograph on the table. "Ever seen that before?"

Linsey looked at the photo. The scene was a typical one of Colorado's mountains. It showed a steep hillside, pocketed with thick stands of conifers, and jagged peaks etched against the sky. No identifiable rocks or buildings. Nothing. Just a rocky mountainside with a scattering of pine, spruce and scrub oaks. She couldn't see anything to identify it or differentiate it from a hundred other photos she had seen.

Beale touched her throat with his knife.

Linsey shot a bewildered look at Darren. His fists were clenched, his body rigid. His eyes narrowed in some kind of warning, but Linsey didn't know what he was trying to tell her.

Beale saw the wordless exchange between them. "Don't get any ideas, dude. We only brought you along 'cause we thought seeing your guts spread all over the floor might help the woman talk."

Linsey didn't know what she should do. Lie? Pretend she had seen the photograph before? "I—I don't recognize it," she stammered.

"How about this one?"

He threw down a second photo. Linsey stared at it. Why would anyone take a picture of an old metal plate with some kind of marking on it? She picked up the colored photograph and held it closer, squinting at it, but she still couldn't read what words had been imprinted on it. "I never saw it before."

"You're lying. Your father took these pictures."

"How do you know?" She glared at him. "And if he did, what are you doing with them?" She put more bravado into her voice than she felt. What did these photos have to do with this bizarre abduction? As an oil company geologist, her father had taken many pictures during the years he worked in Colorado and made investments there. Maybe he had taken these two. But for what reason? Why were they important enough to put her life in jeopardy?

"Turn that one over," Beale ordered, pointing to the mountain scene. "Is that your father's writing?"

Linsey felt a new wash of fear. Her father's left-handed scrawl was unmistakable. Should she be denying everything? Would she make things worse by admitting the truth?

"Your pa was quite a joker. Read it!"

She swallowed to get some moisture into her mouth. "'Visit the family's Sawtooth Fox and look beyond the chimney rocks.'"

"Some funny man, your pa, but we ain't laughing."

Linsey silently read the sentence again, but still without a dram of comprehension. None of the words triggered any memory that would give meaning to the nonsensical sentence. What did it mean? Before she could say anything, she felt the sharp prick of a knife blade at her throat.

"Now, baby, it's time to talk."

Somehow, seeing her father's handwriting sent a jolt of strength through her. He had always given her courage when she needed it. "Get that knife away from my throat!" She saw a spurt of approval in Darren's eyes as Beale hesitated, then lowered the knife. "I never saw these pictures before. Where did you get them?"

"Some guy named Douglas Brady was showing 'em around a Louisiana bar. Bragging about how he and his sisters were going to be real rich."

"Douglas Brady! That's absurd!"

"I'm warning you, baby. You're going to talk, one way or the other."

Jake snickered. "Honey, Beale gets ornery when he gets mad. He'd love slicing a ticktacktoe game on that smooth face of yours."

Linsey blanched.

Beale's fat lips spread in a mirthless grin under his big nose. "You'd better listen to Jake. He's seen some of my handiwork. Now talk."

The moment was such insanity that she couldn't utter a sound. Her thoughts were wildly confused. *Douglas Brady?* The newly found half brother that Kate had called her about? What did that imposter have to do with this? She drew a deep breath. "I don't have a brother," she said as firmly as she could.

Beale only snorted. "See this letter. Took it off the same guy. The handwriting looks just like the stuff on the picture."

He held it close enough for Linsey to see how it was addressed. "A Letter of Intent, to my natural son, Douglas Brady," was what the words said.

The writing certainly seemed like her father's. Linsey felt as if someone had kicked her in the middle of the stomach with a spiked boot. She had been so convinced that the so-called brother was a hoax that seeing evidence to the contrary was a devastating shock. It must be true. *Her father had had an illegitimate son during the Korean War.* The realization blotted out everything else for a moment. Staring at the envelope, she felt utter disillusionment that her beloved father had kept such a dark secret. Anger followed quickly. Something very precious had turned out to be a fraud. Would she have to accept the idea that her jovial, upright father had been a womanizer?

Beale took back the letter, grunting in satisfaction at her ashen face. "Now, start talking. That dumb saying on the back of the photo is a clue, and you're going to explain exactly what it means. 'Visit the family Sawtooth Fox and look beyond the chimney rocks.'"

Darren warned her with his eyes not to say anything.

That was easy. She didn't know anything! None of it made sense.

Beale suddenly grabbed a handful of Linsey's hair at the top of her head.

"Ouch!" she cried as hot fire accompanied his vicious jerk. Tears filled her eyes.

He just laughed, pulled harder, then sliced off a hunk only a couple of inches from the roots. He tossed the foot-long clump of hair onto the table.

Linsey gasped, and one hand went instinctively to the short bristled spikes that were now sticking straight up on the top of her head. The ugly act demoralized her more than the threat of his knife.

"I told you I'm not a patient man. Now tell me what that gibberish means."

"She doesn't know!" growled Darren. "Can't you see that? For Pete's sake, give her a little time to figure it out."

"She knows!"

"No—no, I don't. I've never seen any of this before."

"Family fox? Who's that?"

"I don't know. We had dogs for pets when we were children, just like any other family."

"Chimney rocks?" Beale's knife pricked her throat. She felt warm blood trickle down her neck. The tiny wound smarted. Her heart raced.

"I don't know."

"She'd think a hell of a lot clearer without your knife at her throat," Darren growled.

"You'd better pray that it doesn't take her long, buddy. If you want to stay alive, that is. A few hours we'll give you, that's all. Then we'll treat you and the little lady to a taste of our special brand of persuasion." His heavy-lidded eyes were cold as they fastened on Linsey's pallid face. "Jake's got some tricks of his own that'll make you want to have your throat cut. Got that, honey?"

Linsey closed her eyes and nodded.

The next minute they were gone. Try as he might, Darren's ordered, pragmatic mind could not comprehend such a situation. "Do you know what this is all about?" he asked as calmly as his temper would allow.

"It's a bad movie—and we came in somewhere in the middle. Even those two goons seem like two-bit actors."

"I'm afraid they're for real."

"Well, I don't know what on earth they're talking about. Pictures. Letters. It's all gibberish."

Darren picked up the photo of the small rectangular piece of metal. He brought it closer to his eyes, scrutinizing it carefully. "Can't make out the printing, but it looks like a number, 2065, I think."

"What is it? Do you think it's part of a set?"

"It's hard to tell. Looks old...real old. Somebody's tried to clean up the tag. Probably it was all rusty and bent."

"Why would my father take a picture of that?"

Darren shrugged. "If we knew that, we'd know what our abductors are up to. You sure this scene isn't familiar?" He handed her the other picture.

"I've seen hundreds like it. Every Colorado hillside, ravine and canyon looks like that. I haven't any idea why my father took a picture of this one."

Darren read the sentence on the back. "Beale was right. It sounds like some kind of clue. Why would an old piece of metal be important enough for your father to disguise the location?"

"It doesn't make sense. None of it does. And why would my father keep silent all these years about a son? That envelope was addressed, 'To my natural son, Douglas Brady.'" The hurt Linsey felt was evident in her voice. "And why would he send his illegitimate son these photographs?"

"I don't know, but your brother wasn't too smart, showing them to everyone in a bar. You're sure this is your father's handwriting on the back of the photo?"

"As sure as I can be."

"When did he die?"

"Last spring. He fell while on a hunting trip in the fall. Broke some bones, but no fatal injuries. Then he developed a blood clot in his pelvis and suffered forced immobilization for months. He was in good spirits, and we all expected him to be out of the hospital before long. Then the blood clot traveled to his heart and lungs. Pulmonary embolism, they called it. Instant death."

"My guess is that he sent this stuff to Douglas Brady while he was in the hospital. No telling how Beale and Jake got them from him."

Her eyes widened. "Do you think they killed Brady to get those photos?"

"It's a good guess that he didn't just hand them over." Darren's forehead furrowed. "I just don't understand why your father would code this picture of a metal tag."

"I don't understand any of this."

Darren speculated silently that Linsey's father had expected to be there when his son was introduced to his daughters. "Maybe he was organizing some kind of surprise for the occasion," he offered.

Linsey knew that it was in character for her father to delight in surprises. And he sure had created a humdinger this time. Perhaps he had planned something special to ease the admission of his unfaithfulness and the reality of a son.

"It's the kind of thing my father loved to do," she said aloud. "He loved scavenger hunts, mystery games and the like. I doubt that he would pass up the opportunity to send us on a real treasure hunt." She smiled, remembering all the good times she and her sisters had enjoyed with her father. Picnics, camping trips, Halloween parties, a thousand memories came flooding back. "Yes, he could have planned a treasure hunt."

"Well, I've never heard of anything so stupid in my life," Darren swore. "Telling his family something important in *code*."

Linsey drew away. "My father was not stupid. He was kind and generous, full of fun. Loving and affectionate."

"So it would seem," Darren said sarcastically. "Judging from his romantic tendencies."

"Don't you be critical of my father," she declared angrily.

"I think I have every reason to question the judgment of anyone who lands me in this kind of a mess. And I don't intend to waste my time trying to figure out why your father insisted on playing games or keeping his amorous affairs a secret." Darren got up and began to pace the camper. "We've got to get out of here before those baboons come back. I got a good look at the lock, and I think if I can pry the metal frame loose enough, we may be able to slip something between the bolt and the casting. If I only had a tool.''

"Oh, is that all?'' Linsey said sarcastically, still smarting over his condemnation of her father. Darren's superior, condescending manner infuriated her. "And what kind of a tool would that be?''

"I don't know.'' He emptied out his pockets. Nothing but his wallet, pocket comb, a handful of change and a pair of fingernail clippers.

"I thought all men carried around pocketknives,'' she chided.

"Mine is back at the campsite. I was using it to cut tent rope. What do you have in your pockets?''

"Nothing but a few Kleenex.'' She managed a rueful grin.

"There has to be something in here that we can use.''

He opened all the cupboards again.

Linsey searched the bathroom. Thank heavens, there was no mirror. She couldn't have taken the sight of her chopped-off hair and the dark circles she knew were under her eyes.

"Nothing,'' she reported.

"Well, we're going to tear this trailer apart until we find one.'' A few minutes later, peering under the top bunk, Darren spied a small angle brace, made of iron, which was screwed into the wood at a corner.

"Here it is!'' he said triumphantly. "Just what we need.''

Linsey looked skeptical. It didn't look like much of tool to her. She said so.

He dismissed her pessimistic remark. "It's small...it's iron...and it has a joint we can use.'' He set to work, using the small file in his fingernail clippers as a screwdriver. The miniature file kept slipping, and the screws didn't budge.

It was hopeless, thought Linsey. Time slipped away with frightening rapidity. Every time she touched her hand to the patch of cut-off hair, it was a cue for a surge of panic to sweep over her. They had to get out! She didn't doubt Beale's threats for a moment. The memory of his moist, thick lips and hairy hands brought chills trekking again up her spine.

She wanted to help and kept poking her face close to where Darren was trying to work, and saw that his hands were too large for the space he was trying to work in.

"Let me try." She took the clippers, put the small file into the screw channel and turned. Since her hands were smaller than Darren's, she was able to get a better grip on the tiny file. She managed to give the screw several good turns—then the tiny file broke.

"Damn," Darren swore.

"I'm sorry. I—"

"Not your fault. I think you've loosened it enough for me to work with my fingers. If we can get one screw out—" He grimaced as the metal bit into his hand, but the screw began to turn again. In another minute he had the first screw removed. He used the stub of the broken file to gouge out wood around the other two screws as he lifted the loosened brace. They came loose in half the time.

"Okay, let's give it a try." Darren took the small angle brace and began prying the metal casing that held the workings of the door lock.

Linsey could see why he had been looking for something strong. Anything other than iron or steel would have bent. At first the square metal box wouldn't give at all. Sweat beaded on Darren's forehead as he kept trying to force the small piece of metal under the lock casing. Finally he loosened one corner enough to slip in the angle brace and use it as a lever to pry back the lock.

"Hurry," she urged, biting her lip, frustrated because there was nothing more she could do to help.

He grunted and continued his exasperating task. It took dozens of tries before the casing moved enough to slightly loosen the lock.

"Now for the proverbial credit card." He took one from his wallet and slipped it between the door and the frame. The loosened lock allowed it entry.

Relief sped warmly through Linsey. The door opened—three inches.

Darren swore. "They chained the door shut on the outside."

Linsey bit her lip. After all those frantic efforts, they were as securely locked in as before.

Darren butted his shoulder against the door, but it would not give.

Through the tiny opening they could see the links of chain. "Your hands are smaller than mine," said Darren. "Do you think you could slip the end of the brace into one of those links?" Sweat beaded again on his forehead; deep lines in his face revealed his weariness.

Thank God he was here with her. She resented his chauvinistic attitude of superiority at times but couldn't help but bless a fate that had made him camp where he did. "I'll try."

It was a frustrating, tedious struggle to hook a link through the tiny opening. Several times she thought she had the piece of iron secure, and then it would slip.

"It has to go in far enough for us to twist the link."

"I know," she snapped. He treated her like some imbecile child.

"Try it again," he ordered. "There! You've got it. Keep it in the link. Now all we have to do is twist it enough to force the link open."

"Push! Push!" He put his fingers on hers and they bore down on it together. She felt the link give way and the door suddenly flew open, nearly dumping them onto the ground outside.

They bounded out.

The camping trailer had been parked in a ravine with aspen-covered slopes rising on both sides. Car tracks showed where their abductors had driven away. How far? Were they parked somewhere, watching the camper?

"Let's get out of here. We can admire the view later." Darren urged her toward the side of the gorge, and they scrambled up a rocky slope.

Once they reached the top of the incline, they could see quite a distance. Beyond the rock-ribbed gorge where the camper had been parked, a narrow, meadowlike basin stretched before them, cupped by thickly forested foothills. Red and orange sandstone strata rose high above the green swatch of trees and brought Linsey's eyes upward to barren, crenellated peaks.

"They must have brought us over Redridge Pass from Crystal Lakes," she said with a joyful flash of recognition. "Those are the Sawtooth Peaks." She pointed to twin peaks with sharp, teethlike shapes.

"Sawtooth? Wasn't that one of the words on the photo?

She nodded. "Maybe that's why they brought us to this area. But I don't know what my father meant by a fox."

"You've been here before?"

"Lots of times. Fishing and camping. There's a lodge downstream. About five miles, I think. And Hank Green, a buddy of Daddy's, has a mountain cabin set back in those hills.'' She pointed across a meadow to a thick drift of trees that rose in green-black ridges.

"Which one's closer?"

"Hank's place."

"Let's go." He grabbed her hand. "And pray we make it across that open space without being seen."

"Do you think they're close by?"

"There's only one way to find out. Run!"

Chapter Four

The basin meadow was pocked with ponds of water, some
dammed by beavers and others fed from tiny freshwater
rivulets of melted snow. A midday sun burnished their
faces, and a quickening breeze blew Linsey's hair back
from her forehead as they ran. The exhilaration of being
out of the stuffy camper was intoxicating, and she was glad
that her physical condition allowed her to keep up with
Darren's longer stride.

Spring had not yet come to this mountain valley, and
patches of snow remained in the icy cirques, shaped like
deep bowls, in the Sawtooth Peaks. The air was thin at this
altitude and Linsey's lungs soon began to burn from the
lack of oxygen. The band of trees that offered sanctuary
was farther away than she had thought.

They had covered half the distance when the sound of a
roaring engine broke the stillness. Linsey threw a frantic
glance over her shoulder, just in time to see a motorcycle
leap out of the gorge as if it were airborne. Blond hair
streamed out behind the driver. Jake! Hunched over like
Evel Knievel, he gunned the roaring cycle after them.

The memory of jackrabbits being run to death by a motorcycle gang sent paralyzing terror through Linsey. The
cruel sport had turned her stomach when she had wit-

nessed it one summer. Now it became a horrible reality. They could never outrun the charging motorcycle across this open meadow. Before they reached the shelter of the trees, Jake would be upon them.

"Run! I'll try to slow him down!" Darren shouted as he stopped and prepared to stand his ground.

"You'll be killed!" The man was insane to try and stop the speeding motorcycle. A wooden blockade would have been splintered by the impact. A human body would be pulverized. "You can't—"

"Go!" His eyes were hard as steel. He gave her a rough shove. His face was as hard and commanding as she had ever seen it. His boyish freckles showed darkly on his nose. "Damn it, run!"

She stumbled away, wanting to protest. He was going to be killed. She bent her head and ran. He was sacrificing his life for her, a complete stranger, someone she suspected he didn't really like. Through his efforts they had escaped from the camper. Now she wished they had stayed locked up and taken their chances.

She flung another hasty glance over her shoulder and saw the motorcycle bearing down on Darren at increasing speed. Darren was standing pretty much in the same spot where she had left him. Why didn't he run? What chance did he have against a two-hundred-pound motorcycle? The sadistic Jake would run him over and never stop.

When Linsey reached the band of trees, she turned around and screamed. Putting her fists against her mouth, she watched the horrible scene that seemed to be taking place in terrifying slow motion. "Darren!" she cried. The motorcycle came over a slight ridge, flying into the air. The heavy machine flew several feet and landed only a short distance from where Darren stood apparently waiting to be crushed under its wheels.

Her eyes widened in horror. "Darren!" This time her cry was strangled in her throat. She closed her eyes, knowing that she couldn't bear to look any longer.

The motorcycle's engine died abruptly. No sound came to her ears. Her eyes flew open. She blinked. What had happened? A moment before, Darren had stood in the path of the charging cycle; now he was running in long strides toward her. It couldn't be. Her eyes were playing tricks on her. She was hallucinating. The motorcycle had disappeared.

When he reached her, Darren's grin was real enough. She felt his touch on her arm and heard his heavy breathing. His strong features were unbelievably handsome as she gazed up at him. He was real. Unharmed. Bewildered, she looked back to where he had been standing in the meadow.

"What happened?" she gasped, not believing the miracle.

Before he could answer, she saw Jake's blond head and drenched body slowly rise out of the pond. She began to laugh hysterically with relief. Now she understood. Darren had positioned himself so that when the motorcycle jumped the ridge, it would land in the middle of one of the ponds.

"How could you take that kind of chance?" she asked in a choked voice.

"It was a calculated risk, but I figured it was the only card we had to play. Something similar happened when I was just a kid. Took quite a ducking myself. It's hard to see small ponds hidden in the grass when you're riding fast."

"But you just stood there," she said in amazement. "How could you be sure?"

"I couldn't. But I gambled that Jake would be so eager to catch us that he'd ride recklessly into the middle of those ponds—and he did." Darren's brown eyes glowed with satisfaction. "Our daredevil's going to have his hands full, getting his cycle out of there." Then his smile faded. "We better make time while we can. We've slowed them down at the moment, but they'll be after us again, you can bet on that. Come on. You'll have to make sure we keep heading in the right direction. This is no time to get lost."

Still shaken by the terrifying experience, she managed to assure him that she knew where they were. "I don't think we want to hike up the road in plain sight. We ought to stay in the cover of these trees until we get close to the private road that leads up to Hank's place."

"Sounds good. Let's go." He gave her a confident smile that brought a peculiar tingling inside. Not only was he brave beyond belief, but he could turn on the charm when he wanted.

"Thanks," she said, smiling back at him.

"For what?"

"For risking your life like that."

"Don't tell me you wouldn't have done the same thing if you'd thought of it."

"I—I don't think I could have just stood there like that. I'd have fainted."

"You're not the fainting type, thank God. Now let's quit the chatter and find Hank Green's place."

Compliments seemed to embarrass him, she noted. He didn't want to talk about the brave way he'd stopped Jake. In truth, he didn't want to talk about himself at all. She wished she knew more about him. He was definitely an outdoorsman, not at all the stereotype of a government bureaucrat. Darren obviously felt deeply about environmental issues, and she was certain that he was dedicated to his work. It had been a long time since she'd found anyone to carry on any kind of serious discussion. If they hadn't been locked in this struggle for survival, they might have enjoyed a companionable relationship, but she sensed that the circumstances made him want to be free of her as soon as possible. He was not the type to fit into her life-style of symphonic music, gourmet foods and books on art, nor was she suited to his robust outdoor endeavors.

They had hiked for nearly an hour before Darren called a halt. "How much farther?"

She bit her lip. The never-ending trees were confusing. There was no way to look beyond them and see where they were. Densely needled branches rose in a concealing arch, and tall lodgepole pines stood like an infinity of fence posts. No matter in what direction she looked, everything appeared the same. Trees and more trees.

"I can't tell." Her voice shook nervously. "Without the road and a view of the peaks, I don't know how far we've come."

"We'll figure it out." He touched her cheek with a gentle stroke of his fingers. "You all right?"

"Oh, sure." She gulped. How could she admit her own doubts after his display of courage? "I just wish I knew why they're after us."

"One thing's sure. Whatever it is, they're ready to kill for it."

Kill for it! The reality of his words was stark. Any minute they could be murdered, and they didn't even know why.

Darren glanced up at the deep blue sky that was visible through the canopy of tree branches and noted the sun's position. "We've been heading pretty much straight north."

"Then the road would be to our left," she said.

"We'd better veer in that direction."

"But what if they're watching the road?"

"I doubt that Jake has gotten his cycle out of the pond yet," he said with satisfaction.

"But they have a pickup truck, remember? And they know we're heading in this direction. They could be going up and down the road looking for us."

"We'll have to take our chances. Besides, our luck has been holding pretty good. No reason to think it's going to go bad on us now." Darren gave her a reassuring smile. "Lead on, m'love."

Once more the endearment brought a peculiar warmth under her breastbone. She knew he didn't mean anything by it. He probably called lots of girls, "Love," but at the moment it seemed very special. Once more Linsey thanked a fate that had brought him so precipitously into her life. If only she knew why her father had put her life in danger.

Her thoughts whirled in a devil's wind as they pushed their way through heavy stands of white-trunked aspen, spruce and pine trees. What had been in her father's mind when he took those pictures? And why would he have sent them to a stranger? No, not a stranger, she corrected herself. If Douglas Brady was really his son, then her father had every right to include him in any family affair.

Linsey couldn't still a fresh spurt of anger. She had always been very close to her father, perhaps closer than Kate and Abigail because she had been the eldest, nearly eighteen when their mother died. Never once had she suspected that he had been unfaithful to their mother while she lived. And after their mother's death, her father had never shown any interest in another woman. Linsey had thought she knew him well. Sickened by the insight, she realized that she might not have known him at all.

Lost in her thoughts, she was startled when Darren suddenly stopped, and ran right into him. He pulled her down. "There's something moving ahead."

She bit her lip to keep from spewing out her fears. How could their abductors have gotten ahead of them? The two of them had purposely kept to the woods to avoid the road. How could anyone have seen them weaving their way through the trees? Once they reached the twisting road that led up to Hank's place, they would be vulnerable, but here in this copse of trees, they should be safe.

They crouched and waited. Linsey glimpsed a flash of white in the trees. A man's shirt? Her heart stopped.

Then Darren stood up.

He'd lost his mind. She grabbed his hand to pull him down again, but he drew her gently to her feet. He pointed—and she saw three white-tailed deer leaping through the undergrowth. The animals flicked their mule-like ears and bounded away.

She was so weak with relief that she couldn't give more than a soft chuckle.

"Sorry to give you another scare," he apologized.

She tipped up her head and looked at him. His brown eyes were feathered with dark flecks, and thick auburn eyelashes matched his full brows. She hadn't realized how clear and beautiful his eyes were. For a moment they seemed to draw her nearer. She felt herself responding, leaning slightly toward him, startled by the softness in his eyes. She thought he was going to kiss her; the prospect made her breathing grow shallow and her heartbeat quicken.

He searched her face, and something in it made him withdraw. Without warning a barrier slammed down between them. The softness in his eyes faded. "We'd better get on our way."

She turned away from him, embarrassed and confused. He would gamble his life for her, but he obviously didn't want to encourage any personal relationship. She was furious, both at herself and at him. They hiked in silence until she couldn't stand it any longer.

"Do you think Beale and Jake could have figured out where we're heading?" she asked in a businesslike tone. Darren would never catch her off balance like that again.

"It's a possibility," he said, with what seemed to her infuriating bluntness.

"They couldn't!" she declared, as if he had contradicted her. "Hank has a small place. Halfway up a mountainside. Once we get there we'll be safe."

"Well, then, I suggest we get moving a little faster."

"You think this is all my fault, don't you? You think that I deliberately pulled you into this mess."

"No, I don't."

Her confusion exposed itself in angry indignation. "Well, once we get back to Hank's and notify the sheriff, you can be on your way."

"Sounds good. Did you know that when you're angry, that short shock of hair on the top of your head makes you look like a banty rooster?"

She touched the clump of hair. How dare he make fun of her! "You have the wrong sex," she said sarcastically. "Roosters are male. I'm not."

She brushed by him, new energy in every step.

He laughed as he followed her. "From this angle, there's no doubt about that. That cute little derriere is all female."

He was impossible. Gallant one minute, and irritatingly chauvinistic the next. She'd be glad to see the last of him. Yet she felt both relief and new anxiety when they reached a narrow, graded road that rose from the valley floor.

They cowered at the edge of the trees and scanned the road in both directions.

"See anything?" whispered Linsey.

"No. Do you know where you are now?"

She wasn't sure. It had been a long time, and she had never paid all that much attention to the twists and turns in the road. Intuition seemed to reassure her that the side road that led up to Hank's small cabin was just ahead. In a burst of confidence, she told Darren that they had come out in exactly the right spot.

He chuckled as she tossed her head, as if daring him to disagree. "All right. Let's see if you're right."

They spurted around a couple of curves. With a sigh of relief, Linsey pointed, indicating a narrow-tracked road disappearing into the trees. "There it is. It's not far now."

Hemmed in on both sides by more lodgepole pines, they hiked for a quarter of a mile up the double-tracked road and were almost upon the steep-roofed cabin before they saw it.

"What's the matter?" Darren asked as Linsey suddenly hung back.

She grabbed his coat and pulled him behind some densely needled branches as she peered ahead.

"There's a pickup truck in front," she whispered.

The possibility that Jake and Beale had gotten there ahead of them was like the sudden, deadly flickering of a serpent's tongue. The green truck could be the one that they had seen from the promontory, parked behind Aunt Etta's garage. It had been too dark and too far away to see it clearly.

"It could be Beale's," she said.

"Or Hank's?"

"I think he was driving a Scout the last time I saw him."

"Maybe he bought himself a truck."

"Maybe. Maybe not." They hadn't seen the vehicle that had pulled the camping trailer into the mountain, and this dark green Chevy pickup could well be it, she thought. "Jake could have taken the motorcycle and Beale the truck. He could be inside, waiting," she suggested fearfully.

Darren's eyebrows knit the way they always did when he was thinking.

"What shall we do?" she prodded in a nervous whisper when he didn't speak.

"We'd be fools to march up to the front door and announce ourselves. Let's get closer. Maybe we can get a look in a window."

Staying in the shadows of the trees, they worked their way closer to the cabin and passed within a few feet of the green pickup.

Darren stopped. "Wh—?" she stammered.

"Stay here." Hunched down, he made a quick run to the driver's side of the truck, which faced away from the cabin. Slowly he rose, peered into the window and then ducked again. He grinned broadly and gave Linsey a quick wave of his hand.

She darted to his side and hunched beside him.

"The keys are in it," he whispered. Putting his hand on the door handle, he eased the door open. "Get in. Stay low."

She slid across the seat, keeping her head down. The window on her side was open. What if Beale saw them? Terror prickled the skin on her neck, and the memory of his curved knife washed all moisture from her mouth.

Darren slipped into the driver's seat. No movement from the house. No sign that they had been seen.

"Hurry," she croaked.

Darren turned the key and the starter ground loudly but the engine wouldn't catch. Pumping the gas pedal he swore, and laid a heavy hand on the starter button.

Linsey held her breath, praying silently.

At last the motor sputtered, coughed and started.

Darren had just rammed in the clutch and shifted, when the double barrel of a shotgun came through the window on Linsey's side.

"Hold it right there, or I'll blow your heads off."

Chapter Five

Linsey's eyes followed the gun barrel up to the man's face. His mouth fell open. "Well, I'll be jiggered. If it ain't Linsey Deane, trying to make off with my truck."

She was out of the door in a second, laughing and hugging him. "Hank. I'm so glad to see you!"

"What are you and this fellow doing in my truck?" Hank lowered his rifle and scratched his head of thinning gray hair. As tall as Darren, his rangy build was spoiled by slightly rounded shoulders. He wore overalls, faded to white in places, and a plaid shirt open at his tanned neck.

"We didn't know it was yours. Oh, Hank. I'm sorry." The poor man looked absolutely bewildered. "You'll never believe what's happened."

"What is it, honey?" Clumsily he patted her shoulder and squinted at Darren, who was sliding out of the truck. "This fellow giving you a bad time?" Hank looked ready to raise his shotgun again.

Linsey laughed. "No. He's a . . . a friend."

Darren held out his hand. "Darren McNaught. We can explain, Hank. No offense intended. I know how it looks."

"What it looks like is you two were making off with my truck," Hank said bluntly.

"We didn't know it was yours," Linsey began again. "We thought—"

"Why don't we go inside and we'll explain everything!" Darren said, interrupting her.

"Sounds fittin'," Hank said, still eyeing Darren with suspicion.

Linsey slipped one arm through Hank's. "It's so good to see you again. You look just the same. Wonderful!"

He gave her a crooked smile. "Only handsomer?"

"Definitely."

"Well, I can return the compliment, honey. You're prettier than a field of bluebells with them eyes of yours. I remember when you three girls used to be wilder than Indians. Guess you've all turned into ladies now. Haven't seen Kate and Abigail for a pack of Sundays, either. How are they?"

"Fine. Abigail's busy with her job at the Colorado Historical Society. And Kate's been having a ball water-skiing in Hawaii, and who knows what else. She's staying with Aunt Etta in Crystal Lakes right now."

Hank grinned. "Henrietta. Now there's a gal that could turn this bachelor into a lapdog."

"You?" Linsey laughed up at him. "You're sweet on Aunt Etta?"

He looked a little sheepish. "Could be...but I'd have to get in line. How many husbands has she had by now?"

"Four, but you could be the fifth."

He shook his head. "She probably already has somebody lined up." He opened the screen door. "Well, here we are. Home, sweet home."

The small cabin had one main room, a tiny kitchen, a bedroom and an outhouse. Linsey remembered it well and nothing seemed changed. The cabin was bachelor quarters and looked like it. The same deer antlers hung on the wall beside a faded calendar picture. Homemade chairs and tables were of rough-hewn pine. The familiar smell of Hank's pipe was another memory from the past. Linsey stood in the middle of the floor and looked around. Then it hit her.

"You don't have a phone." What a fool she was, not to have remembered. Her worried eyes fled to Darren's face. "We should have gone to the fishing lodge."

He gave her a reassuring smile. "We made it *here*." His emphasis on the last word was clear; they might not have made it to the lodge.

"Yes." She drew a deep breath of relief. He was right. "If we had headed in any other direction, Jake might have overtaken us on his motorcycle."

"There wouldn't have been any ponds to trap Jake with a dunking, that's for sure. I think coming here was the best decision. We can ask Hank to drive us to the lodge."

"No use going to the lodge for a phone," said Hank.

"Why not?"

"Closed down last winter. Mel and Judy Johnston had to file for bankruptcy. The whole thing's in receivership. Too bad. They was a real nice couple."

"Then I am glad we came here," Darren said. "If the lodge is closed up, we would have been vulnerable going there. How far to the next phone?"

"All the way down to Spruce Junction."

"How far is that?"

Linsey knew from Darren's tone that he was impatient with Hank's slow drawl and curt answers. She smiled inwardly. Nobody was going to rush Hank. He talked when he wanted to.

"About thirty miles as the crow flies...longer up and down these twisting mountain roads. What's got you all fired up about a phone?" He squinted at Darren as he placed his gun in a rack that held a couple of other hunting rifles.

"We need to call the sheriff."

Hank nodded, as if the request was an ordinary one. "Guess we can arrange that."

Nothing seemed to rile him much, thought Darren. Anybody else would be demanding all kind of explanations, but not this slow-moving codger. In spite of his impatience with Hank's ambling ways, Darren couldn't help but like him. "You'll drive us to a phone?"

Hank lighted his pipe and took a few puffs before he nodded. "We can run down to the junction in my truck. Say, Linsey, honey, you look awful peaked. How about some of my venison stew? And I've got sourdough biscuits to go in the oven. You two hungry?"

Three meals of bread and water made their answer a resounding, "Yes."

Linsey sent Darren an anxious look. "Do you think we should take the time?"

Darren eyed Hank's gun rack. Then he grinned. "Let's eat."

Her eyes crinkled with a smile, and Darren had to agree with Hank. No field of bluebells was as blue as those eyes. Even with a slight tinge of blue shadows beneath them, her oval face was the kind models would envy. Back there in the woods, he had almost pulled her into his arms and kissed those provocative lips of hers. When she had looked up at that moment, he hadn't been able to still the sudden flood of desire. Fool that he was, he had wanted to kiss and caress her and feel her sweet length pressed against his own. The memory of that urge made him feel guilty as hell. She was vulnerable. After all she'd been through, her defenses were down. Beale's cruelty had set her up to respond to any sincere affection, and he had almost taken advantage of it.

"Is something the matter?" She had been watching his face, trying to read his expression.

"No." He came out of his reverie. "Sorry, just thinking."

"They must have been long, long thoughts," she teased. "I've never seen you glower like that."

"Just giving myself a lecture."

"Do you do that often?"

"Not often enough, it seems." Even now he wanted to put his arm around her as they walked to the kitchen, but her touch was beginning to drive him crazy.

Hank chatted to Linsey about the good old days as he put food onto the table. "Remember the time we all went down to that beaver pond and one of you girls fell in?"

"Kate. Only I think it was deliberate. She thought she could see where the beaver lived if she jumped in. Thank goodness we got her out with only a soaking. I gave her a beaver book for Christmas, but she said it wasn't the same as seeing things firsthand."

"You were the bookworm. I remember that. Always reading or writing something. Well, here you be. Sink your spoon into this." He handed her a steaming bowl.

Darren groaned as he breathed in the wonderful aroma from his ample serving. "I think I've just gone to heaven."

Linsey took one mouthful and decided she had never eaten anything so delectable as Hank's stew. Even though she fancied herself a gourmet cook, she found the simple fare absolutely mouth-watering. Vegetables and chunks of meat swam in venison gravy, and hot biscuits dripped with butter and honey. Both she and Darren shoveled in the food, as if Hank might change his mind and take it all away. They smiled at each other as they ate furiously, like the famished fugitives they were.

Hank poured mugs of coffee from a blackened coffee-pot and then leaned back in his chair, watching them with a puzzled expression on his face. "Well, now, I reckon I'm a bit curious to know why you two came sneaking around here like polecats raiding a henhouse. Whatcha up to?"

Linsey's face lost all color. She set down her coffee so abruptly that the liquid spilled onto the plastic tablecloth.

Darren said quickly, "Actually we're not up to anything, Hank. We're trying to get out of the clutches of some guys named Beale and Jake."

"You're not going to believe what happened." Linsey's voice was shaky. Darren reached across the table and took her hand for a moment, giving it a reassuring squeeze.

"Shall I tell him, or do you want to?" Darren asked.

"I will." Linsey took a deep breath and began with the attack upon her at the house. "I came in the front door and those two goons were there!" She told Hank how they had jumped her and how she had escaped through the bathroom window.

"Hurrah for you!" Hank clapped his hands. "I always knew you were as smart as a polecat."

"I got away on Calico and rode to the ridge above the house. That's where I met Darren. He was camping out up there and came back with me to the house, thank heavens." She gave him a grateful smile.

"What happened next?" Hank prodded.

"We saw the men drive away and we thought it was safe to come back. We looked the whole house over. I was worried about Kate, but we didn't find anything to indicate she'd been hurt. Her car was gone. We thought the men had gone for good, but they jumped us in the garage, hen chloroformed us. And when we came to, we were in a camper parked in a ravine about five miles from here.''

"That's quite a yarn," said Hank, rubbing his whiskered chin, skepticism evident in his hazel eyes. "Couldn't have spun a better one myself."

"It's true," she insisted. "The camper had iron slats like venetian blinds on the windows. We couldn't get out. Then these guys, Jake and Beale, threatened to harm us if I didn't tell them what they wanted to know."

"And what might that be?"

She drew the two photos out of   jacket pocket. "Have you ever seen these before?"

Hank took out a pair of cheap Ben Franklin glasses and peered through them. "Nope. Can't say that I have. What s this thing?" He tapped the photo showing the metal tag.

"We don't know. It has some indented numbers. #2065, we think."

"Read what's on the back of this one," Darren instructed, turning over the mountain scene.

"'Visit the family's Sawtooth Fox and look beyond the chimney rocks.'" Hank peered over the half glasses resting on his nose. A faint smile hovered on his lips. "Sawtooth Fox. I reckon that's me."

"What?" exclaimed Darren and Linsey together.

"Yep. Fox—that's the name your pa always called me when we was in Korea together."

"I don't believe it," Linsey declared with a laugh.

Darren couldn't stifle his excitement. They had stumbled on the first clue to this bizarre puzzle. "Why would Linsey's father put your name on the back of that photo, Hank?" he asked eagerly.

"Beats me." The older man frowned and pursed his lips as if thinking hard.

"You must know," insisted Darren, trying not to be too impatient.

"Nope. How'd those fellows get ahold of these pictures?"

Darren watched the deep hurt spring into Linsey's eyes, evidence that she was fighting the acceptance of her father's infidelity. With her tousled hair and wide blue eyes, she looked like a child someone should take into his arms and hug. He settled for a hand squeeze.

"We don't know," she said in a firm voice, her emotions outwardly under control.

Darren admired the way she was able to look at a problem directly, without flinching.

"They showed me these two photos and a letter my father had sent to Douglas Brady."

"Who's Douglas Brady?"

"My half brother. Kate called from Aunt Etta's and told me that my father had had an affair during the Korean War and fathered a son by an American nurse. That's why I went to Crystal Lakes, because Douglas Brady was supposed to show up in a day or two." She kept her eyes fixed on Hank's weathered face. "I told Kate I was sure it was a hoax, but now...after seeing the letter, I don't know what to think. Do you know anything about this, Hank?"

He peered at her over the rim of his glasses. "Well, now, Linsey, honey, your pa and I were only together at the end of the war. I don't know what went on before that. Ronald Deane was my best friend, you know that. When he died, I lost a part of myself. But I never pried into his personal affairs."

Linsey's eyes narrowed. Hank's gnarled hands trembled slightly as he took off the glasses and stuck them into the pocket of his shirt.

He's lying, thought Darren. Probably Ronald Deane swore his buddy to secrecy. Hank wasn't going to tell Linsey anything about her newfound half brother. Well, Darren couldn't blame him. She was the kind of girl any male wanted to protect.

Hank took out a pipe and started working it. "You know, come to think of it, your pa was acting kinda mysterious on that last hunting trip. I caught him grinning like a Cheshire cat several times. Didn't know what he was up to. You know your pa, Linsey. He loved being mysterious. Always playing games and planning surprises. Anyways, after the accident, him falling like that, I plumb forgot all about it."

"About what?" prodded Darren. He could see Hank's mind working like the slow ticktock of a clock.

"Well, now, he was talking to me about joining in some kind of doings...can't rightly remember what he said. But he gave me one of his business cards."

"Business cards?" Darren echoed.

"What for?" asked Linsey. Why would her father give Hank something like that?

"Don't rightly know. Was puzzled at the time. I just glanced at it. Had something written on the back. Your pa told me to keep it but didn't say nothing else. I wonder where I put that thing?" Hank scratched his head, and Linsey and Darren exchanged exasperated looks.

"Please remember, Hank," pleaded Linsey. "It might be important."

He took some more puffs on his pipe. Then he shook his head. "'Fraid it's long gone, honey. I've used that camping equipment a dozen times since then and never ran across it. Never have been much good keeping track of things." Then he smiled at Linsey as if to make up for her disappointment. "I know where the chimney rocks are, though."

"Where?" asked Darren. They had visited the Sawtooth Fox. Now the second part might start to make sense. *Look beyond the chimney rocks.*

"There are some sandstone rocks on the top of a hill not far from here. Your pa and I used to ride horseback up there."

"Do you think he left some clue in those rocks?"

"A clue? Like a treasure hunt, you mean?" Hank chuckled. "Wouldn't that just be like your pa? Well, I guess we could take a look around."

Linsey shook her head. "No. I think we should drive to the junction and call the sheriff. That's the sensible thing to do. I'm uneasy about those brutes catching up with us."

"Well, now, I think we could hold our own if those varmints show up. How are you with a rifle, son?" he asked Darren.

"It's been a while since I handled a gun," Darren admitted. "But I used to be a pretty good shot. Won a couple of turkeys for Thanksgiving at a turkey shoot."

Hank grinned a yellowed smile. "Sounds good enough to me." He handed Darren a rifle from the gun rack.

"What do you think, Linsey?"

She hesitated.

Darren knew that the sensible thing to do was get back to Crystal Lakes and chalk the whole thing up as a bizarre adventure. There was no need for him to get further involved. Better to back out of this thing right now. He wasn't about to get involved with a gal like Linsey Deane, who obviously came from a cultured background. They had nothing in common . . . except the abduction that had thrown them together. Yes, the sensible thing would be to turn the puzzle over to the authorities and forget it.

Whatever old man Deane had had buzzing around in his brain had nothing to do with Darren McNaught.

"It wouldn't hurt to take a look around," he heard himself insisting.

"Well, I'm game if you are. I'd really like to know what this is all about."

"We can clear it all up for the sheriff. Save him a lot of questions and hassle," Darren said.

"And your curiosity needs to be satisfied." She grinned.

"Frankly, yes," he said, returning her smile. "I can't go off to the wilds of Canada without knowing what this is all about. We seem so close to finding out something, I think we should give it a try."

"I want to get the whole thing straightened out as quickly as possible myself."

"Just let those polecats come snooping around, and I'll give them a seat full of buckshot," Hank bragged. "Come on. I've got horses in a small pasture behind the house. We'll take ourselves a little ride up to the rocks and see what your pa left for us." He chuckled, as if he hadn't had so much fun in a coon's age, stuck a big cowboy hat onto his head and led the way outside.

They saddled up and left the small corral. With the two men riding shotgun in front and behind her, Linsey relaxed and gave herself up to the excitement of finding out what her father had meant about the chimney rocks. He had wanted them to come to Hank, the Sawtooth Fox, probably to get another clue that Hank seemed to have lost. They might never know what that was.

The horses puffed their way up a steep incline layered with rocks and dotted with white-trunked aspen and forest-green conifers. It was a ride Linsey had never taken before, and when they came out on top of a ridge that dropped away thousands of feet below, she caught her breath.

"Wow!" Darren exclaimed after he helped her down from the saddle and they stood looking at the vista stretching below them.

"Well, there they be." Hank pointed to a mass of jagged sandstone rocks, which were piled up like giant chimneys along the edge.

"'Look beyond the chimney rocks,'" Darren quoted. "That must mean that whatever we're looking for, Ronald Deane left in the midst of these rocks."

"What are we looking for?" Hank asked bluntly.

"Darn if I know," Darren admitted. "What do you think, Linsey?"

Her father's message was as obtuse and meaningless to her as to anyone else. More confidently than she felt, she said "If we're in the right place, he might have hidden a clue or written another message on one of the rocks."

"All right. Let's have a look," Hank suggested. He muttered something about pure foolishness and stomped away. He hiked to the rocks farthest away, Darren disappeared into the midst of another half dozen, and Linsey took the ones nearby.

What could it be? Why had her father arranged for them to come up here? The questions were like a record in her mind, playing over and over again. Under, around, over, between cracks, into the piles of loose rocks. None of them escaped Linsey's scrutiny. And she found nothing. Absolutely nothing.

She sat down on a rock. The lack of success was disappointing and frustrating, but somehow she would figure this thing out. Her father had always complimented her on her quick mind. He certainly was putting her mental faculties to the test now.

She heard steps and started to turn around.

"Don't move!" Darren shouted, some distance behind her.

His commanding tone left no room for argument. She froze.

Then she heard it. A deadly, warning rattle. *Rattlesnake!* Just behind her head. The reptile must have been sunning on the rock she was using as a backrest, only a few inches from her neck. Linsey had learned enough about snakes to know from the rattle that it was coiled and ready to strike. Screams sprang into her throat and she wanted to run, but the command in Darren's voice held her rigid and waiting.

His footsteps crunched on loose rock as he came closer. He raised his rifle. The deadly snake was inches from Linsey's head, ready to sink its poisonous fangs into her neck. He had no choice, he had to shoot it, but a near miss would blow Linsey's head off. He took steady aim and pulled the trigger. The snake flipped up in the air.

Linsey screamed as the reptile fell at her feet. Nearly a yard long, the rattlesnake had a bloody stump where its head had been.

Hank came running.

"Well, I'll be— Look at the diamondback, would you. Land's sake, you're some shot, mister." Hank looked admiringly at Darren, as if really seeing him for the first time.

Darren eased Linsey onto the ground a few yards away from the dead snake and sat down beside her. He held her close. "I was afraid you were going to move before I could get a good aim." His voice was shaky.

She had trouble getting air up from her lungs. "I hate snakes," she finally said; it was an understatement.

"That skin would make a pretty belt," he teased, trying to lighten the moment, although he was still shaking inside. He would never forget the fright of seeing her small head inches from the coiled snake.

"Ugh." She shivered. "I don't care to have a souvenir, thank you."

His arm tightened around her shoulders. "I'm sorry to put you through another ordeal."

"You didn't put me through it. You saved me from getting a snakebite. I owe you another grateful thank-you."

"Any time I can be of help," he quipped, smiling.

"Seriously, I don't know how to express my gratitude for...for all you've done." She didn't want to let her emotions get out of control, but wanted him to know how much she appreciated what he had done to help her. "I can't bear to think how this whole thing would have turned out without you. It's selfish, but I'm glad Calico dumped me at your feet."

"So am I," he said quietly, tightening his grip again, so that her head rested against his shoulder.

Hank sat down on a nearby rock and took out his pipe. "Don't this beat all? We didn't find nothin' in them rocks. Haven't got a whisper of an idea what my old buddy was up to."

The words echoed in her mind. *Beyond the chimney rocks.* Linsey looked out over the mountain valley far below them. On a wide spread between the forested mountains several buildings dotted the landscape—a ranch-style house, a large barn and numerous corral fences. They all looked like toy miniatures from the height of the chimney rocks ridge.

"Whose place is that?" Linsey pointed below.

"Carrie Bates. A gal who used to run the best dude ranch in these parts. Been kinda ailing lately, though."

Look beyond the chimney rocks. Like forked lightning the answer flashed into Linsey's head. Was that what her father meant? That ranch far below? It *was* beyond this high ridge of piled-up rocks. Excitement raced through her. "My father knew her?"

Linsey read her answer in the expression that flickered across Hank's face. It told her more than she wanted to know. Ronald Deane had known the woman—well.

Carrie Bates. Linsey turned the name over and over in her mind as they returned to Hank's place and unsaddled the horses. She was unusually quiet as they left the corral and walked back to the house.

Darren was aware that a struggle was going on inside her, so he wasn't surprised when she asked, "Hank, will you drive me over to Carrie Bates's place?"

"I think we should get to a telephone," Darren countered rather dogmatically. "We gave it a good try, Linsey, but the time has come for us to turn the matter over to the sheriff. Let him figure it out. No sense in us risking our necks, running around trying to second-guess your father's little games."

She leveled large eyes at him. "No one's asking you to risk your neck any further, Darren. I appreciate what you've done, I really do, and I understand your wanting to put this all behind you. You've got a seminar to go to, and this crazy nightmare of mine has intruded upon your life long enough."

He gave an impatient wave of his hand. "Listen to me! I was willing to investigate the chimney rocks because I thought we might find a quick answer to this thing. And it was almost a disaster. A rattlesnake was inches from poisoning you." He softened his tone. "Linsey, we know those two goons are out there somewhere, ready to jerk you back into their snare at the first opportunity. Can't you get it through that pretty head of yours that it's *you* I'm thinking about?"

"I'm sorry if I seem ungrateful, but I have to see this thing through. Why did my father want us to meet Carrie Bates?"

"Maybe he didn't. We don't know for sure that's what he meant by 'Look beyond the chimney rocks.'"

"There's only one way to find out, isn't there?" she responded with a stubborn jut of her chin.

He couldn't help but admire her courage, even when it exasperated him. "I don't think we should take the time to investigate Carrie Bates."

"I thought you wanted to solve the puzzle."

"I do, but I don't want to risk your neck to do it."

"Hank will protect me, won't you, Hank?" She sent him a pleading look that would have melted the strongest male into soft butter.

"Sure, honey. But all this palavering is just wasting time." He eyed the western horizon, where the sun was descending in a wash of color. "Going to be dark soon."

"Then we'd better head for the junction and call the sheriff," Darren insisted.

Hank looked from one stubborn face to the other. "Why don't we just kill two birds with one stone? Go to Carrie's house and call the sheriff from there?"

"She's got a phone?" both asked together, then laughed.

"Sure 'nough. Guess we better take these rifles along, in case we meet somebody on the way."

For a moment Linsey almost gave in to Darren's insistence that they give the whole thing up, but her stubborn streak overcame her fright. They seemed to be so close to the answer. She had to know what her father had wanted her to find.

"Let's go see what Carrie Bates has to say about all of this."

Chapter Six

A dim light beside his hospital bed threw weird shadows upon the ceiling as Douglas opened his eyes. Dangling tubes and bottles crisscrossed in cobweb patterns against the walls, and he blinked gingerly to bring the room into focus. The wild pain had receded from his head, but it crouched somewhere beneath the bandages, ready to pounce and shatter his consciousness once again. He dared not move, not even when a nearby voice breathed a sigh of satisfaction. He heard the whisper of soft-soled shoes and the quiet opening and closing of a door.

Time blurred. A gray-haired man dressed in white bent over his bed. "Well, now, you've decided to wake up, have you?" he said in a cheery voice. "Nasty bash on the head. Lucky that someone found you when they did. Want to tell me what happened?"

Douglas blinked. Deep furrows creased his forehead.

"You were found unconscious beside your car. The car was a rental, and you had no identification on you. The helicopter rescue squad brought you to a Denver hospital. What's your name?"

His brain seemed detached from his body, and he couldn't work his mouth. A groan was somewhere deep in his chest.

"There, there. Don't worry. It'll all come back. No need to fret. There's all the time in the world."

But there wasn't time. That much he knew. A fluttering of panic brought the pain from its hiding place, and his head shattered into jagged shards. He struggled against a mounting sense of urgency. The shadows on the ceiling grew darker and finally disappeared in a floating darkness that drew him away from the edge of memory. Away from danger.

Douglas slept.

LINSEY SAT RIGIDLY between the two men in the pickup. She kept her eyes fixed straight ahead on the twilight tunnel of trees. As headlights sliced the sides of the road, wild creatures sent bushes quivering as they fled. Every movement brought a stab of terror to her chest. She feared that two human predators might be waiting around every curve, and her nervousness increased with every jolt of the pickup. Hank's hunting rifles seemed to offer less protection out here in the vastness of the night.

Hank chatted easily with Darren, spinning tales of hunting and fishing. "There was one time I 'member when this trout broke my line five times before I caught the old boy."

Their voices flowed over Linsey as background noise to her dark thoughts. When she had gazed upon Carrie's place from the top of the ridge, it had not seemed far away, but that was as the crow flew. Since dark they had been climbing seemingly unending layers of wooded hills. An hour and a half had passed, and they still weren't there.

"Hold on," Hank warned. "There's a rough part here."

The washboard surface sent Linsey bouncing against Darren. He put out an arm to steady her in the seat, grinning as she bobbed up and down with every bump.

"He wasn't kidding, was he?" she managed, returning Darren's smile. She was aware of the firm thigh pressed against hers, reassured by the warmth of his body that radiated strength and virility, and had to still an impulse to rest her head against his shoulder. Such an overture would surely not be welcome. Even though there had been times when he was gently affectionate, most of the time he remained distant and guarded. She didn't know whether this was his attitude toward all women or just herself. Someone must have hurt him deeply, she thought.

"Now I know what riding a bucking bronco feels like," he said when the road finally smoothed out. "You all right?" he asked Linsey.

She nodded. Acutely aware of his vigorous profile and the firm hand he had on the rifle resting at his side, she felt at once guilty and relieved that he had not taken off at the first chance. He had wanted to go to the sheriff and be done with the whole thing, including herself; that much she knew. It had been selfish of her to insist that they go to Carrie's ranch first, but she was convinced in her own mind that "Look beyond the chimney rocks" meant that they were supposed to go to the ranch.

"What was that deep sigh about?" he asked.

"I was just thinking how inconsiderate it was of me not to agree to go to the junction. My family troubles have kept you from your own plans long enough. It's just that I can't let go. Not yet."

"It's all right. I understand." He gave her a wry smile. "I'm out of the mood for camping, anyway."

"Maybe another time."

"Yes…another time." His gaze swept her face, then he quickly looked away.

Linsey smothered another sigh. Once they talked with Carrie Bates, they might find out why her father had taken those photographs and sent them to a perfect stranger. No, not a stranger, she corrected herself. Douglas Brady might be her father's son. Her half brother. Her father had kept his existence a secret all these years. She had loved her father very much, but the picture of Ronald Deane that was emerging was of someone she didn't even know. Not only had he been unfaithful to their mother but it seemed that he had been more than a casual friend to Carrie Bates.

"A wooden nickel for your thoughts," Darren whispered.

"It's supposed to be a penny."

"I know, but I'm a cheapskate."

"All right, I'll take a wooden nickel."

"Can I charge it?"

She laughed and felt better. "Sorry. No credit."

She went back to her thoughts, and didn't find them quite so heavy as she thought again about her father and the bewildering surfacing of unexpected facets of his life. After Kate's call telling her about Douglas Brady and before leaving for Aunt Etta's house at Crystal Lakes, Linsey had taken her key next door to their neighbor, Becky McDougal. Linsey had sought reassurance from the old family friend that her father had been just what he had always seemed—a dedicated family man.

Becky had been on her knees in her garden when Linsey came through the gate that linked the two properties. Somewhere in her sixties, Becky always wore size 44 jeans and a man's sloppy shirt that hung halfway to her knees. An expansive smile in a round face matched her ample figure. "What's the matter, gal? You look like a critter whose tail's caught in the barn door," she greeted Linsey.

"I got the weirdest call from Kate."

Becky chuckled. "What's that scalawag sister of yours up to now?"

Linsey told her. "It's ridiculous. It's someone trying to finagle their way into the Deane money. And that sister of mine is ready to welcome him with open arms. Daddy would never keep that kind of secret. He was about the greatest father that ever lived...."

"But he was a man," Becky finished, leaning back on her haunches and looking up at Linsey. "A fine figure of a man. Personable and handsome enough to catch any gal's eye. I bet in a uniform, Ronald Deane was something to see."

"But he wasn't interested in any woman but Mother. He *can't* have been."

"Now, don't get yourself riled up. Sure as you try to put someone up on a pedestal, girl, they're bound to fall off. Your pa was flesh and blood. And things happen during wartime."

"He was true to Mom, I know he was. He never looked at another woman...not even after Mom died. We girls were his whole life. How can you suggest differently?"

"Land's sake, honey. I don't know if he sowed a few oats now and again. But he never neglected your mother, God rest her soul, nor you girls. I can still hear y'all giggling over some game. Always organizing some kind of party or another, your Dad was. He went all out for Halloween. Remember the witches' house he made in that old shed?" She chuckled. "That was really something. Skulls, wet spaghetti for brains and cooked rice as lice. Liked to scare me pink when I stuck my hand in that slimy jello he told me was blood." She laughed again. "Good father, he was." She peered up at Linsey. "That's what you have to remember."

Linsey didn't like the way Becky looked at her. She stiffened as if a cold, cold draft had hit her neck. Was there a warning in those round, candid eyes? "I know what my father was like," she snapped. "He was a loyal father and husband."

Becky shrugged. "Are you going to Crystal Lakes to check out this half brother?"

"No," Linsey lied, angry that Becky had only added fuel to her worries. "I'm just going to take a few days' vacation."

She sighed deeply as Hank's truck bounced her from side to side. Now she was paying for her pride. That little lie had kept people from missing her.

"Are you sure you're up to this?" Darren asked, looking down at her. An unexpected huskiness in his voice caught her unaware. It betrayed a deep concern, a personal empathy, and a loving gentleness that she had not seen before. From the first, Darren McNaught had made it clear that she held no personal attraction for him, and most of the time he looked at her as if something in her manner or appearance distressed him. Now she was startled by an expression that softened his mouth into a tender smile. "I think Hank should take you home. I want you safe."

A peculiar tingling spiraled through her. His bold coloring and strong features combined in an assault of masculinity that filled her senses. A shock of wavy hair fell onto his forehead, softening the lines and planes of his face. Why had she thought his features too craggy to be handsome? "I feel safe," she said softly, surprised at her answer. It was true. Here in the warm interior of the truck with him at her side she felt protected.

"That shows how confused you really are," he teased.

Hank gave Linsey a yellowed smile. "Relax, honey. T'ain't a varmint alive that can outfox old Hank." He chuckled. "I'd forgotten all about that nickname. Imagine your pa remembering after all these years." He began to reminisce about the Korean War and the close buddies he and Ronald Deane had become.

Branches scraped the side of the truck as it careened from side to side through the dark tunnel of trees. Darren was right, thought Linsey. They should be heading in the opposite direction, toward lights, people, the authorities and civilization. Instead they were maneuvering over a switchback road between Hank's cabin and Carrie's ranch. If Jake had recovered his motorcycle from the pond, he might be on the move again. And there was Beale, with his curved knife and his pickup. Linsey touched her hand to the stubby shock of hair on her head. She shivered.

"I'll be golldarned!" Hank swore, peering into the rearview mirror.

"What is it?" Darren asked quickly.

"Car lights. Can't you see them flickering over the top of that last hill?"

"Maybe it's just some other campers," Darren said in a reasonable tone as Linsey caught her breath.

"Don't get many cars wandering around after dark in these parts," Hank countered. He braked suddenly and started maneuvering in the narrow road.

"Why are we turning around?" protested Linsey. It seemed insanity to be heading back toward the approaching lights.

"If they see us on this road, they can follow us straight to Carrie's. There's no turnoff between here and her place. But there's a road at the bottom of this hill that turns northwest and goes halfway up one of them Sawtooth Peaks. If we fool 'em into thinking we've gone that way, they'll have a nice long ride with nothing to show for it."

Hank brought the wheels as close to the drop as he could, then inched the truck around in the narrow road until he could head the vehicle back down the twisting road the way they had come.

"Do you think it's them?" Linsey asked Darren.

"I wouldn't take any odds that it isn't. Whatever they're after, it's something important enough for them to go to all the trouble of fixing up that camper and bringing us way up here. Doesn't strike me that they're going to give in easily and let us get away." He tightened his grip on the rifle.

They roared back the way they had come. When they reached the bottom of a steep incline, Hank took a curve on two wheels. He grunted in satisfaction and slowed down. "We want them critters to get a glimpse of our car lights."

Linsey and Darren twisted around to see out the back window. The pair of lights darted behind them like twin fireflies through heavy stands of conifers and grew into round eyes as they came closer and closer.

"They're going to catch up with us!" Linsey exclaimed anxiously.

"Nope," Hank said laconically. "If it's your friends, we want to let them get a good piece down this road before we lose them."

Darren peered out the side window. "I can't see anything but a dry creek bed on one side and a sheer mountain cliff on the other."

Linsey's nails bit into her flesh as she clasped her hands. They were creeping along so slowly that she was certain the vehicle behind would run over them at any moment.

"Hold on! Here we go." Hank doused the car lights, turned the steering wheel, and the trunk plunged off the road and down an embankment. It rattled across the dry, rock-pitted creek bed like a bronco rearing on stiff legs.

Linsey bounced high enough to hit her head on the roof of the pickup. She was certain the truck was going to shake apart as it jolted from side to side, but it lurched out of the creek bed on the other side and Hank braked in a band of trees.

Darren shot a look at the full moon, half hidden by whorls of drifting clouds. It was bright enough to highlight any chrome on the truck, and lights from the approaching car might hit the truck's mirror or hubcaps in a betraying reflection.

"Come on, get out." Hank opened the driver's door on the side away from the road.

"Why?" Linsey protested. She felt much safer in the truck.

"Don't want to be trapped inside if they spot us."

She didn't argue. There was no doubt in her mind that Hank had earned his wily nickname.

"You two duck down behind the back," he ordered. "I'll take the front. Get ready to shoot, Darren. We may have to spread a little lead around if they see us."

Linsey stayed close to Darren as he hunched behind a rear wheel.

"Here they come," said Hank in an excited tone.

He's loving this! thought Linsey. He sounded young again, keyed up. War must get into some men's veins, she thought, praying that there would be no need for the Fox to prove himself.

The sound of an engine grew louder.

"Is it Beale and Jake?" she whispered.

"Can't tell," Darren answered, peering around the wheel.

Linsey saw the sweep of headlights along the side of the road as the vehicle came closer. If it veered in this direction, the pickup would be clearly seen. She remembered

Beale's cold eyes and vicious smile and clamped her mouth shut to keep her teeth from chattering.

"It's a pickup truck," said Darren as the car pulled even with their hiding place. "Could be theirs."

She stopped breathing, her ears listening for any break in the engine's rhythm.

She heard Darren let out the breath he had been holding.

"It's gone."

They waited a few more minutes to make certain it didn't turn around and come back. Then Hank gave a victorious, "Yahoo!"

"Did you recognize the truck, Hank?"

"Nope, and I know about every truck for miles around. It's them, all right. I'd bet my buttons on it. Only strangers would head up that road this time of night."

"Won't they notice that they're alone on the road?" Linsey asked anxiously.

"Nope. Sides of the mountain keeps out any view of what's ahead or behind until they hit timberline," Hank assured her. "Come on. Let's get this baby back on the road."

They climbed back into the pickup. Hank had to grind the starter a terrifyingly long time before the motor caught. Every minute Linsey expected to see returning headlights as the other truck came back. Hank sent his pickup bouncing across the rocky creek bed and headed up the road the way they had come. "We lost 'em good," he gloated.

"Pretty tricky," agreed Darren. "I can see why they called you the Fox."

Hank grinned. "I could tell you some tales...." He glanced at Linsey. "Well, maybe some other time. We're almost there...another ten minutes."

"I hope we've done the right thing coming here," said Linsey, shaken by the nearness of their abductors.

"Won't hurt nothin' to see what Carrie has to say. We'll call the sheriff, talk to Carrie, and see if we can't make some sense out of all of this. You're sure you don't know what your pa had in mind, Linsey?"

"I'm completely bewildered. Mailing photos to a son we never knew he had. Writing clues that would lead us to Hank and then on to Carrie Bates. It's crazy."

"Sure beats me," said Hank. "But then, your pa always was one for playing games." His voice blended with the monotone of the truck's laboring engine as he related the story of some foolish wild-goose chase or other that he and Ronald had managed to persuade their army sergeant to undertake.

Linsey's thoughts flew ahead to the woman they were about to meet. Her father must have known Carrie Bates ever since he started hunting in the area, she reasoned, since Hank had said Carrie furnished packhorses and ran a dude ranch. And yet, during all those summer vacations they'd spent fishing in this area, her father had never once mentioned Carrie Bates. Why had he been so secretive about her? And why did she seem to be at the center of this nightmare?

Darren was asking himself the same questions. If they were right about the chimney rocks clue, then Carrie Bates had information that might clarify exactly what Ronald Deane had found in those photos, and why their abductors were ready to kill them for it.

"Are we about there, Hank?" Linsey asked anxiously.

Darren glanced out the back window to make certain no one was following. It was pure idiocy to be wandering around on these isolated roads with Beale and Jake on the hunt for them. Trying to solve this bizarre puzzle was just asking for trouble…and Lord knows, they'd had enough of that already. He was a fool for hanging around any minute longer than necessary. The first opportunity, he was on his way back to Crystal Lakes.

He glanced at Linsey's petite frame beside him, and a protective instinct mocked his decision to leave her as soon as possible. She was one gutsy gal. Begrudging admiration for her mingled with other disturbing feelings that made nonsense of his outward indifference. He'd better get his emotions under control fast or he'd find himself in another impossible emotional tangle. So he was relieved when Hank said, "There's Carrie's place," and pointed ahead as they came down a switchback road.

Clouds had thinned in front of the moon, leaving the night clear. Filtered light bathed the sprawling buildings below.

"The place looks all dark," said Linsey. "Maybe she's not there." New uneasiness flared unbidden as Linsey realized they might have wasted precious time coming here.

"Oh, Carrie's there all right. Never goes any place, no more. Closed up the ranch, she did. Got rid of all her stock. Ever since Ronald's death she's been ailing fast. She's home, all right."

"I think you're right," agreed Darren. "There's a light at the back of the house."

A new anxiety brought dryness to Linsey's throat. *How well had Carrie Bates known her father?* What sort of woman was she?

Hank's pickup took the last hairpin curve, its wheels spitting gravel. A level road ran under a wrought iron arch bearing the legend, Bates Dude Ranch. Corral fences hemmed in the road on both sides as it ran straight toward the main house.

I should feel relief, thought Linsey. Instead, an un-named premonition prickled her skin like a sudden cold draft. She had never in her life experienced any psychic tendencies and had always felt a slight contempt for those who claimed them. Yet now apprehension tugged at her senses as the pickup approached the large, stone house, as if she glimpsed something in the future that was as real as the breath in her body. The chill ran bone deep. She shivered. "We shouldn't have come!" she said.

"What is it?" Darren asked quickly, aware of her shudder. "Do you see something?"

She shook her head. "No, it's not that."

Instead of chiding or reminding her that he had advised against coming here, Darren's glance went over her white face. "What is it?"

"I don't know. I just feel that . . . that we took a wrong turn somewhere. That something terrible is going to happen."

Hank just snorted. "Now, don't go borrowing trouble, honey. No reason to get yourself in a stew. We done the right thing coming here."

"I hope you're right." Her lips were stiff, and moisture was gone from her mouth.

Hank drove around to the back of the house and gave a couple of toots on his horn. "You'll like Carrie." He got out of the car, his hunting rifle in hand, and walked to the back door of the house.

Darren helped Linsey out. "Don't look so scared. I bet she's a nice lady." He gave her a reassuring grin.

At Hank's knock, a light came on in the porch.

Linsey involuntarily grabbed Darren's hand as they waited. "I don't want to meet her," she said to him in a low, half-scared voice.

"Why not?" Darren raised an eyebrow. "I thought that was why we're here. You're not much good at hiding your curiosity, you know. I saw the look on your face when Hank let it be known that your father and Carrie Bates were well acquainted. I think you're harboring some kind of adolescent jealousy because your father may have had a sweetheart you knew nothing about."

"It's not that," she declared. But was it? No, she didn't think so. She was mature enough to accept the fact that her father might have had a love affair. No, it was something else. Some nebulous, frightening presentiment.

"Well, we're here now." Darren squeezed her hand. "Let's find out what she knows—if anything."

The door opened, and the puzzled expression of the woman they saw there eased into a smile when she saw Hank. "What a nice surprise."

"Hi, there," said Hank, going into the house.

Linsey and Darren followed him into a large warm kitchen with knotty pine walls and a brick fireplace.

"Carrie, this here is Linsey, Ronald's oldest girl, and her friend, Darren McNaught."

Linsey was prepared to meet a big, horsey woman, so she was startled to find herself looking into a pair of soft, smokey-blue eyes framed by gray-threaded hair the color of pale flax. The woman's tall, slender figure was snugly clad in jeans and a jersey blouse printed with yellow daisies. The sun had wrinkled her tanned face, but there was youth in the smile and affection in the impulsive hug she gave Linsey. "I'm so happy to meet you."

Linsey flushed, embarrassed for no good reason.

Carrie shook hands with Darren, and Linsey knew from the way his face softened into a warm smile that he too was surprised to find Carrie Bates so fragile and charming.

"We need to use your telephone, Carrie," said Hank. "Some funny business going on."

A frown crossed Carrie's face and then disappeared. "The phone's in the hall, Hank. Help yourself."

"Be back in a minute," he said. "You two can fill Carrie in on what's happening." He ambled out of the kitchen.

The friendly woman smiled at Linsey and Darren. "I just made a whole pot of coffee. Can't get used to making just enough for one. How about some sandwiches? Could you stand a bit to eat? I was just thinking I should be fixing something for myself." She laughed. "It's nice to have company. After so many years of cooking for ranch hands, I hate eating by myself."

"That would be very nice," Darren said and smiled. "We had some of Hank's stew for lunch, but my empty stomach's making rumbling noises now."

"Let me help," Linsey offered, forgetting her earlier uneasiness. Her premonitions must have been way off base. There was nothing about Carrie Bates to inspire anything but friendliness. "Could I freshen up first?"

"Sure. Bathroom's through that door on your right."

Linsey found it and eyed the pretty blue-and-cream shower stall with envy, but settled for a nice hot scrubbing with a soft, soapy washcloth. Gingerly she washed off the dried blood where Beale's knife point had pricked her skin. For a moment she leaned up against the sink and fought for composure. The wave of nausea passed. She found a rubber band in a tray of bobby pins. She brushed her hair to the top of her head, making a coil over the stubby ends left by Beale's knife.

When she returned to the kitchen, Carrie and Darren were chatting easily.

"So you're from Canada. I spent a summer in Montreal," Carrie said. "Loved every minute of it. Beautiful lakes and forests. Beautiful country. I took a boat trip through the interior. Have you ever been there, Linsey?''

"No, it's a place I've always wanted to see...someday."

"Maybe you can come visit me?" Darren's eyes met hers.

For a moment she thought he was teasing, but his eyes were quite solemn.

"Maybe." Although chasing a man was something that went against her pride, under other circumstances she might very well plan such a vacation—to see the scenery, of course.

"You ought to go, Linsey. If you think the Rockies are spectacular, you should see some of the Canadian mountain ranges."

Darren frowned. "Canada's got the same environmental problems as the U.S. Something's got to be done to stop industrial pollution from fouling the air and killing the wildlife. I've been assigned to a U.S.-Canadian joint task force. We'll work to get a handle on the acid rain problem."

"And what brings you to Colorado?"

"A seminar in Crystal Lakes. I ran into Linsey—no, let me correct that. She ran into me." His grin teased her. "Fell off a horse right at my feet. I just had to tag along with her to see what would happen next."

"Campers who pitch tents on other people's land must expect the unexpected," Linsey chided Darren.

"I guess you're right. Now I know what the saying, 'Adventure is the result of bad planning' means."

They laughed together; Carrie would have never guessed from their light banter that they had been drugged, abducted, threatened and pursued by armed men before they reached the door. Linsey could hardly believe it herself. Sitting in the comfortable kitchen as Darren charmed

Carrie with his easy, confident manner made all the preceding events seem too melodramatic to be real.

Carrie smiled at Linsey. "Well, it's certainly nice to meet both of you. Linsey, you don't know how much Ronald talked about you and your sisters." She chuckled. "Your father bragged that his daughters were the smartest and prettiest, and took top ribbons in whatever they did. He kept clippings of every one of your piano recitals."

"He did?" Linsey couldn't remember that her father had ever expressed any great interest in her music. She was beginning to wonder if she knew him at all. "He always encouraged me, but I'm surprised to learn that he had that kind of interest. Classical music was not a love of his. Nor fancy cooking, either. He used to tease me about working in the kitchen all day to create something he couldn't pronounce."

Carrie laughed. "Do you know that when you had recipes printed in a gourmet cookbook, he ordered me a copy?" She looked sheepish. "I have to confess I never tried any of them. My ranch hands wouldn't eat anything they couldn't drown in salt, pepper and ketchup. And I've never taken any blue ribbons in cooking, but I used to love to try all different things." She sighed. "Since my health has gone bad, I haven't had much of an appetite for anything."

This mention of her health caused Linsey to notice that Carrie moved about the kitchen at a controlled, slow pace that indicated she might be in pain. Hank had said Carrie was "ailing", and Linsey felt a rush of compassion for this woman she had just met.

"Let me chop up those vegetables," Darren offered. "I'll show you a prizewinning salad."

"Don't put any fingernails in it," chided Linsey as he whacked a knife upon a chopping board.

"Good protein." He grinned at her, and she swallowed the impulse to tell him he was holding the knife the wrong way.

Hank came back just as they put the food on the table. "The sheriff's out of town. Due back in the morning. I talked to Sam, his deputy. Sam said they'll check out Dead Horse Gulch first thing to see if the camper's still there. Told us to stay here tonight. The sheriff'll come out and talk to us tomorrow. Hope that'll be all right, Carrie?"

"Wonderful. I love houseguests. It gets pretty lonely here all by myself. Now, tell me what this is all about."

Darren stopped Hank from answering. "I think we ought to do justice to this food first. We're all a little uptight. A full stomach will help us keep things in perspective."

"I agree," Linsey said, exchanging knowing glances with Darren. He didn't want Carrie upset any more than necessary. His empathy toward the sick woman was so obvious that Linsey chided herself for thinking that he was insensitive. Even though she was anxious to pump Carrie for information, she knew that Darren was right not to spoil the meal their hostess had fixed for them.

Darren asked Carrie questions about the dude ranch as they ate.

"My father bought it when this part of Colorado was really a remote part of the state. People from New York thought they were in the wilderness when they vacationed at our place. We had a string of forty horses at one time." She laughed and color came back into her cheeks.

The older woman must have been very pretty once, thought Linsey. Her father must have sat in this same kitchen, laughing and talking. A lump rose in Linsey's throat.

Why hadn't he told them about Carrie? They would have understood his need for female companionship. How close had they been? Friends? Something more? From Hank's manner, she guessed that Carrie and her father had been lovers. The thought made her angry, not because her father had found someone to love, but because he had kept it a secret.

Hank started talking about some of the pack trips he had led into the mountains. "Them city fellers couldn't hit a wild turkey flapping in a barrel. 'Course, Ronald and I showed 'em how it was done. Every year we'd take a bunch of them greenhorns all over these mountains. Nigh on ten years, eh, Carrie?"

"My father's been coming here for ten years?"

"Only the last five, regular like," Carrie said as if answering her real question. Her warm eyes met Linsey's gaze. "He really appreciated your staying in the family house with him. You were a great joy to him, Linsey, . . . but . . ." She hesitated, as if searching for the right words. "But he was lonely, and so was I."

Hank cleared his throat, as if embarrassed by the sudden turn in the conversation. "Well, now, I think we'd better be telling Carrie what this is all about. Dropping in on her like this must have set her curiosity a-twitchin'. Right, Carrie?"

She set down her fork, having eaten very little of the food on her plate. "Yes, I must confess I am."

"Well, Linsey's got some pictures to show you."

"Pictures?" She looked bewildered.

"A couple that Linsey's father might have taken," said Darren.

Carrie frowned. "I'm not sure I can be of help. Ronald didn't share all that much of his life with me."

Hank leaned forward. "You ain't gonna believe this story. Some guys kidnapped her and Darren, held 'em in a camper till they escaped and made it to my house."

"What?" Carrie's horrified expression drained away what little color there was in her cheeks.

Linsey hastened to ease the fright she saw in the older woman's eyes. "They didn't hurt us. Just took a swipe out of my hair."

"Oh, my goodness. Why? What did they want?"

"Show her the pictures, honey," Hank said. "See if she knows what your pa was up to."

Linsey laid the two photos on the table and watched Carrie's face closely. The woman looked at them for a long time and read the writing on the back. Her forehead furrowed, and she caught her lower lip in her teeth.

"Have you seen them before?" Linsey asked.

Carrie shook her head.

Linsey was about to challenge her. She was lying. Something in the nervous flicker of her eyelids gave her away.

Darren leaned forward. "But you do know *why* Linsey's father took the pictures, don't you, Carrie?"

She moistened her lips. "Yes."

"We was right?" Hank slapped his leg gleefully. "Good old Ron gave us the right clue. Well, I'll be jiggered. Carrie knows all about this."

For a moment she didn't speak. Then Carrie leaned back in her chair. She sighed deeply. "I'm afraid I do."

Linsey's breathing grew short and shallow as she waited. A kitchen clock ticked loudly in the silence. She fixed her eyes upon Carrie's face. "Please tell us."

For what seemed like an eternity, Carrie stared over Linsey's shoulders at some invisible point as if weighing her response. Then she smiled at her unexpected guests and said pleasantly, "Why don't we take our coffee into the sitting room? We'll be more comfortable there."

Hank said something under his breath. Linsey smothered her impatience. Darren politely pulled out Carrie's chair and loaded the cups onto the tray she handed him.

Carrie clearly wasn't going to talk until she was ready, Linsey realized. Whatever knowledge she had would be given at her own pace. One thing was certain—Ronald Deane had confided in Carrie Bates.

Their hostess led them through an archway into a long living room, pleasantly furnished in western style with deep, cushioned chairs and a couch placed comfortably in front of a huge rock-faced fireplace. "Would you light the fire, Hank? I'll be back in a moment."

Darren and Linsey sat down at one end of a long sofa and he put down the tray on a smooth slab of polished wood that had been fashioned into a coffee table. Linsey glanced curiously around the room. Varied paintings on the wall, an assortment of books, and albums of popular and classical music stacked near a stereo indicated that here was a woman of eclectic tastes. With mixed emotions, Linsey wondered how many of the things her father had given Carrie.

"Your eyes are popping with excitement," Darren said in a soft voice. "I hope you're not going to be disappointed."

"Whatever we find out will be better than ignorance. I just can't believe that my father kept Carrie a secret from all of us."

"Maybe he was intimidated by his daughters."

"You have to be kidding!"

"No, I'm not. Whether you know it or not, you could intimidate any man on almost any level you chose."

"Me?" She gave a laugh. "Maybe Abigail. She's one impressive gal and has always left Kate and me a little in awe. If she were in this situation, I bet she'd have the answers and the solution already laid out in her mind. And Kate." She laughed. "Heaven knows what Kate would do. You really must meet my sisters." Then she caught herself. "Sometime."

"I'd love to."

His hand found hers, and she was grateful for the way his fingers curved gently in a firm hold. His touch was infinitely disturbing. For a moment they looked at each other. Feelings that Linsey had been trying to deny swelled like an incoming tide. The sensation was frightening, and she stiffened in an attempt to resist it as she pulled her hand away.

Carrie came back into the room, carrying something wrapped in a striped tea towel. She stopped in front of the couch and loosened the cloth. "Your father gave me this."

Linsey gasped.

A beautiful, shiny bar of gold bullion gleamed back at her.

Now Linsey knew what had put her life in jeopardy. GOLD!

Chapter Seven

"Holy Jehoshaphat!" exclaimed Hank. "Would you look at that!" His rounded eyes feasted on the gold bar.

Carrie laid it on the coffee table and then eased herself into a nearby chair. "I'm glad to get out from under the responsibility of keeping it in the house. Ronald told me there was more where this one came from."

Darren gave a long, low whistle.

"Holy cow!" Hank swore. "You're sure that's what my old buddy said?"

Carrie nodded. "He gave me the gold bar and made me promise not to tell anyone about it until he gave the word."

"Where did he find it?" Linsey was finally able to speak.

"I don't know, but it's from a shipment of gold intended for the Confederate army. Wagon #2065, he said." She pointed to the picture of the metal tag. "I bet that came off the lost wagon. You can barely make out the numbers."

"Lost wagon?" repeated Darren.

"Oh, my gosh!" Linsey gasped. "You don't mean my father really found it? The lost wagon of gold?"

"Found what? For heaven's sake, tell me what on earth a Confederacy wagon #2065 has to do with all of this," Darren demanded in an exasperated tone.

Hank laughed. "Well, don't this beat all. That son of a gun found gold up in them Colorado hills, after all."

Linsey took a deep breath. "It's an old legend, Darren, like the Lost Dutchman Mine in Arizona," she explained.

"That old coot!" Hank laughed again. "We talked about it plenty, but nobody really believed that old story."

Darren looked impatiently at Linsey. "What story?"

"During the Civil War, Confederate sympathizers working in the Colorado goldfields sent several wagons loaded with gold bullion to the South to help the rebels' cause," Linsey told him. "According to legend, one of the wagons was lost or hijacked before it left the Rockies. Treasure hunters have spent their lives looking for the lost wagon down through the years."

"I know there's a bunch of Southerners who come to Colorado every year looking for it," said Carrie.

Linsey nodded. "My sister got acquainted with them. They're quite serious about the hunt, and so was my father. He roamed all over these mountains in his job as geologist, and he used to joke about hunting for the lost wagon, but we never took him seriously."

"Good old Ron must have found it, all right," cackled Hank. "Where's the rest of it, Carrie?"

"I told you, I don't know. Really, I don't."

"He must have told you something," Hank insisted.

"No, he didn't. When I asked Ronald what he was up to, he just gave me a secret little smile. He was as excited as a school boy with a secret, I can tell you that. He told me I'd find out in good time. You know how he was. Full of life and always dreaming big dreams. I just laughed with him.

He seemed to be getting such a kick out of the whole thing that I just went along and kept the gold.''

"When did he give it to you?" Darren asked.

"Just before that last hunting trip when he got hurt. He brought the bar here to the ranch and made me promise not to tell anyone about it. He told me he wanted to set up some kind of a family treasure hunt."

"A treasure hunt?" echoed Hank. "Why'd he do a fool thing like that?"

"He never expected it to turn into a deadly game," Carrie assured him.

"Did he tell you what the clues meant?" Darren asked hopefully.

"No. When I visited him in the hospital, I asked him what I should do about the gold, and he told me to keep it. I remember there was a glint of excitement in his eyes when he told me that he was working out things while he was laid up." Carrie bit her lip. "Of course, Ronald thought he'd be out of the hospital in a few weeks. We didn't know—" she faltered "—that a blood clot moving to his heart would kill him."

"Rotten luck," Hank muttered. "Who'd think a couple of broken bones would cause something like that?"

Carrie took a deep breath. "Anyway, he died before he could carry out his plans. Ronald didn't show me the photos or tell me where the gold was hidden. I'm sorry. Apart from what I've already told, I'm as much in the dark as the rest of you."

"He must have taken a picture of the metal tag and the mountain where he found the wagon," Hank reasoned.

"And set it up so we were to go to Hank's and then come here for the next clue," Darren speculated.

Linsey nodded. " 'Look beyond the chimney rocks.' A very clever clue." Her father had always been very cre-

ative. She knew he must have worked on the clues to keep
the treasure hunt moving. What next? she wondered.
Ronald Deane had set in motion a series of events that kept
going like a runaway train after his death.

Hank puffed on his pipe. "Don't that beat all. Ron
never said one word to me. Nary a hint. He was all excited
about something on that last camping trip we took together. I know that," he said. "He gave me that card of his
and told me to put it in a safe place." He scratched his
head. "Gosh dern it, can't rightly remember what I did
with it. Do you suppose it's important?"

"It might be," said Linsey. There was no telling how
elaborate her father's planning had been.

"It might be another clue," Darren said.

"You think so? Reckon I should have stuck it in my
wallet instead—" Hank's voice broke off. He lifted his
eyes in surprise. "Instead of sticking it in the compartment of my Scout. I 'member now."

"Then you still have it?" Linsey asked eagerly.

"Nope." He took several more puffs on his pipe and
squinted against the smoke. "Sure wish I did, but I traded
in the Scout for my pickup."

"Didn't you transfer the stuff from one glove compartment to another?" Darren inquired. "That's what most
people do when they get a different car."

Hank cocked his head. "Don't rightly 'member. Guess
I could bring in the stuff, and we could have ourselves a
look." He cackled. "Gold. A whole wagon load of it. Sure
looks like my old buddy stumbled onto something pretty
important."

*Important enough for treasure hunters to kill us to get
it*. The unspoken thought was contained in the look that
Linsey and Darren exchanged.

Hank ambled toward the door. "I'll take a peek in the truck and see what I can find. Be back in a minute."

While they had been talking, Darren's hand had found Linsey's. His fingers curled around hers, bringing warmth with his touch. "You all right?" he asked.

"Just a little stunned. My father has turned a parlor game into a deadly hunt. Where will it end?"

"Ronald would be devastated to think he had put your life in danger, Linsey," said Carrie. "I just don't understand how it happened. How could those terrible men have gotten Ronald's photos?"

"If we knew that, we might be able to make sense out of this nightmare. But at least we know what Beale and Jake are after," Darren observed.

"If we're right in thinking my father found the Confederate wagon, we're talking about a fortune in gold bullion."

"And they need you or your sisters to decode the clues. Nobody else would know about it."

"What about Douglas Brady?"

"It's possible," he admitted.

Linsey turned to Carrie. "Did you know that my father had an affair with an army nurse during the Korean War? And that he fathered a son?"

The only sound for a long moment was the spitting of the fire. Linsey waited, watching Carrie's face.

Finally she nodded. "I think he was tired of secrets. All those years he kept his life compartmentalized. I know he never told you girls about me. It didn't matter when I was healthy and busy with my own life. Your father loved me, and that was enough. I really didn't want to leave here, and there didn't seem to be any place for me in your home. You were content there, Linsey, and he didn't want to disturb you by bringing another woman into the house."

"How was I to know he was ready to marry again?" Linsey couldn't keep the anger out of her voice. "Did he think I was so set in my ways that I would reject a new wife? When my mother died, I took over running the household. My sisters left, and I kept the family home intact for him as much as for myself. How dare he insult my devotion by keeping his true feelings hidden from me?"

"Easy," Darren cautioned. "I'm sure he was only thinking of your happiness."

"Yes. He always put you girls above everything. If I had remained physically strong, we would have gone on as always. But when my health began to fail, Ronald asked me to marry him so he could take care of me. It was then that he told me about his former love affair. I knew there had been a child."

"He told you about him. Why wasn't he honest with us?" Linsey's anger flared up again. "He should have told us years ago that we had a half brother."

"Ronald was afraid to let you find out that he wasn't the perfect man all of you idolized." Carrie smiled wanly. "He had his faults like anybody else. It was easier to put the past behind him. Your mother never knew about the infidelity, and he decided that no good would come of telling his daughters."

"But to deny his own son all these years!" Linsey protested. "Kate called me and told me that Aunt Etta had heard from our half brother, and that he was coming to Crystal Lakes to see us. Abigail and I didn't believe it for a minute. We've been the victims of confidence games before, and we decided this was just another attempt by a con artist to get his hands on the Deane investments. Abigail talked me into going to Aunt Etta's to make sure that Kate didn't land us all in a mess. She's gullible as they come, and I went to Crystal Lakes to prove them wrong. Only it turns out that the joke's on me. I guess there really is a half brother. It would have been better if we'd known.''

"Yes, but hindsight is twenty-twenty vision, Linsey. Ronald must have decided to bring his children together, but he ran out of time. You haven't told me what his illegitimate son has to do with all of this.''

"One of our abductors showed me a letter, addressed to 'My natural son, Douglas Brady.' I think it was my father's handwriting, but I can't be sure.''

"A letter addressed to Ronald's son? But how did that man get it?'' A puzzled expression put creases onto Carrie's forehead.

"That horrible man, Beale, claims that Douglas Brady was showing the letter and the photos around a Louisiana bar. They must have taken them off him.''

"Linsey and I couldn't figure out why. We didn't know what they were after,'' admitted Darren. "But now we do.''

"A wagon full of gold bullion would be worth a fortune on today's market,'' said Linsey. "No wonder they're ready to kill for it.''

Hank whistled as he came into the room. "If that gold really came from the lost wagon, my old buddy found himself a treasure, all right.''

"Maybe he was just playing some kind of joke. Pretending this bar came from the lost treasure. What do you think, Linsey?''

She closed her eyes for a moment. She didn't know what to think. Maybe her father had conceived an idea for a real treasure hunt—and maybe not.

"I think Ronald was sincere,'' said Carrie. "I think the treasure hunt is for real.''

Hank threw a handful of papers onto the coffee table, sat down on the floor and began sorting through them.

"Lemme see what I can find in this mess." He fumbled through crumpled receipts, automobile registrations and miscellaneous bills. He squinted at bits of paper, smoothed them out, and then tossed them aside.

Hank must use his glove compartment as a catchall, Linsey thought, as she helped him to look through the mess. Some of the dated stuff was three years old. It would be a miracle to find anything in all that junk.

Hank proved her wrong. "Lookee here!" He triumphantly held up a small white card. "I'll be goldarned if it ain't the one that Ronald gave me. Got something written on the back of it, too." He squinted at it, then handed it to Linsey.

Darren and Linsey silently read the card together.

"What does it say?" asked Carrie, obviously trying to read their expressions. The question was in her eyes. Surprise? Relief? Disappointment? Linsey wondered, glancing at the older woman.

"It's another clue," Linsey said. "Another obtuse, incomprehensible rhyme. 'Pass Along The Family Tree and Raise a Glass to History.'"

Hank scratched his head. "Don't make no sense to me."

"Why would a man who found a fortune in gold bullion want to play games?"

Linsey sighed deeply. "It's just the kind of thing my father would do. But he would have never guessed the vicious turn of events his game would take. I know he planned to be with us every step of the way, laughing at our mistakes, encouraging us, beaming when we were successful. All of us having fun." She looked at Carrie. "I couldn't figure why the clue sent us here, but now I know. My father chose this way to bring us all together. Sending us here to your ranch was deliberate. He wanted us to meet you."

Carrie nodded. "How different things would be tonight if he were here. He would never have wanted to put your life in danger," she agreed. "Thank heavens, you made it safely here. You can relax now. In the morning you can tell Sheriff Wooten everything."

Darren squeezed her hand. "He'll know what to do."

Hank relighted his pipe. "Well, now. I don't know if that's such a good idea."

"Why not?" asked Linsey.

"Well, the way I see it, your pa wouldn't want someone else to get there ahead of his girls. You see what I mean?"

"No. What are you afraid of?"

"You show them pictures around, and you'll have more hunters on these mountains than peas in a pea patch."

Nobody spoke for a moment.

"I think he's right," Darren said. "This whole thing has to be handled very carefully. If there really is a treasure, and if your father found it, and if we have clues to where it's hidden—"

"A lot of 'ifs'," said Linsey.

"It'd be better if we could figure out the thing ourselves." Hank chomped on his pipe. "You ought to know what your pa meant, Linsey, honey. Just think on it a bit."

Linsey read the card again. "'Raise a glass' might refer to a toast," she speculated.

"Did your father have a favorite one?" asked Darren.

Linsey shook her head. "Not that I can think of. Do you know of one, Carrie?"

Carrie admitted she'd never heard him make a toast of any kind. "He just drank his beer and licked the foam off his lips." Her smile was pensive.

"What about 'family tree'?" Hank prodded.

Darren gave Linsey an encouraging smile. "Is there somebody famous or infamous in the Deane genealogy?"

Again she shook her head. "We had a grandfather who was a judge on the Colorado supreme court, and a great-aunt who ran a bawdy house in Alabama. Other than that, I think we're a pretty boring family. I haven't a foggy notion what my father was referring to by 'family tree.' The whole thing's gibberish," she said impatiently.

"Maybe there was a Southerner in your family?" suggested Carrie. "Maybe Ronald was referring to him. Someone who was looking for the gold—or maybe accused of being one of the men who was involved in its disappearance."

"I can't think of anybody in our family but Aunt Etta, my father's sister, who might know something about a family tree."

"Let's ask her," urged Hank.

"She's away on a cruise. But I'm going to call Kate and Abigail." Linsey got to her feet. "It's time they knew what's going on."

"Good idea," agreed Darren. He watched her leave the room, admiring her straight little back and graceful carriage. He had to acknowledge that he felt an indefinable sense of loss whenever she was out of sight. His feelings were mixed and at the same time contradictory. He was both thankful and regretful that his responsibility for Linsey was over.

Hank started telling Carrie about an old treasure map that he'd once bought from an old prospector. Darren only half listened as his thoughts careened in every direction. Some sensible inner voice admonished him that tomorrow he could return to his seminar and go on to Canada with a clear conscience. Linsey would be in good hands with Hank and Carrie. It was stupid even to think of continuing any contact with her. He had been waiting for a long time to get back on track. He'd be stupid to get involved with another female who could put new shackles on him, especially one like Linsey who obviously enjoyed classical music, good art, literary books, and fine food—things he'd never had time to learn about or appreciate. His favorite music was the sweet tones of a wailing guitar, and he appreciated a Rockwell print as much as a Degas painting. There was enough beauty in a sunset and a diamond-studded ski slope to stir his blood. With Linsey Deane he was out of his cultural depth in a good many ways, and he was glad he'd held his feelings for her on a short rein.

She was back in a few minutes with an exasperated expression on her face. "Nobody answers at either number. Abigail's probably still in Washington, but I wonder where on earth Kate is?" Her eyes widened. "You don't think they went back after her?"

"No, I don't," Darren declared flatly. "Remember Beale said one sister was as good as another. They caught you instead of Kate when you wandered into their clutches first. Wherever your sister is, she's probably a whole lot safer than you have been. Now quit worrying. I suggest we all get some sleep, and we can work everything out in the morning, before the sheriff gets here."

"Yes, of course," Carrie agreed. "That's the sensible thing to do. Take any bedroom upstairs that you want. I have a small one on the first floor at the back of the house so I don't have to climb the stairs. The rooms are all laid out. I hope you all have a good night's sleep." She smiled at them without getting up.

"Thanks so much for your hospitality," said Linsey. Carrie's pallor and lassitude hinted at a deep-seated illness. Compassion washed over Linsey. "I'm so glad my father sent us here. I'll bring my sisters to meet you."

"I would like that. Have a pleasant night. After what you've been through, I'll bet you won't open your eyes till morning."

"Every muscle in my body thanks you for a nice warm bed."

"The blue and white bedroom at the top of the stairs has some night things in the drawers and some of my clothes in the closet, Linsey. Please feel free to help yourself. There's another one for Darren across the hall. My bedroom is downstairs, and there's a guest room for Hank on this floor, too."

Impulsively Linsey bent over and kissed Carrie's wan cheek.

Darren took Carrie's hand and squeezed it. "You're an angel, letting us fall in on you like this."

She smiled. "I told you. I'm happy for the company."

Hank stood up. "Let me take this stuff into the kitchen for you, Carrie." He collected the coffee mugs on a tray.

"Thank you, Hank. I think I'll sit here by the fire and read for a while."

"Good night, then," Darren said.

"See you in the morning." Linsey turned to Darren. "Shall we find those bedrooms?"

He took her elbow as they went up the stairs to a wide hall that ran the width of the house. They stopped in front of the first open door and peeked in. A pretty blue and white bedroom furnished in an old-fashioned style was a welcoming sight, and a half-opened bathroom door promised the luxury of a hot bath.

"I'll take this room," said Linsey. "And it looks like there's another bedroom right across the hall." Her voice trailed away. She wanted Darren near her, but wasn't going to ask him outright to choose that room.

"I could stay closer than that if you want me to."

"Like outside my door?" she quipped.

"No, like inside."

Was he teasing or serious? "I don't think that will be necessary, but thank you for the gallant offer. You— you've been wonderful," she stammered.

"It wasn't hard to play Knight to The Rescue. You bring out that kind of feeling in a man, you know."

"I do?" she asked, puzzled. "My sisters are the ones who have feminine appeal. I'm . . . I'm just sensible."

He rested one hand on the door frame behind her head and looked down at her. "I have perfectly good eyes. I see a very attractive woman who exudes femininity like perfume. There's a fragility about you that is very deceptive."

"Really?" Her heart was spinning like a raft heading over Niagara Falls.

"No one would expect to find iron-ribbed stubbornness and courage in such a petite package. You were very, very brave today."

"Thanks for coming here with me. I know that tomorrow you'll want to get back to Crystal Lakes. I'm sorry to have intruded into your life like this."

Her blue eyes gazed up at him with a vulnerable air. Fool that he was, he knew he didn't want to leave her. "Yes, that's the sensible thing to do. Get back to my seminar and my job. But I don't feel sensible." Slowly he bent his head toward hers.

She did not move back but waited, looking up at him.

Purposefully he reached out and pulled her into his arms. She looked a little surprised, but did not pull away. Her lips were as soft and pliable as he had imagined, and the sweet length of her body pressed against him stirred him even more than he had expected. He forgot his resolution to stay clear of such a tender trap. A pull like a magnetic field flared between them, and he felt her rise onto her toes. Their lips met again. This time a surge of desire sped through him with such force that he drew back like someone who had touched his finger to a flame.

He dropped his hands to his sides. "I guess this is goodbye, then," he said huskily.

She nodded.

"Call me if you need me."

She wondered what he would do if she confessed that she needed him very much, that the deep feelings he had aroused in her were making a mockery of her ordered life. He would most likely be embarrassed by such a confession, and it would unfairly put him under more obligation than he already felt. "Good night," she said in a formal tone.

"Leave your door open," he ordered.

Her eyes questioned him, hoping that no bold invitation lurked in her expression.

"In case you have a nightmare—or something," he answered briskly, then disappeared into the room across the hall.

Fluttering feelings stayed with her while she showered and as she slipped into one of Carrie's high-necked flannel nightgowns and climbed into the high bed, which had deep springs and a thick mattress. She let out a blissful sigh as she burrowed beneath the quilted covers. Darren's kiss still lingered on her lips. Fatigue, warmth and physical exhaustion drew her into a deep sleep.

SHE MUST HAVE been asleep a couple of hours when shots rang out on the floor below. Fright surged through her as she tried to remember where she was. Then it all came back. Instantly she was on her feet. Beale and Jake! Her abductors had come to Carrie's house! Hank's trick had not worked, after all. Somehow the kidnappers must have followed them here.

She saw Darren streak by her bedroom door with a rifle in his hands.

"What's happened?"

She followed him, nearly tripping on the too-long nightgown whipping around her legs.

"Stay back!" he yelled at her as he raced across the hall into the living room.

But it was too late. Through the open living-room doors she saw Carrie's crumpled body on the floor. She had fallen forward out of her chair and was lying apparently lifeless in a pool of blood.

Darren ran over and knelt down beside her body. Linsey held her breath, but she knew even before Darren shook his head that it was too late.

"She's been shot," he said. "At close range."

Anger surged through Linsey, coating her shock with rage. No one deserved that kind of death, and especially not a sweet, tender person like Carrie. "Why? Why?"

Darren's hands were clenched as he stood up.

"There's Hank," said Linsey, pointing outside. The front door was open.

"Stay here!" Darren ordered, but Linsey ignored him. She was right at his heels as he crossed the hall and went out the door.

Hank, half dressed, was on the porch, with his rifle clutched in his hands.

"Did you see who did it, Hank?" asked Darren, searching the shifting shadows, keeping his rifle leveled in shooting position.

"No, they got away. I was sleeping in a room behind the kitchen. The front door was already opened when I ran into the hall with my gun. I heard 'em take off. Dang blasted, I didn't even get off one shot.''

"Carrie's dead," said Linsey as they went back inside.

"Them low-down, murdering critters," Hank swore. "I thought I heard something. A half hour ago, my hunter's ear warned me there was movement outside the house. If I'd gotten up then…" He shook his head. Tears glinted in his eyes and he wiped them away.

"It must have been Beale and Jake," said Darren.

"But why would they kill her?"

"I don't know. She must have been sitting in her chair reading when they broke in," Darren conjectured. "There was an open book on the floor beside her."

"The gold," said Linsey in a near whisper.

"What?"

"Did they take the gold bar?"

Hank swore.

"Let's have a look," Darren suggested.

Linsey sat down on the bottom step. She didn't have the stomach to go back into the living room again. She was not surprised when Darren came back a moment later and said, "It's gone. It was on the coffee table when we all went to bed. But it's not there now."

"They killed her and took it!"

"Do you think they were after me?"

"Seems reasonable. I guess we weren't as clever as we thought. They followed us here. Came in, saw Carrie, grabbed the gold and fled."

"It must have happened that way," she agreed.

"I'm betting they'll try again," said Darren.

"Holy Jehoshaphat. We've got to get out of here." For the first time Hank sounded worried. "I'll call the sheriff and tell him we're coming. You two get dressed."

"Shouldn't we stay here? Wait for the sheriff?" she protested.

"Nope, we'll be safer in the truck," said Hank. "They could set fire to this place and force us out. Darren and I can shoot their heads off if Jake or Beale try to stop us. With us going down the road in one direction and the sheriff coming from the other, we'll trap the murdering thieves! They ain't gonna kill Carrie and get away with it."

Linsey's mind wouldn't function.

She went back upstairs and dressed mechanically. Before going to bed she had laid out one of Carrie's cotton blouses to wear under her jacket, thankful to have something to wear instead of her dirty pullover.

"All right, let's go," said Hank when the three of them had gathered in the kitchen.

"What about Carrie?" asked Linsey. "It doesn't seem right just to leave her."

"Nothing ain't gonna harm her now. Slowly dying, she was," said Hank. "Anyways, she's out of her pain now."

"We put her on the sofa and covered her with a sheet," said Darren. "That's the best we can do until the law gets here. She'd want us to get you out of danger."

"I guess so," Linsey said reluctantly.

With guns loaded and ready, the three of them hurried out of the house and into the truck. The foreboding she had felt about coming to Carrie's ranch had proved valid. She should have heeded the premonition. Carrie might still be alive if she had.

Hank drove recklessly, sending wheels skidding close to the edge of the mountain road in the dark. Linsey cried out in fright as the truck squealed around a curve and one wheel seemed to hang in midair.

"Slow down, Hank," Darren ordered. "Won't do Carrie any good now if you land us at the bottom of one of these ravines."

"This thing's got me so het up, I want to lash out at somebody," the other man admitted, easing the pressure off his big boot on the gas. "Sure misjudged them varmints."

"They must have doubled back, followed us to Carrie's, and waited until they thought we were all asleep," Darren speculated.

"And when they saw Carrie sitting there reading, they shot her." Linsey almost choked on the words.

"And stole the gold bar," added Hank, tight-lipped. "Well, we'll get it back for you, honey."

"I don't care about the gold! I wish my father had never found it."

"Too late for that kind of wishing, honey. Your pa sure stirred up a hornet's nest with this little game. I never figured it was anything like this when he was looking so smug on that hunting trip. He shoulda told me what he was planning."

"Somebody should have talked some sense into him, all right," Darren growled.

Linsey started to answer him, but at that moment lights from behind hit the truck's rearview mirror.

"Well, I'll be jiggered. How'd they get behind us?" Hank exclaimed and stamped on the gas. They had passed the junction where one road led to Carrie's place and the other up Sawtooth Peak. "They must've been waiting for us."

"Where's the blasted sheriff?" Darren swore. "How far is it to the junction? You think we can outrun them?"

"Sure 'nough!" Excitement laced Hank's voice. "Nobody knows these roads better'n me. A glimpse of our taillight is all they'll get."

The promise was short-lived.

With a loud bang, the front left tire blew. Hank fought for control. The truck swerved, skidding dangerously. High speed and the narrow road sent the truck plowing down a deep embankment—into the solid trunk of a ponderosa pine.

Chapter Eight

The jolt shot Linsey headfirst toward the windshield. If Darren hadn't flung out an arm in time, she would have gone right through. The pickup truck behind them on the road gunned its engine.

"Get out!" shouted Hank. "Run like hell. Give me your gun, Darren. I'll keep 'em busy till you two get away." He was out of the car, a rifle under each arm, and running low along the side of the road toward the truck that was screeching toward them. Moonlight spilled upon the ground, giving an eerie illumination to the scene.

Any hope that it might not be their abductors faded as Linsey glimpsed Beale's thick form as he leaped out of the Ford truck the minute it stopped. A bullet from Hank's rifle into the door stopped the brute from coming after them as Darren shoved Linsey ahead of him up a rocky embankment.

An exchange of gunshots sent fiery tongues sparking into the night. Beale and Jake must have waited just out of sight for their prey to run right into their net again, thought Linsey. Maybe they had even set something on the road to blow the tire. How long could Hank keep shooting? And what would happen to him once he ran out of bullets?

She ran beside Darren up a rugged incline. In her panic she lost her footing, and would have slipped back to the bottom if Darren hadn't caught her around the waist. "Easy—hurry!"

A contradiction in terms, she thought, gasping for breath. They scrambled up a shelf of rocks cut deep into the narrow ravine. Her hands grew scratched and began to bleed as she clawed her way upward, often on all fours.

The capricious moon took that particular moment to come out from behind fast-moving clouds. It shone down upon them as they mounted the steep cliff, highlighting them like two black bugs against the gray limestone back-drop.

They heard a wild exchange of gunfire. Beale shouted something, then the night fell deadly quiet. *They've killed Hank!* Sobs caught in Linsey's throat.

"Keep going!" Darren commanded, as all strength seemed to go out of her. "We're almost to the top!"

"I can't." Horror engulfed her. First Carrie and now Hank, murdered!

"Move!" Darren gave her a shove upward, then scrambled over the top of the ridge himself. They ran a short distance, then he grabbed her hand and pulled her down into a thicket of scratchy junipers. They were out of sight and range of the gunman below and would be able to hear anyone climbing after them. Maybe Beale and Jake hadn't seen in which direction they had run, Darren thought hopefully. Hank had kept them pretty busy until . . .

"Hank," she echoed, as if reading his thoughts. "They shot him."

Darren's mouth hardened. "He gave us a chance to get away. We can't blow it. Come on."

They plunged through the trees as fast as the darkness would allow. Just when they needed moonlight to give them some visibility, the moon deserted them, like a spiteful creature playing hide-and-seek behind the clouds. When the pine, cedar and spruce trees thinned out, interlacing branches of aspen saplings clung to their arms and legs and scraped their faces.

"Maybe they won't come after us," she gasped, fighting her way through the thicket.

"I'm not betting our lives on it. Keep moving."

"Beale's too fat to climb that cliff," she insisted, knowing she was acting like a child, starting some insane argument in order to avoid the truth.

"Jake isn't."

"But maybe they'll give up," she argued stubbornly. *Carrie and now Hank.* Where would it end?

The flicker of a flashlight behind them was their answer. It was probably Jake. He was agile enough to climb the steep incline. Darren swore under his breath, and Linsey felt pure anger rise like bile into her throat. She had never felt the urge to kill before, but it was there now. If she had had a gun, she would have stayed her ground, turned around and pulled the trigger.

They fled like helpless creatures being harrowed by a vicious hound, lurching breathlessly through the underbrush, weaving between the trees and stumbling over dead logs and dried branches. The noise they made pinpointed the path of their escape in the echoing night. Owls hooted, and night creatures scurried away from their loud thrashing. In their mad flight, they almost fell when the ground suddenly sloped drastically under their feet. The sound of rushing water greeted them as they stumbled down a steep fault in the mountain.

At the bottom of the ravine they discovered a wide stream flowing swiftly through a rock-pitted channel. Spume from white water splashed around glistening black stones and tumbled over fallen logs that were half submerged in the water. Linsey and Darren looked frantically upstream and then down. The white-foamed water rushed past steep cuts in the mountain, with no bank in either direction on their side of the stream. The only way to run was back up the slope into the arms of their pursuer. They were blocked. Trapped!

As if to accentuate their plight, a tiny circle of light flashed through the trees high above them. Purposefully a flashlight's orange glare moved downward, coming closer and closer to the spot where they stood helpless on the edge of the stream.

Darren swore, feeling Linsey's hand tremble in his. His mind raced. No chance to get by Jake if they tried to retrace their steps.

"What can we do?" asked Linsey in a deadly calm voice as if she already knew the answer.

His eyes scanned the opposite bank that offered a thin, rocky passage along the water's edge. "We have to get across."

"How? It's too deep and too fast for wading," she protested. A hundred times as a child she had been lectured about the treachery of these ice-cold, swift mountain streams. Accounts of drownings involving careless fishermen were common. "It would be pure suicide to wade into those waters."

"And suicide—or worse—not to. See those rocks?" He pointed to some boulders that lay scattered in the water.

"They're wet and slippery."

"Some of them are close enough to step on."

"But they don't go all the way across."

"We'll have to jump to the log that reaches halfway."

She gulped back her horror. *Rounded wet rocks, and a decayed log.* Darren was insane. But he was also correct. The river was their only chance.

"I'll go first. You follow my footing."

"What if you fall in?"

A flicker of amusement touched his grim mouth for a second. "In that case, use your own judgment."

He stepped out onto the closest rock, and water surged over the tips of his boots. His long leg reached out for the next rock and the next one.

Linsey stood mesmerized. She couldn't do it. The rocks were too far apart, the white-foaming stream too fast. She wasn't a water lover under the best of conditions, and this crazed, roaring mountain stream made an outright coward of her.

"Come on!" shouted Darren from midstream. "Move, Linsey, move!" He stood there waiting, balancing on the slippery rocks in the middle of a foaming cauldron.

"I'm coming." The words were feebly spoken, drowned by the roar of surging water. She couldn't risk his life by standing there immobilized by fear. Linsey stepped out onto the first rock and then the next. The third was a stretch for her legs and for a moment she tottered, afraid to reach out to it.

"Linsey!"

His voice steadied her, she lurched across the space and put both feet onto the same glistening rock. Now the roar of the stream was deafening. Looking down was a bad mistake, she realized, as she stared at the maelstrom circling the rock on which she teetered. Moonlight caught the rampaging waters, creating a liquid sculpture. Sparkles, glints and silvery swirls were hypnotic, rushing, changing, leaping, flowing, surging, and splashing her feet in a diabolical frolic. How pretty it was, she thought on some de-

Return this card **TODAY** to qualify for the $1,000,000.00 Grand Prize **PLUS** a Cadillac Coupe de Ville **AND** over 5000 other cash prizes!

If offer card is missing, write to: Harlequin Reader Service® 901 Fuhrmann Blvd P.O. Box 1867 Buffalo NY 14269-1867

DETACH ALONG DOTTED LINE

tached level, schooling herself not to close her eyes for even a second. She must not give in to the vertigo that was threatening to engulf her. She forced herself to look away from the water. The moving flashlight was halfway down the slope. Once Jake came out of the trees, he would see them.

Frozen in the middle of the stream, Linsey watched as Darren reached the fallen log and crawled along it toward the other bank. How had he managed to jump far enough from this rock to reach the fallen tree trunk? From where she stood, she could not see any bridge of rocks that reached that far. Too late, she realized that she had not watched him carefully enough. Where had he stepped? The distance was too far to jump. She'd never make it. "Darren!" she screamed. "It's too far."

He reached the bank, turned, motioned frantically with his arms and shouted something that she could not hear over the thunder of the stream. An expression of pure terror crossed his face as the flashlight's beam caught her.

Now she had no choice. She leaped toward the log—and missed it! She cried out as she fell into the churning waters. The shock of the ice-cold water took away her breath and almost smothered her as she went under and was caught in the swiftly rolling current. The force of the water tumbled her over and over, beating at her like some fiendish masseur as it carried her downstream.

Gulping in the icy water, Linsey flailed her arms, but her grasping fingers found no purchase in the swiftly moving waters until, by some miracle, she grabbed a submerged root that reached outward from the bank. Clinging to the gnarled root with both hands as the frigid water tugged and pulled at her, thundering loudly in her ears and filling her mouth and eyes, she managed to raise her head. The hold she had on the twisted wood kept her from being swept downstream, but the root was wet and slick and slowly slipped through her hands. A few more seconds and the struggle would be over. Her strength was going, and the temperature of the water numbed every inch of her body. She did not even feel the firm hands on her until she was dragged out of the water.

"Darren." His name almost stuck in her throat as he carried her behind some boulders about fifteen feet down from where she had fallen in.

He stripped off his coat and wrapped it around her shivering body. He had seen her go under and then come up only a short distance away. Like a madman he had leaped over boulders and tumbled debris until he reached the spot where she lay half-submerged in the stream. For a split second she almost floated away from him, then he had her, before the force of the tumbling waters pulled him in, too.

"Linsey...Linsey, love." He pushed back drenched tendrils of hair from her face. Her lips were blue, and water glistened on her eyelashes. The last few minutes had proven how precious her safety was to him. With her wet hair plastered around her face and her clear complexion as white as chalk, she laid low the defenses he had tried to raise against her. He swore at himself for not having taken better care of her. She would have raised a fuss, but he should have carried her piggyback across the blasted stream.

He held her close and tried to warm her with his body heat. Rubbing her cheeks with his hands, he sighed with relief as color returned. No sign of their pursuer. After seeing Linsey tumble into the water, it wasn't likely that Jake would follow. For the moment they were safe on this side of the stream, Darren thought with relief.

"What were you trying to do—drown yourself?" His tone was scolding, but his eyes caressed her face.

Her teeth chattered. "The damn log...was too far away."

"Didn't you see me step on a couple of rocks just under the water?"

She shook her head.

"Well, no matter. I don't think Jake will try to cross where we did. Not after seeing you fall like that. And there's no way he can follow us unless he manages to get across. I think we ought to follow the water downstream. That's what you're supposed to do if you get lost. And we are lost, aren't we?" His eyes questioned hers. "Do you know where we are?"

She shook her head. "This isn't the stream my father used to fish. It's on the wrong side of the road. I don't have any idea where this one comes out."

"We could stay here until daylight, if you'd rather."

The offer was tempting. She was tired and frightened, and the chance to close her eyes and sleep against Darren's chest offered a pleasant prospect. She liked the way his arms went around her and the way he cuddled her as if she were something fragile. Being comforted and looked after was very nice. Very nice indeed. The usual need to assert her feminine independence was not exactly strong at the moment. Then she felt him shiver and realized that he was almost as cold and wet as she.

"I think we should keep moving." She withdrew from his arms and stood up. The night air hit her wet clothes, and even the warmth of his jacket couldn't dispel a bone-deep chill. "Let's get walking so I can warm up."

They hiked along the stream until a narrowing in its channel forced them upward. The curtain of night faded to a gray swath of dawn—and then they saw it.

A weathered miner's shack was perched high above the stream, close to a pile of rock tailings. The sight was a familiar one to Linsey. The Colorado mountains were pocked with old mine shafts and cabins left by miners who had hoped to find rich veins of gold and silver. This one looked absolutely inviting.

"Do you want to hike up to it?" asked Darren, "or try to get back to the stream?"

"I want to get warm."

"If we stop, we lose time," he warned.

"I know, but that tumbledown shack is so beautiful."

He laughed at her wistful expression. "All right. Let's see what creature comforts lie under that sagging roof."

They hiked up to the small structure. A rough-hewn door hung lopsidedly on dangling hinges, and Darren had to lift it in order to push it open.

Not a very promising welcome, but the inside was better, he decided with relief. "Someone's obviously used the place in the not so distant past," he said.

"A stove!" she cried and squealed with delight.

A small wood stove sat in one corner with a blackened smokestack sticking up through a hole in the roof. A pile of dirty sheepskins lay in one corner beside some cut wood. On a homemade shelf pounded into the wall Darren found a glass jar. He held it up triumphantly. "Matches. How about a fire, m'lady?" he asked in a polite tone.

"Thank you, kind sir." She giggled, feeling slightly tipsy from too much stress and too many physical demands. "Can I help?"

"No."

She dropped onto the pile of sheepskins and leaned her head against the log wall. Would she ever be able to get up again? Exhaustion overrode her fear, even though she knew they should keep moving. With millions of dollars in gold at stake, Beale and Jake weren't going to give up. They would comb this area until they found her. And when they did, Beale's knife would enforce their demands. She shivered. They thought that she was the key to learning where her father had found the missing wagon. *Pass along the family tree and raise a glass to history.* She closed her eyes and the rhyme repeated itself like a broken record, over and over again. Carrie... Hank.

"I've got the fire going." Darren gently took her hand. "Come on, you can sit in front of it and dry out. Take off that blouse and jacket. They're drenched." Before she could protest, he quickly stripped off the garments and handed her his jacket again. "Your pants are almost dry... so you can leave them on."

"Thanks."

He grinned at her sarcasm and hung the denim jacket and cotton blouse on nails behind the stove. Then he spread out the sheepskin and sat down beside her.

She stretched her hands toward the stove. They felt stiff and clumsy. "I wonder if I'll ever be able to play a Chopin concerto again," she said, flexing her fingers.

"Chopin? Is he the guy who never finished anything?"

She laughed. "I assume you're referring to Schubert's *Unfinished Symphony.* Not much of a classical music lover, I gather." For some reason disappointment accompanied the realization. It made clear how far apart their life-styles were. "Don't you ever go to a symphony?"

"Nope. I don't like dressing up like a penguin and sitting in an auditorium filled with a bunch of people too polite to yawn."

"You're serious, aren't you?" she said, appalled. One of her greatest pleasures was listening to a good symphony orchestra.

"I can never find the melody in all those flute trills and crashing cymbals," he confessed.

"Your ear needs educating."

"Maybe. Give me a good dance band anytime. Do you like to dance?"

"Not anymore. I'm not the *Dirty Dancing* type."

"I bet you would be, if you'd let yourself go."

"I never 'let myself go,' as you so crudely put it."

"You're a bit of a snob, you know."

"I am not!" Her anger flared up once more.

"All right . . . all right!" He held out his hands in a gesture of surrender. A quirking at the corner of his mouth hinted at a suppressed grin. She looked like a ragamuffin, yet they could have been sitting in the Waldorf Astoria instead of in a tumbledown miner's shack. In spite of everything that had happened, she still wouldn't let down the barriers. She needed educating herself. He knew it would never happen but wished he had a chance to get her onto a dance floor, to slide his hands along her back, pulling her close enough to rub her smooth hips against his own as they swayed to sensuous music. He'd show her what music was meant to be.

She closed her eyes and once more leaned back against the wall.

"Don't frown like that," he chided.

"I always frown when I think."

"Puts wrinkles in your forehead."

"I'm trying to figure out the clue Dad left with Hank. I have the feeling that it would make perfect sense, if I could just put it in the right context."

"And you can't?"

"Nope. Family tree . . . that's a real stumper. As I said before, nobody's ever done a genealogy on the Deane family, but the clue must be there somewhere. I wish Aunt

Etta weren't so far away." Linsey smiled. "She's a great gal, in her sixties, and been married four times. She owns a lot of land around Crystal Lakes. When the ski developers came in, she sold some of it for big money. She and Kate are a lot alike."

"Tell me about Kate. Maybe I'll tumble onto something."

Linsey smiled. "My youngest sister graduated from college with a degree in sociology. She's been a television weather lady, a radio deejay, a ski instructor in Aspen, a model for bathing suits in California, and a photographer's assistant in New York." Linsey laughed. "Name it. Kate's done it or been there." Then she sobered. "I hope to heaven she's all right."

"From what Beale said, they had your aunt's house staked out for her, but you walked into the trap instead. Do you think Kate might have understood the clues your father left?"

"Better than me? I don't think so. Kate doesn't have that kind of mind. Abigail would be better at deciphering Dad's messages. She has an analytical mind and handles all our business matters. Very much in charge of her life. Our abductors would have been better off snatching her, except that she'd have escaped, of course. Instead they got me," she said ruefully.

"I'm glad. And I can't imagine either of your sisters handling this situation better than you have."

She looked at him in surprise. "I thought you didn't like me."

"I don't." He kissed her lightly on the forehead. "But for some reason, I wanted to do that from about five minutes after I met you. You have lovely blue eyes that snap when you're angry and a mouth that begs to be kissed." He sighed. "You reminded me of someone I cared a great deal about once. Unfortunately that wasn't a good memory."

She stiffened. "And who was that?"

"Her name was Laura. She's the kind of woman who turns a man's heart inside out."

The edge of regret in his voice chilled the warmth that his touch had invoked in Linsey. "You loved her very much."

He nodded. "So much that I accepted a boring job in Washington for five years, because that's where she wanted to live."

"And—?" Linsey tried to keep her tone light.

"Oh, she's still there. Only with someone else. She left me as soon as a richer prospect came along. And I gladly accepted a new assignment that will take me out of the country."

He's running away, Linsey thought, and the only attraction she held for him was her resemblance to this Laura. The bizarre happenings that had thrown them together had weakened his defenses. A normal reaction for a man and woman who had been thrown together in the kind of dangerous intimacy they were sharing. Her own emotions were in as much of a tangle as Darren's. If they didn't get back to their normal lives soon, they might both do something foolish. These amorous stirrings for Darren McNaught had best be left unnurtured, she thought, attempting to school herself. "Is there anything in this place to eat? I fancy myself an accomplished gourmet cook."

He groaned. "I'm a meat and potatoes man myself. I don't like guessing what's lurking under the hollandaise sauce."

"Your palate needs educating as well as your musical tastes," she said flatly and began searching in a couple of stacked-up orange crates that must once have served as a crude pantry. A lone bent can of pork and beans remained in the bottom section. She held it up. "Do you want it hot or cold?"

"Hot, please, and served with garlic bread and barbecue ribs drowning in rich tomato sauce."

"No problem. I make delectable, dark molasses-baked beans," she assured him. Then she frowned. "How do I get the darn can open?"

"What, no can opener? How badly prepared you are, my dear."

"Sorry, no can opener. No knife. No...hold everything. Victory is ours!"

"What is it?"

"One half of a pair of scissors. I bet we can poke a hole with this."

"And then what?"

She looked at him quizzically.

"How are you going to eat it? No spoons, no forks."

Cocking her head to one side, she thought for a moment. "Chopsticks?"

He laughed. "And here I thought you were going to say fingers. Of course, I should have known better. You—using your fingers!"

"Don't scoff. You're looking at a champion finger-looter of peanut butter and jelly. Used to hide behind the kitchen door with a jar and stuff myself. I was a chubby little kid."

He chuckled. "And then you grew up—with all the curves in the right places."

She flushed under his admiring glance.

They ended up scooping the beans out of the can with a couple of flat sticks. They chatted easily about wonderful meals they'd both enjoyed in San Francisco, New York, and other places that both had visited.

"My sister lives in Florida," he volunteered.

"You have brothers and sisters?" she asked. He had not talked about his own family.

"One sister, Penny. Great gal, married to an engineer who works for Martin Marietta on the space program. They have four little girls under seven." He laughed. "What a gaggle of strawberry-blond cuties. I took them all to Disney World on my last visit. You should have seen me trying to keep up with them on Magic Mountain and the other fantastic rides. They were still going strong when I took them home to their mother, stuffed with ice cream, sticky with candy, and arms loaded with balloons and toys. We had a great day." He chuckled at the memory.

The affection in his voice was obvious. He loved kids. One more thing she knew and liked about him. They shared some childhood escapades in a comfortable companionship. Sitting in front of the radiating little stove, half lying on the pile of sheepskin, Linsey couldn't keep her eyes open, and her heavy lids finally closed in sleep.

Hours later she awoke with a start from a bad dream and sat up. Her breathing was rapid and her heart raced in fright. With relief she saw that Darren was stretched out on the floor asleep, but still the dream wouldn't let her go. Beale and Jake had pushed her down a deep hole and she couldn't get out. They were shoveling dirt in on her when she had jerked awake, screams caught in her throat.

"What's the matter?" Darren sat up and put an arm around her trembling shoulders. "It's all right...it's all right."

"Beale and Jake were burying me alive. It was awful. I couldn't breathe, and they kept laughing and throwing more dirt."

Darren swore. "Those swine are going to pay for this." He glanced out the half-open door. "It's midafternoon.

We've got to get moving again. Too dangerous to linger too long.''

She nodded, wide-awake now, but the fear that caused her heart to race wasn't from a dream that could be sloughed off. It was real. The brief respite they'd had from danger was over.

"Get dressed. I'll be back in a minute. I don't think staying with the stream is the best way. Not unless the canyon widens. But I'm going to take a quick look." He tossed her the dry blouse.

He went out the door and for a moment she just sat there, hugging his jacket around her. Although she was lost in the long arms and large shoulders, the jacket had the warm feel of his arms. She heard him coming back, guiltily took it off and quickly buttoned up the blouse.

The door opened. She turned as Darren's shadow drifted across the floor.

Only it wasn't Darren!

Her stomach plunged in a sickening dip to the soles of her feet.

Beale stood in the doorway.

"I'll be damned if it isn't our pigeon, waiting for us in a nice little coop." He laughed as he pointed an ugly revolver at her.

Chapter Nine

Linsey gave a cry and bounded to her feet.

Beale remained just outside the door and shot his gun into the air. He must be signaling to Jake, Linsey thought, panic-stricken at the sight of her abductor on the doorstep. The revolver's loud report echoed down the mountainside and between the canyon walls. Beale's bulk filled the doorway, and Linsey's frantic gaze swept the small cabin for a means of escape or a weapon.

"Don't try it," he warned as he came in slowly, his ferret eyes surveying the small interior and his finger poised ready on the black revolver. His gaze swept from corner to corner, over the small stove, orange crates, the pile of sheepskins, then settled on Darren's jacket lying on the floor. "Where's lover boy?" he asked.

A spurt of relief went through Linsey. They didn't have Darren. Some acuity born of desperation made her lie. "He left me! Ran off! Dumped me to save his own skin." She tossed her head in an angry gesture. "The coward said he could get away faster by himself. Left early this morning, he did."

Beale grunted.

She couldn't judge from Beale's glare if he was buying her story or not.

"It's true," she insisted, maybe a little too emphatically. If they thought he was already gone, they wouldn't go looking for him. She had never considered herself much of an actress, but the motivation for putting on a good show had never before been this strong. "I begged him to take me with him," she wailed, "but he said I'd slow him down."

"Smart man. He had no business getting in the middle of this in the first place. Jake's pretty steamed up about the way he tricked him. His motorcycle's still dripping. I wouldn't want to be around if he ever gets his hands on that dude again. He don't take kindly to someone messing up his cycle."

"Well, he's gone," Linsey said firmly.

"Why'd you have to drag him into this?"

"I didn't have any choice. Anyway, it doesn't matter now. He won't be back."

"We should've wasted him right off," grunted Beale. "Wasn't my idea to bring him along, but the boss thought he might be useful as a little persuasion. Now, I guess, I'll just have to persuade you all by myself." His lips gleamed wetly.

Linsey backed up. "Wait. I know what you're after. Gold. You think my father found that lost Confederate wagon. But he didn't."

"Liar. Save your breath, lady."

"It's true. He was just playing a game. It was all a joke." She gave a false laugh. Her mind scrambled at high speed for some way to outwit him. Physically she didn't have a chance, but mentally she might spurt ahead far enough to confuse him. "My father loved to play tricks on the family. He just pretended to find a gold bar, and he fixed up those photographs to look like the real thing, and he—"

"Don't take me for a fool! Your pa found the bullion, all right. Says so right here in this letter." He jerked an envelope out of his pocket and waved it at her.

Linsey's heart plummeted in a sickening sensation. She'd forgotten about the letter addressed to Douglas Brady. "It's a forgery," she said quickly.

He smirked. "It's got Ronald Deane's signature on it."

"Let me see it."

"No tricks." Beale's eyes narrowed in a warning. "All this chasing around gets me riled up, you get my meaning? I aim to gentle you one way or another, honey."

Reaching out her hand as far as she could in order to avoid getting any closer to his bulldog frame, she took the envelope that was addressed to Douglas Brady. With trembling hands she pulled out a letter. Beale had not lied. It was signed by her father. As Linsey read it, her chest tightened in a surge of conflicting emotions.

To My Beloved Family:
I hope that my daughters, Linsey, Abigail and Kate will understand the unusual circumstances I have chosen to introduce their half brother to the family. After many agonizing years of wrestling with my conscience, I have decided to acknowledge the son I fathered during the Korean War. Because I already had a wonderful wife and young family at the time of his birth, this baby boy was put out for adoption by his mother and until recently I had no knowledge of his whereabouts.

In order to make up for years of neglect, I have arranged for him to share equally in the sudden wealth that has recently come into my hands. In an unbelievable happenstance, which I have chosen to keep a secret, I uncovered the lost Confederate wagon with its load of gold bullion. The idea of bringing my children together in an unusual way appeals to me, and I am sending Douglas two photographs and this letter with an invitation to participate in an exciting adventure. A treasure hunt! I'll be watching all of you as my children follow the clues I have carefully placed to lead you to a very real pot of gold. Good luck. I love you all.

Ronald Deane.

The letter was typewritten, but her father's familiar signature sprawled across the bottom of the letter. His fun-loving personality came through the words. How ironic it was, thought Linsey, that the family adventure he'd planned to bring them all together had set in motion a series of murderous events.

"Give me the letter. That's your pa's signature, isn't it?"

"Maybe," she said as she handed back the letter. "Or maybe it's a forgery. You're all chasing some mirage."

Beale made a rude noise in his throat and spat onto the floor. "Quit lying, baby doll."

"How'd you get that letter?"

"None of your business."

"You killed Douglas Brady, didn't you?" Even as Linsey voiced the question, the memory of Carrie sprawled in her own blood was answer enough. "You murdered him to get the pictures. Just like you killed Carrie for the bar of gold."

Beale only laughed at her angry accusations, as if her tirade amused him. "You must have me mixed up with somebody else. I don't know any dude named Douglas, I ain't got no bar of gold, and I don't believe one word that comes out of your pretty mouth. But I'm going to give you a chance to save your own neck."

Beale and Jake could have seen Darren leave the shack. Her mind raced. Maybe it was already too late for Darren to get away. Beale could be pretending not to know where Darren was, playing cat and mouse with her. Jake could be after Darren this very minute.

"Don't plan on lover boy coming back to rescue you," Beale said with a smirk. "It's just you and me, baby."

She glared at him. "I told you that this is all a mistake. And you're going to be in plenty of trouble with the law if you don't quit threatening me!"

"Let's quit wasting time," snapped Beale. "You and me both know your father found the gold, and we're going to have our own little treasure hunt. Beginning right now!"

Linsey watched his knife replace the revolver. The sight of its gleaming curved blade brought back the memory of terror when its sharp point had bitten into her neck and cut off her hair. He waved it in front of her and she backed up, watching it as if it was something alive, ready to spring at her.

"You're going to tell me where your dad stashed that wagon of gold," he growled menacingly. "Talk, sweetheart."

"He never found a wagon of gold. It was all a game. A pretend game."

"The letter says there's a pot of gold."

"I don't know what that letter's all about. It could be a fake. How do I know you didn't write it yourself and forge my father's signature?"

"It's real, all right. Now where's the gold?"

He took a threatening swipe at her face with the blade.

"I can't tell you something I don't know!"

"We'll see about that."

She met his beady eyes, glare for glare. She had been drugged, shot at, nearly drowned, and seen two good people murdered. She had taken enough! And even though her life was in danger, she refused to knuckle under and beg this killer to spare her. Courage that had lain dormant in her well-ordered protected life and never put to the test, suddenly surfaced. She drew on that strength now. Even though it appalled her to admit it, she would kill Beale if given the chance. She owed Carrie and Hank that much—and maybe Darren!

"Guess I'll have to help you remember." Beale jabbed toward her stomach with his knife, forcing her backward. His thick knuckles whitened in a tense grip, as if anticipating the thrill of plunging the blade into her soft flesh.

Linsey's mind raced for some means of defense, but she had only her fists to flail against his barrellike frame. Her back was flattened against the crude log wall as he pressed her into a corner.

"All right, talk." Like a two-hundred-pound football guard, he planted himself in front of her, his foul breath bathing her face. "Where'd your father hide that gold?"

"I don't know."

"I'm out of patience, lady," he growled, "You've run us all over the place, and I ain't got any more time to play games. Either you tell me what I want to know, or I slit your throat here and now."

She swallowed hard. "I can't talk with my throat slit, so I don't think you'd be stupid enough to do that."

He grasped her cotton blouse by the collar and ripped it nearly to her waist. She staggered forward, trying to get by him, but his rough hand shoved her back against the wall. "That's only the beginning."

"Let me go!"

He pointed the curved blade in front of her face so that it followed her as she turned her head from side to side. He won't kill me, she kept reassuring herself. He's just bluffing, trying to scare me. She was scared, she admitted to herself, but she wasn't going to let him know it. What was a torn blouse, anyway? She pulled it together and glared at him, refusing to watch the point of his knife coming closer and closer to her neck.

"You got guts, I'll say that for you. Too bad you don't have the sense to go with it. Why don't you smarten up?"

"I'm smart enough to know that you need me—alive."

She heard a sound outside the door. Darren! He'd come back. She opened her mouth to warn him.

Beale slammed a thick hand over her mouth.

Darren, don't come in, Linsey silently pleaded as the door slowly opened.

Beale swore and removed his hand.

Jake stood in the doorway, breathless, his lean face flushed.

"Where have you been?" Beale demanded.

"All over the place." He grinned at Linsey cowering in the corner. "Well, lookee who showed up."

"Didn't you hear my signal? I fired my gun."

"Nope, I was searching along the creek. How'd you find her?"

Beale kept his knife poised at Linsey's throat. "Smoke. I smelled wood burning, followed my nose and found our little pigeon snug and waiting. I left the truck on the ridge above."

"Where's the guy?"

"She says he's took off, but that's his coat on the floor. I don't think he'd go without it. Get outside and watch for him. He'll be coming back. When he does, waste him."

"Right!" Jake said excitedly. His pale blue eyes fastened on Linsey.

"Git!" ordered Beale.

Jake didn't move.

Linsey held her breath. The atmosphere was suddenly charged and snapping as if with static electricity.

"I'm tired," said Jake, defying Beale's glare.

"Who's giving the orders here?"

"Ah, Beale, have a heart. I must have walked miles chasing them down to the stream. T'ain't fair."

"I'll tell you what's fair. I'll peel your hide if you don't get out of here and look for that dude. He's around someplace."

Linsey said, "No, he isn't. He's gone. A long time ago." If Jake believed her, maybe she could keep Darren out of danger. "He left me. Ran off to save his own skin."

Jake believed her. He seemed relieved. "No sense chasing him if he's long gone."

"She's lying, you dumb oaf. Don't you see what she's doing? Trying to keep us from looking for him. She's playing you for a fool."

"No need to call me names," said Jake, as if hurt by Beale's attack.

"You're not stupid, Jake," said Linsey, smiling at him, trying to play off one against the other.

"Did you hear what I said?" Beale growled menacingly. He lowered the knife from Linsey's throat and half turned toward Jake.

"I don't know why you get all the fun, Beale," the youth protested. "I could make her talk."

The way he said it made Linsey decide that she might be better off taking her chances with Beale.

"Git, before I carve you up like dog meat," Beale warned. "You know what someone looks like when I get through with 'em. I'm not nice when I lose my temper." His eyes bore into Jake's as if to accent the warning. "Now get out of here. Find that guy. Kill him and hide his body. I'll take care of the girl."

Linsey's hopes for a confrontation that would take their attention off her faded when Jake nodded. "I'll find him, Beale." He went through the doorway, his rifle ready in his hand.

Darren! Where was he? New anxiety colored Linsey's thoughts. He must have heard the shot and known their abductors had found them. Without a weapon he couldn't challenge them directly. Had he gone for help? Was he hiding outside, waiting for a chance to jump their abductors? Her mind scrambled her thoughts like Ping-Pong balls bouncing off a hard wall. She tried to grab one, only to have two more bewildering ones come at her.

Beale's eyes had turned hard. He was all business. "Last chance." He waited.

Her brain refused to function. She stood rigid as he poised the edge of the knife's blade over the crevice of her breasts. Beale's eyes glittered with anticipation. The hungry look chilled her bones. She'd have to try and bluff him.

"All right! I'll tell you," she said with a rush.

"I thought you would."

Linsey put a hand against her forehead. "Oh, I feel faint." She let her legs go limp and slumped to the floor, knocking over one of the orange crates.

"Don't take me for a fool," growled Beale. "Get up now—before I lift the scalp off your head." He kicked the orange crate, scattering the empty can of beans, eating sticks, and the homemade can opener.

Linsey played for time. Lying on the floor, she saw the broken piece of the scissors just inches from her hand. Had Beale seen it, too?

"Get up!"

"Please, please, don't hurt me," she pleaded, acting as if she were terrified. Her mind raced as she cowered on the floor, playing for time. "I'll tell you, honest I will." Her fingers slipped closer to the scissor blade. "The Sawtooth Fox was the man in the truck...."

"The cowboy who kept shooting at us?"

She nodded. "He was my father's buddy in Korea. They were good friends and went on hunting trips together. He was with my father when he fell." She managed to thrust out her hand and cover the blade. It felt small and harmless. Unless she could stab Beale in some place like the throat, the wound would be inconsequential.

Beale jerked her up. She kept the hand holding the broken blade behind her back. If she had to take Beale by surprise, she would only have one chance. Her mind refused to contemplate what would happen if she failed to incapacitate him.

"Now, where were we?"

"I was going to tell you where the gold is, but blood always makes me weak. That's why I almost fainted. You see—" She brought her arm around, but her attack was not quick enough.

"Wh—?" He swung up an arm in time to ward off the blow. The piece of iron went into his forearm instead of his throat. It penetrated his skin, but his heavy jacket weakened the thrust of the blade. She knew that it had only gone halfway into his flesh.

"Ouch!" Still, the pain was enough to make him drop his knife. A red flush of anger blazed in his flat face as he jerked the pointed steel out of his arm.

Linsey lunged past him. She was halfway to the door when he threw himself at her in a tackle. He connected with her lower legs. She went down. His weight knocked the breath out of her. Gasping for air, she tried to wriggle out of his grasp, but he pulled her to her feet.

"You little—"

She butted her head into his stomach.

Gasping for breath, he doubled up.

She darted away. In her haste, her feet got tangled in Darren's jacket that was still lying on the floor. She was trying to regain her balance when Beale's open hand caught her on the side of the head in a vicious blow.

She fell forward and hit her head on the side of the stove. A kaleidoscope of colors revolved before eyes that wouldn't focus. Her arms and legs seemed alien appendages. Bells rang in her ears. Voices came in watery waves.

"What did you do to her, Beale? Is she dead?"

"No, stupid, she's not dead."

"What's the matter with your arm? It's bleeding all over the place."

"I know. Hurts like the devil, too. She stabbed me."

"You shoulda watched out for her."

"Don't tell me what I should have done," snapped Beale. "I'll get her for this, believe me."

"What happened to her?"

"I hit her good and she fell. Hit her head on the side of the stove."

"We better get out of here fast," argued Jake. "I couldn't find the guy. He got away. He'll alert somebody, for sure."

Beale swore. "The boss isn't going to be happy about this."

"We did the best we could," Jake whined.

"He's not going to believe that."

"Maybe we can get her to talk before he shows up."

"You can bet on it," said Beale. "The only safe place to keep her now is at the chalet. When I get her there, I'll make her pay for her cute little tricks."

Linsey tried to raise her head, but it wanted to loll to one side. She had trouble focusing her eyes.

Beale picked up Linsey's jacket and threw it at Jake. "Put that on her. And we'd better take the one the guy left. Don't want any signs that they've been here."

Jake stooped and braced Linsey against him as her head tipped to one side. "She's knocked senseless, Beale. The boss ain't gonna like that. How she going to tell us anything now?"

"Don't worry. She'll talk. Now carry her out of here."

Jake put her arms into the sleeves of her denim jacket and buttoned it. She felt like a disjointed doll. The wires between her limbs and her brain were down. The blow to her head had made her as limp as a dishrag. Now she knew what fighters were talking about when they said somebody was punch-drunk.

"Hurry it up!" ordered Beale.

Jake tried to lift Linsey to her feet, but her legs buckled.

"She can't walk."

"Then heave her over your shoulder and carry her!" ordered Beale. "The truck's not far. Gimme your rifle. I'll go first, just in case that guy's still hanging around."

Darren was out there, thought Linsey hazily. Or was he? Had he gone for help? Maybe he was hiding somewhere. She ought to scream to warn him, but there was no breath in her lungs as she dangled over Jake's shoulder like a sack of potatoes, head down, bouncing against his back with every step.

The ground spun dizzily. Every step Jake took up the rocky path was an eternity of torture.

"The truck's parked at the top," said Beale.

"She's heavier than she looks," Jake complained, puffing from the climb.

"Quit griping. It's your fault that they got away in the first place. You should have easily overtaken them on your bike."

"I told you. I was riding too fast to see that pond."

"I'm tired of your excuses. This time I'll see to it that she stays exactly where we put her."

When they reached the pickup, Jake lowered her to the ground. Linsey thought he was going to throw her into the back with the camping stuff, but he shoved her into the cab. Beale slid into the driver's seat, and Jake pressed closely against her on the other side. He put an arm around her shoulders.

"Save it!" snapped Beale. "Leave the woman alone."

"I was just holding her up," protested Jake, removing his arm.

"Get your gun out and be ready to shoot," ordered Beale. "We might run into her pal."

Jake glowered but did as he was ordered, rolling down the window and keeping his rifle ready for firing.

Linsey knew she must keep alert so that she could prevent Jake from shooting straight. No telling where Darren was. If given the chance, she might be able to get Jake's gun away from him. This hope was foolish, but she clung to it as she tried to force some rigidity into her limbs.

At one time the crude road must have led down to the mine workings, probably to carry out the ore, Linsey reflected. Beale was concentrating on his driving. Forcing her gaze out the window, she squinted to stop the enveloping vertigo. She must try to stay alert to her surroundings. Apparently Beale had followed this old road to a point above the shack. She remembered he'd told Jake that the smell of smoke had led him down to the old miner's shack. Their lovely warm fire had betrayed them.

The truck lurched forward and gained speed, bouncing down the road away from the cabin. If Darren had watched her abductors carrying her off like a sack of potatoes, there was nothing he could do about it now, she realized. In a very genuine way she was glad that he was no longer a part of this nightmare. From the beginning it had been only an unlucky happenstance that had put him in the middle of things. He deserved to get on with his life.

Her blurred vision took in endless layers of mountains, ravines and cliffs as the generic mountain scene swept by the windows. No one would find her in this wilderness. Newspapers were full of stories about victims of foul play who were never found for years after they were killed.

"You had to do it the hard way, didn't you?" Beale snapped, lashing out at her as if reading her thoughts. "We had you all set up nice in that camper. Went to a lot of trouble, we did. You could have made it easy on everyone. But no! You caused us all plenty of trouble."

And got Carrie and Hank killed. Linsey bit her lip. These heartless murderers would kill her, too, as soon as they realized she honestly didn't know where the gold was hidden. Her only hope was to keep up some kind of pretense, to feed them erroneous speculations—enough to lull their suspicions and keep herself alive.

"You're going to tell us what your pa scribbled on the back of that picture," Beale declared. "We're going to lay our hands on that gold, or you're not long for this world."

They didn't know about the last clue, "Pass along the family tree and raise a glass to history." Even in her present foggy state, some recognition tugged at her. "Family tree…family tree…family tree." Like an incantation the phrase mingled with the loud ringing in her ears. Why did comprehension dangle just out of reach? She would gladly tell them where the gold was, if there was a chance she could bargain for her life. She leaned her head against the back cushion. She knew she should be trying to remember where they were taking her, but her eyes wouldn't focus properly. The blow to the side of her head had affected her sight and equilibrium. She prayed it was only temporary.

"The boss ain't going to like this," Jake said. "Taking the pigeon to his place."

"We don't have no choice. Anyway, it won't be for long. We've gotta move quick. No telling how soon that guy will be spouting his mouth off."

"Hell, he won't find his way out of these mountains for days, if he makes it at all," Jake said with a chuckle. "By then it'll be too late. We'll have the gold and be out of here."

Linsey closed her eyes. Jake was right. Darren could be lost for weeks. Because the Rocky Mountains were layered, mountain ranges rose and fell, one following the other, cut up and sliced by streams and lakes, crisscrossed by deep valleys and a myriad of ravines, vaulting cliffs and jagged peaks. Treacherous and beguiling, they demanded a high toll. Many people who went into the mountain wilderness prepared, never came out alive. And Darren wasn't even prepared. No food, no jacket, exhausted from running and lost in an area that was completely unfamiliar. Just thinking about him left her with a deep sense of emptiness.

The motion of the truck increased Linsey's dizziness, but she kept trying to keep some sense of direction. They had left the Sawtooth Peaks behind and were climbing a twisting Jeep road. Distance was difficult to judge because the road constantly circled back on itself. Like a rag doll she sat slumped between the two men, wondering how far they had come from the miner's cabin—and from Darren.

They had driven for nearly an hour when Beale made a sharp turn and sent the truck at a nearly perpendicular angle up a steep rise. Rocks spun out from under the wheels as he gunned the engine and the truck plunged into a thick stand of trees. Two worn tracks twisted and turned through a canopy of needled branches, and finally leveled out in front of a mountain chalet that lay hidden in the dense infinity of trees at the base of a high cliff.

Linsey squinted, trying to bring into focus an A-frame house; its steep roof slanted almost to the ground. The redwood exterior was well preserved, and a second-floor balcony flaunted red and blue deck chairs. The mountain home had a fairy-tale charm in this isolated setting. Decorated eaves along the roofline, flowering pots and shutters lent a beguiling charm like the witch's house in *Hansel and Gretel*, Linsey thought. Indeed, this mountain home reeked of danger just as deadly as the cannibal old witch who'd fattened innocent children for Sunday dinner.

Beale drove the truck under a wide carport at the side of the house.

"Shall I take her upstairs?" asked Jake hopefully.

"The boss won't want blood all over his pretty house," said Beale grimly. "We'll tie her up out here."

"But—"

"Shut up. Get me some rope out of the back." Beale pulled Linsey across the seat and out the driver's side. Her legs went out from under her, and he dragged her over to a post that held up one corner of the carport. Propping her against it, he tied her hands behind the post, giving the knot an extra jerk that cut the circulation from her hands.

She winced as he stood erect and glared down at her. Blood made an ugly stain on his sleeve. "Baby, we're about to have a party... and you're the honored guest."

Jake snickered.

''First we've got to tend to my arm. I don't want the damn thing to get infected. I need some disinfectant and a bandage. She'll wait. Won't you, honey?''

Linsey closed her eyes and leaned her head against the post.

Beale laughed and muttered something that made Jake laugh.

She heard retreating footsteps and the slam of a door. She had a few moments' reprieve. Weakly she pulled at her bonds, knowing she didn't have the strength to break a single thread, let alone a thick knot of rope. She turned her head gingerly.

''Ouch!'' A thumping headache crashed in a painful rhythm inside her skull, but her vision was almost back to normal. At least she thought it was, until her gaze traveled over the truck's bed; she saw the camping stuff in the back begin to move.

A piece of canvas rose and bellowed out as if wind were caught beneath it. Her eyes widened, and she caught her breath in a shallow gasp.

Chapter Ten

She must be hallucinating. It couldn't be.

A shock of red hair appeared from under the camping tent.

"Darren!"

He gave her a crooked grin, grabbed up his jacket from where Beale had thrown it, leaped from the truck bed and glanced hurriedly into the cab. No keys. He knelt beside her.

"We'll have to run for it," he whispered as he untied the knots. Her cheek was bruised and her lovely eyes were slightly glazed. Anger knotted like a steel cord in his stomach. He had never felt such rage. For a moment it blotted out rational thought, and he had to clamp a tight control on his emotions. They had to get out of here. Doing it would demand some kind of miracle.

"They're in the house," she whispered.

"I heard. What did you do to Beale?"

"Stuck our can opener in his arm," she said proudly. "Almost got away, too. Worst luck, I tripped on your jacket. Then Beale knocked me down and I hit my head on the stove. Still kind of dizzy, but my eyes are focusing now."

"Where are we?" he asked as he pulled the ropes from her hands and ankles.

"The boss's place...whoever he is. Fancy Swiss chalet, but I've never seen it before."

They sent quick searching looks in every direction. The house was set against a steep cliff, so there was no way to escape from the back. High windows that rose to the second floor gave a panoramic view of the front, if they fled that way. The house was protected in a half circle of vaulting cliffs that formed a cul-de-sac. Only a narrow opening at the front allowed passage into the enclosure, and it was shut off by a high barbed wire fence.

"What do you think?" whispered Linsey. "That way?" She pointed to the west side of the house.

Darren's eyes narrowed as he registered the formidable cliffs and the exposed front. There seemed to be only one choice for immediate sanctuary, a thickly wooded area that reached one side of the carport. Thick stands of trees and large boulders offered temporary concealment, but little more.

He nodded. "That way. Can you walk?"

She nodded, staggered, then almost crumpled to her knees. He took a firm grip on her waist, and they ran as best they could away from the house.

"I thought you'd gotten away. Why didn't you? Jake said he couldn't find you."

"I was up on the ridge when I heard the shot. Before I could start down to the cabin, I saw Jake. He was poking his gun into every bush and rock pile along the creek. I knew I had to find a hiding place before he saw me."

"And you climbed into their truck." Linsey laughed. "I never thought of that once. You sure surprised me when I saw that red head of yours pop up."

"It seemed to be the best hiding place for the moment. When I saw them coming to the truck with you, I just stayed hidden."

They had only gone a short distance when the stand of pine and aspen trees ended. "Look at that!" Darren exclaimed, pointing in exasperation.

Beyond the trees, a narrow expanse of ground was covered with tumbled rocks that rose abruptly to meet high cliffs. They raised their eyes to a sheer rock wall that circled in both directions to the narrow fenced-in opening. No place to run. No time to go back and attempt an escape down the road that was blocked by the high fence.

"We're trapped, aren't we? Like in a cattle chute."

"I guess that's as good a description as any," he agreed. "We'll have to find some place to hide. They'll be looking for you soon."

"Hide here? Almost within hearing distance of the house?"

"No other choice. Besides, those wobbly legs of yours wouldn't let us run very far... or very fast."

Linsey wanted to deny it, but she knew it was true. Her equilibrium wasn't back yet.

Frantically they looked about for a place of concealment. Heavy rocks had fallen from the face of the cliff, tumbled down upon a rocky slope and lay piled up in haphazard, natural sculptures.

Darren eyed some large rocks, where dirt had collected and small junipers had taken root. "Come on."

"Those scrubs aren't high or thick enough to hide a jackrabbit," Linsey lamented as they circled the huge boulders. Time was running out. Beale and Jake would be after them any minute. Their captors would know that the cul-de-sac formed a natural coop. They'd be after their pigeon in an instant.

Four huge boulders leaning against each other caught Linsey's eye. The way the rocks were piled up, there was a small enclosure in the midst of them about six feet off the ground. "What do you think?" She pointed to the opening in the pile of rocks.

At first he didn't understand. There was no space to hide behind them.

"See, the way those boulders have fallen, we can climb into the middle of them."

He grinned. "And put some brush over the opening. Smart girl."

"It's a small space," she warned. Once again she was thankful for her small frame.

"You first." He cupped his hands and gave her a lift upward.

The slanted, uneven opening was even smaller that it looked from below. Ducking her head into her pulled-up knees and wrapping her arms around them, she scooted back into the opening as far as she could. Darren would have to be a contortionist to fit into the space that was left.

"I'll get some brush." He looked around. Only a few dwarfed bunches of tiny grasses and weeds grew on the rocky slope. He needed branches and twigs. "Hurry," urged Linsey in a muffled voice. Her cramped position was already bringing pain to her legs and back. How long would they have to stay here? Maybe not long, an inner voice mocked her. Beale and Jake might find them right away.

Darren spurted toward the edge of the trees, picked up several small pieces of dry branches, and was running back when he heard a shout go up from the house.

Linsey heard it, too. The human hounds were loose again.

Darren tossed the branches up to the roo... ing and followed. He grunted as he folded up ... frame as best he could and squeezed in beside Lin... Peering through his pulled-up legs, he reached out and placed the dry branches over the opening.

"What do you think?" whispered Linsey.

"Good," he lied. He despaired to see how little concealment the few branches provided. At least another half dozen more were needed to do the job. He feared that anyone looking directly into the opening could easily see them crouching there, but he wasn't going to tell Linsey that.

Her breath came in strained gulps. He knew she must be frightened and didn't blame her. Instead she gave him a weak smile that didn't stay on her lips very long.

There wasn't enough room to put an arm around her, so he gripped her hand firmly and gave it a reassuring squeeze. That crazy patch of short hair stood straight up on the top of her head, one cheek was swollen and discolored, her beautiful eyes were pained and shadowed, yet he had never felt such tenderness for her, such caring as he did at that moment.

Why had he ever thought she was like Laura? They weren't remotely made of the same stuff. Laura would have given up at the first sign of unpleasantness, weeping and wailing and blaming everyone else for her predicament. They were both petite and feminine, but Linsey's physical fragility was girded with mental and emotional steel. She was a fighter, stubborn, obstinate, yet utterly desirable—a combination to beguile any man.

It would be tempting to try to fit her into his future, if they ever got out of this. That thought was quickly followed by more realistic considerations. It was absurd to think that she'd move to the Canadian prairie, just so that he could pursue his own career. It wouldn't be fair to ask her, and he wasn't getting sidetracked again. He had already learned that lesson. But at the moment there was only one overriding demand—staying alive.

Tension built with every uneventful minute that passed. After that first shout, nothing. What were those murdering brutes doing? Why weren't they trying to find Linsey? The silence didn't make sense. Sweat beaded on his forehead. The cramped position sent pain up his long legs and into his bent shoulders.

"See anything?" she whispered. The opening was blocked by his hunched figure.

He shook his head.

"Maybe they've given up?"

He shook his head, then stiffened. A quiet snap of a branch resounded in his head like a shot. He warned her with his eyes. He hoped their whispers hadn't betrayed their hiding place. A stalker! Very close.

Linsey pressed her fists against her mouth to muffle her breathing. Beale and Jake must have known she couldn't go far in her condition; they must be stalking her like hunters after a wounded animal, silently, furtively, not crashing about like a couple of wild boars. They were wily, shrewd and practiced in their cruelty. She shivered, remembering Beale's anger and his promises of "persuasion." If he got his hands on her again, nothing would stop him. She had humiliated him by getting away, and the next time there would be no teasing pricks of his knife while he played with her. She felt her breathing grow shallow and her heartbeat quicken, both signs of a rising, almost unbearable tension.

Darren moved his head slightly so that he could peer through the thinly stacked branches. His heart lurched al-

most to a stop and his mouth went dry. He ...
hand a warning squeeze.

Jake stood quietly in the shadows of the trees.

Darren's eyes fastened on the hunter, wondering what to do if he raised his gun and fired at them. Jake hadn't seen them. Not yet.

Jake maintained a listening stance, holding his rifle in readiness. Even the primitive instinct of a deer or elk would have been deceived by his motionless watchfulness, thought Darren. No wonder they hadn't heard the blond gunman's approach. He blended into the shadows and became a part of the natural backdrop.

The skin crawled on the back of Darren's neck. He knew that Jake was scanning the cliff behind them, because the other man's head was tipped back. If he lowered his gaze slightly, his attention could easily fasten on the tumbled rocks and piled-up boulders. Darren cursed himself for not deciding that they should take their chances out in the open, where he might have jumped the gunman. It had been pure stupidity to trap themselves like this. Jake could shoot them as easily as squirrels in a cage. As if to verify Darren's fears, the youth slowly raised his gun and took aim. Darren stopped breathing, forcing himself to remain frozen in position. Waiting. Darren watched Jake's gaze pass over the boulders where they were hiding, as if he were tracking something in the rocks above them.

What did he see? Darren mentally thanked God for whatever it was. For the moment, it had taken Jake's attention away from their hiding place.

Jake fired, and the sound of the rifle's shot reverberated against the cliffs.

Linsey jerked instinctively. Darren tightened his handclasp in warning.

He continued to watch Jake. For a moment the gunman just stood there, looking up at the cliffs, following something with his eyes. Then he swore and lowered his gun. From his expression Darren knew he had missed his target.

"Where is she?" Beale crashed through a nearby stand of trees and followed Jake's gaze to the rocks above. "You didn't shoot her, you fool?"

"Nope. A bobcat!" Jake said excitedly. "A huge son of a gun. Standing up on that ledge like he was king of the hill. I almost got him, too. Wow, what a fur rug he'd have made."

"You blasted idiot!" Beale swore. "It's your hide that the boss will stretch for a rug if you let the woman get away."

"Aw, she can't get far in her condition. We'll get her all right."

"Not if you waste time playing the great white hunter," Beale snapped. "Now tend to business for once in your life. If she came this way, she's hiding behind some of these boulders. Check 'em out! Use what little brains you have."

Jake scowled at the tongue-lashing and mumbled something about searching the cliff.

"There's no way she could climb out of here," countered Beale. "And I was looking out the front window all of the time you were fixing my arm. I would have seen her if she had run that way. You circle around. I'll check close to the house. She couldn't go far on them shaky legs of hers."

"Maybe she was pretending not to be able to walk. Besides, how'd she get free of them ropes, Beale? You must have fouled up on the knots." He needled the older man with obvious satisfaction.

"Them ropes were tight. Can't figure it ...
won't get away from me again, I'll promise you tha...
I ain't putting up with your stupidity, either. Now, fin...
her." Beale stomped away, leaving Jake scowling and
glaring at his back.

Darren squeezed Linsey's hand once more in warning as
the pockmarked Jake turned. Once more he glanced up at
the spot where he had presumably seen the bobcat, then
shrugged. Darren didn't dare move as much as an eye-
lash. The moment stretched into an agonizing eternity as
Jake's searching eyes came lower and lower. His gaze
seemed to linger for a second too long on the piled-up
boulders and the few pieces of dead wood feebly obscuring the opening between them.

Linsey felt Darren stiffen. She closed her eyes tightly.

Rocks crackled under Jake's boots as the gunman began walking toward their hiding place.

Darren's impulse was still to try to jump the hunter, even
though he knew that Jake would be able to get off a shot
before he hit the ground. Thank God, Jake wasn't looking high enough to see them yet. His interest was on the
single rocks tumbled at the base of the cliff, as if he
expected to find Linsey lying behind one of them.

Linsey moved and Darren gripped her hand even tighter.
He knew that one sound, one movement, would betray
them.

Jake was very close now, ready to pass within a few feet
of them. If he lifted his head only slightly, he would see
them cowering in the tiny rock enclosure above him.

Hope spurted through Darren. Jake kept his gaze on the
ground, cautiously approaching each sprawled boulder.
The top of his straggly blond head went by the opening of
their shelter.

They listened to his footsteps crunching on rock as he continued along the foot of the cliff back toward the house. After a few more long, long moments, he shouted something to Beale.

Like hunted animals caught in a burrow, Darren and Linsey remained stiff and quiet. Even though they exchanged smiles of relief, they didn't move. Caution overrode the pain in their cramped bodies. Maybe Jake would circle back. When they heard a motorcycle gunning away from the house, Darren sighed in relief. At least Jake had extended the range of his search.

"Come on, m'love. Let's get out of here."

"Is it safe? Beale's on the loose."

"I don't think they'll search this area again for a while." Darren helped Linsey out of the rocks.

He held her in his arms for a moment. "Nice going. I never would have seen the hiding place. I'm glad I brought you along."

"Don't you have that backward? I brought you along, remember?"

"No matter," he said and smoothed her hair away from her cheeks. "We make a good team. Now all we have to do is figure out how to get out of here before they come back." They sat down behind another large rock. "I'm gambling that this is safe enough for a moment. You stay here, and I'll take a look around."

"No. It's too risky. I don't want you running into Beale."

"We can't just wait for them to search the whole area again, or sooner or later they'll find us. We have to get out of here."

Gently he took her head between his hands. Such tenderness welled up in him that for a moment he couldn't speak. Lightly he kissed her trembling mouth, then smiled

reassuringly. "I'll be careful. I'm not going ᴛᴏ
m'love," he whispered huskily.

"That might be a good idea," she said softly, in a practical tone, hiding the sudden buoyancy his kiss had engen-
dered. "You might be able to get away by yourself."

"And in the meantime?"

"While you go for help, I'll play hiding games with these
guys."

"I won't take that kind of gamble. I'm staying with
you." He kissed her eyelids and then the tip of her nose.
"And here, have a snack while you wait." He reached into
a pants pocket and drew out a small cellophane sack filled
with jelly beans.

Her eyes widened in disbelief. "Where did you get
those?"

He grinned. "I stopped at a 7 Eleven store...."

"And robbed them. You've been holding out on me."

"Nope. Found them in the camping stuff in the truck.
Nothing else I could lay my hands on, without moving
around too much."

"Beans for breakfast. Jelly beans for supper. What a
rut." She managed a weak chuckle.

"Nag, nag, nag," he teased, popping a few into his
mouth. "Stay here. Don't move until I get back."

She managed to keep her anxiety below the surface as he
quietly slipped away. Thank heavens the roaring in her ears
had faded; only a dull ache still sat like a tight cap over her
skull. Her jaw hurt when she chewed on the jelly beans,
but the intake of sugar was well received by her empty
stomach.

She glanced up at the sky. The last splash of sherbert
colors in a sunset was fading. The day was nearly gone.
Long shadows stretched away from the rocky cliff, and
already Linsey felt the warmth of the rocks receding. What

were they going to do? She looked up at the sheer rock walls above her. They might be able to get halfway up, but not even an experienced rock climber with the proper equipment would try such an ascent. The only possible retreat was back toward the house—and into the clutches of the men who were looking for them.

Darren's promise to be back in a minute had been a lie. He was gone a long time. Had he been caught? She hadn't heard any gunshots, but that didn't mean anything. Beale could have stabbed him with a knife or bashed in his head. What should she do? Darren had told her not to move, but waiting was pure torture. Anxiety built with every passing minute. Why didn't he come?

Where was he? Feeling steadier on her legs, she eased herself up from behind the rock. A glimpse of movement in the shadowy trees made her drop back. Who was it? Darren? Beale? Someone else? Her heart pounded as footsteps crunched closer to where she crouched.

Darren dropped beside her. "What do I see the minute I leave the trees but that rooster topknot of yours popping up?"

She smiled broadly at him, delirious with relief. "It's you."

"Of course it's me." He looked puzzled. "Did you think I'd decided to try and go for help? I told you, we're sticking together."

The promise made her feel deliciously warm and happy. "What in heaven's name took you so long?"

"I was trying to find a way to get by the house and down the road, but it's no go. The house is built up against the cliff, and there's only a narrow exit from this natural bulwark. With cliffs behind us and on both sides, we're penned in as effectively as in a box canyon."

"There has to be a way," she said with her usual stubbornness.

He sat down with his back against a rock and looked upward. "See that first ledge up there? It's quite wide and runs horizontally along the rock shelf."

"The one that's only about a thirty-foot jump from here?"

He nodded. "If we could get up there—"

"Simple. All we need to do is suddenly sprout wings and fly up to it," she chided, wondering why he was so serious about a ledge that was completely beyond their reach.

"That's where the bobcat must have been," he continued, ignoring her tone.

Suddenly Linsey's interest was piqued. "That means the animal must have found an access to it."

Darren nodded, not understanding completely what had put that glint of excitement into her eyes.

"An animal couldn't leap that high from the ground. So he must have found a way to it that we can't see," she reasoned.

Darren looked at her with open admiration. "The animal didn't run down here, or Jake would have taken another shot."

"There's no sign of him still on the ledge, so he fled somewhere," she said triumphantly.

Darren grinned. "And if he didn't come down—he must have gone up!"

"Elementary, my dear Watson," said Linsey with a quiet laugh. "There must be an exit from that ledge."

"And a means of escape for us. Now the question is, how do we manage to get up there?"

Linsey's eyes circled the rock enclosure. The steep cliff walls were uniform all the way around and absolutely defied any means of scaling them without rope and pitons.

"Wait a minute," said Darren. "I took a look behind the house, and there's a place where water has worn a trough into the sandstone. I dismissed it, because it didn't offer any hope of climbing clear to the top of the cliff—but it might allow us to climb as far as the ledge."

"Right behind the house?" Her eyes widened. "Where they can look out the window and see us?"

"They can't be everywhere at once."

Climbing around on the sheer face of a cliff was not the kind of thing that excited Linsey under the best of conditions. With two gunmen taking shots at them while they tried to find hand and footholds in the crumbling shelves of sandstone, the prospects of success were infinitesimal.

"Well? Are you game?" Darren asked.

"What if we run into the bobcat once we get up there?" she parried.

"I know it's not much of a choice. Either the bobcat or Beale."

"In that case, the choice is easy," she said quickly. "Let's climb."

"It's almost dusk. I doubt if they'll search this area again until morning. We'd best stay here."

"All night?"

"All night. I think it would be better to try to escape just before dawn. Give you a chance to recuperate a little. It's not going to be an easy climb."

"I'd rather go now," she insisted stubbornly. "And take my chances."

"Of falling?"

"I'm not going to fall. My equilibrium is back. Worrying and freezing all night is not going to improve our chances one bit."

"You sure grab the bit in your mouth, don't you? Headstrong as they come." Even as he chided her, there was a begrudging admiration in his tone. "All right. We'll have to head toward the back of the house."

She groaned.

"Once we start up the draw and reach the ledge we'll be visible to anyone below. There's absolutely nothing to hide us on those rocks. We'll be as exposed as the bobcat was," he warned.

Linsey had already visualized their vulnerability. She knew he was trying to lay out all the cards, and she appreciated his honesty.

"Twilight will give us some protection, but we can't wait until it's completely dark. We have to have enough light to walk safely on the ledge. Still want to try it?

She nodded. "Yes." Anything was better than cowering against these rocks, waiting for Beale to find them.

"Good. Let's go."

She didn't know whether it was physical weakness or fright that made her legs rubbery, but her optimistic assurance that she was just fine was soon put to the test as they inched along the base of the cliff, threading their way around fallen piles of rocks and slipping on loose stones that cracked despite their cautious steps. The closer they came to the house, the louder her heartbeat banged in her throat. The sun had disappeared, but a graying twilight remained.

A light shone in one of the lower-floor windows.

Darren motioned to her to stay hidden as he peered from behind a rock near the back door.

Her ears strained to hear any betraying sound. Was someone outside the house? Watching? Waiting? Icicles trickled down her spine. At any moment, their chance for escape could be a lost hope. Maybe Darren was wrong. Maybe there wasn't any place they could climb up to the ledge, and if they did succeed, they might get stranded thirty-five feet above the ground and not be able to go either up or down. She could imagine Jake's glee as he took shots at them as if they were targets in a shooting gallery.

"Listen," Darren hissed.

Linsey's turbulent thoughts were punctuated by the sound of a roaring engine. Jake's motorcycle. He was coming back. They froze in a spot only a few feet behind the carport, hidden in a cluster of rocks and juniper that filled the space between the log structure and the cliff. Close enough to breathe gas fumes from the motorcycle as it roared to a stop, Linsey realized as her stomach turned over with sudden nausea.

They could observe Jake through the prickly branches as he strode toward the side door of the house. How could he miss their presence a few feet away? This was the second time he had walked within inches of them without sensing their hiding place. Jake definitely was not psychic, thought Linsey in a moment of pure thankfulness.

The moment the door closed behind Jake, Darren grabbed Linsey's hand and they fled to a spot beyond the house, where heavy rains had worn a sloping gully into the sandstone.

Linsey glanced upward and saw little reason to be optimistic. The rock surface was uneven and indented, but it provided only a precarious foothold in the shelves of layered rock. Only the thought of Jake and Beale almost within breathing distance sent her upward with an assumed air of confidence.

Starting ahead of Darren, she lost her footing almost immediately, sliding back down the face of the rock. Quickly he bent his head and braced her on his shoulders to stop her slide.

"Steady!"

Under different circumstances it would have been laughable. He gave her a helpful push with one hand and she started up again.

"Take your time," he said, but both knew that every minute was precious.

Every time a rock skittered out beneath their feet and tumbled its way to the bottom, the sound seemed as loud as an avalanche.

"Both gunmen must be in the house, or they would have heard it," Darren whispered as new tension built in him.

Adrenaline propelled Linsey upward at an amazing speed. "We're almost there."

She hauled herself up onto the wide ledge they had viewed from below. She couldn't believe their success, but their triumph was short-lived. A burst of light from an outdoor lantern mounted at the side of the house flooded the area behind the house and halfway up the cliff, making Darren and Linsey clearly visible to anyone who might be looking up at the high ledge.

"Lie down," whispered Darren.

Linsey stretched out on the rock with Darren beside her. They lay there motionless, trying to quiet their shallow breathing.

A door banged. Then silence.

Night air cooled by snow-filled cirques dispelled the warm temperatures of the day and Linsey shivered. Darren put an arm over her back as they lay there, facedown on the rock ledge. She could feel the rise and fall of his chest and the rapid beat of his heart.

Cautiously he raised his head, searching below in the radius of light that circled the house. Jake! The youth was standing outside the side door that opened onto the carport, just waiting, a rifle in his hands.

"Get moving!" Beale shouted from inside the house as the door was jerked open. "And don't come back until you find her. She has to be somewhere between here and the locked gate."

"What if she climbed over?"

"Hell, it's seven feet tall. Blood would have been all over those barbs. She didn't leave. She's here."

"Can't we wait till morning? She ain't gonna go nowhere."

"And take a chance on her doing something dumb?" Beale spat. "She's our ticket to good times, remember?"

"Why don't we go back and get another one of them sisters?"

"We don't have time, stupid! This has already taken too long. We gotta find that dame, or Linquist will pay us off—and I don't mean in money."

The door slammed.

Darren saw Jake move out of the light into the shadows, heading toward the front of the house. "This is our chance," he whispered. "We can follow the ledge before it gets too dark to see."

"Jake?"

"He's gone around front."

"Beale?"

"In the house."

Darren held Linsey's hand as they began to navigate the narrow ledge that ran horizontally in front of them. Stealthily, cautiously, they moved away from the house below and headed for the place where Jake had shot at the bobcat.

Linsey knew that if they knocked any rocks loose now, Jake would hear them. Twilight was deepening, but it was still light enough for him to make out their figures if he looked up from the bottom of the cliff. This whole scenario of their escape was built on a lot of unproved suppositions, a calculated risk.

Darren was thinking that Linsey's idea about the bobcat had been brilliant, but only time would prove how right her speculations had been. All they knew for certain was that Jake had fired at the bobcat...and missed. Where had the animal gone? Maybe it had a lair in the rocks and hadn't fled to the top of the cliff at all. This possibility stopped Darren in his tracks. Were they going to come face-to-face with a wild animal protecting its lair?

"What's the matter?"

He moistened a dry mouth. They were committed to this avenue of escape, good or bad. They couldn't slide back down the hill and try something else. Only a half hour of dusk remained. If they didn't find a way off this ledge soon, darkness would trap them until morning.

"Do you see something?" Linsey asked again, wondering why he had stopped so abruptly.

Darren shook his head. He wasn't going to tell her that they might be attacked by a wild animal at any moment.

"Isn't this just above where we were hiding?" asked Linsey, looking down and seeing the piled-up boulders.

Darren nodded. "I don't see how he got off the ledge from here. Let's keep going."

She was about to express her despair that her brilliant idea had served only to strand them thirty feet above the ground, when Darren suddenly pointed ahead. "You were right, m'love. Look!"

She blinked. The bobcat had not gone up—but through the rock.

"See, there's a deep fissure in the cliff, where the rock layers have parted."

"It looks like only a crack," Linsey protested. "How could anything squeeze through that?"

"Stay here and I'll have a look."

"No. We'll both look."

He put his arm around her waist without more argument. The gray sandstone reflected what little light there was left in the sky. They pushed into a jagged, narrow passageway that ran deep into a gigantic upheaval of rock that had undoubtedly been belched up from the earth's fiery core centuries ago.

"The passage is getting narrower," he warned as he twisted and turned.

"I hope the fissure doesn't run out before we reach the surface."

"If it does, we'll have to go back—"

"To where?" she asked. They both knew the answer to that.

Many times they had to turn sideways to slip through a needlelike crevice and even humped over like frogs to get through some of the openings. Every moment they expected the way to be cut off.

Linsey was startled when the sky suddenly came down to meet them. She didn't realize that they had been climbing steadily all the time.

"Hallelujah!" Darren breathed, looking straight up. The top of the cliff was only a few feet above them.

"We made it," she breathed. "We made it!"

They sat down on the promontory and just looked around in astonishment. They were high above the house and their abductors. They had escaped. Joy colored Linsey's cheeks; she felt like singing and dancing.

Darren put an arm around her shoulder, laughing in that deep, soft way of his. "This calls for a celebration. Let's build a nice fire...."

"Is it safe? Beale said that smoke brought him to the cabin."

"No smoke is going to float down from here, nor be seen either. We'll build it over there against the rocks. I kept some of the matches from the cabin. I'll do dinner. We'll have ourselves a nice little feast."

"Feast?" she echoed, smiling.

"Something you've never had before in all your culinary achievements."

"Let me guess." Her forehead wrinkled, then she laughed. "Hot jelly beans."

Chapter Eleven

Muted hospital sounds had become a familiar accompaniment to the daily routine that Douglas discovered seldom varied. He could keep his eyes closed and still know everything that was going on. First came the sound of breakfast carts moving down the hall, followed by the rattling of trays being distributed or collected. Soft-soled shoes whispered in and out of rooms as nurses and attendants dispensed medicine and carried out morning duties. Gurneys rolled swiftly down the corridors, taking patients to and from surgery. Douglas was grateful that his concussion was mending without the need for an operation on his skull. A mixture of smells was familiar, too, most of them antiseptic and medicinal. For that reason he was startled when a delightful scent of roses unexpectedly reached his nostrils. He opened his eyes.

A young woman breezed into the room with a huge bouquet in her arms. Abundant blond hair spilled over her shoulders onto a silky red dress as she dashed to his bedside and gave him a hug.

Douglas winced with pain.

She stared into his eyes. "You are Douglas Brady, aren't you?"

He frowned and then the puzzlement eased. *Douglas Brady.* Relief sped through him. "Douglas Brady," he said in wonderment. "That's my name."

"Hi! I'm your half sister . . . Kate Deane."

He frantically searched her face, hoping to experience some flicker of recognition. The pretty woman was a complete stranger. "Do I know you?"

She looked at him strangely. "No, we've never met."

He felt some semblance of relief. "Then how—?"

"The hospital was trying to get in touch with Aunt Etta and reached me instead, when I got back from a hiking trip. Somebody found a slip of paper near the spot where you were mugged. It must have slipped out of your pocket. Anyway, it had Aunt Etta's name and telephone number on it."

Aunt Etta? Kate Deane? Douglas closed his eyes against the confusion that was beating at him like a whip made of nettles. It was no use. The blow on his head had left him with disjointed pieces of memory that refused to mesh. What was it he was trying to remember? This strange woman was tied in with a sense of urgency that made his heart pound and his mouth dry, but he didn't know why or how. "I can't even remember why I came to Colorado . . . but it was something important." He grabbed her hand. "Something's wrong. Terribly wrong."

She looked a little frightened at his wild manner. Her smile wavered as she patted his hand. "I'm sorry you were mugged. Not a very nice welcome, I'm afraid, but it won't be long until you remember everything," she assured him. "As soon as the doctor says you can leave the hospital, I'll take you to Crystal Lakes. I'm anxious for you to meet Linsey and Abigail."

Douglas echoed the names. "Linsey? Abigail?"

"Two more half sisters," Kate explained. "Linsey, the oldest, lives in the old family home in Boulder. I stopped there before I came here, but the neighbor said Linsey is away on a short vacation, which probably means a gourmet cooking seminar or a series of lectures on Bach. My other sister, Abigail, is in Washington on business, so I'm a welcoming committee of one."

The names were beginning to seem slightly familiar—Linsey, Abigail, Kate—but he didn't know in what context. Like unraveled threads, the names dangled loosely in his memory. Somehow he knew that he was supposed to meet them—but why? A sense of desperation colored his struggle to collect all the unanswered questions and arrange them into some meaningful pattern before it was too late. Too late for what? The answer escaped him.

CRISP, FRIGID night air was warmed by early sunlight spreading across the high plateau where Linsey and Darren had slept in a hollow under an outcropping of rocks. Weary from continuous flight, they had given into the demands of body and spirit and had slept heavily.

During the night, Linsey was aware of Darren getting up to feed the fire, but when he lay down again and drew her against the warmth of his body, she promptly went back to sleep. Her mind was numbed by the harrowing succession of events that had threatened their lives. For the moment they were safe. She couldn't think beyond that. Like soldiers in combat, they had survived the last battle and must renew their strength for the next one.

When she first opened her eyes, a benign suspension of thought kept reality at bay. Her back and buttocks were cupped against Darren's front, their bodies pressed together like two spoons. Her head lay on the pillow of his forearm and was cradled by his other hand as it fell across

her breasts. Like a warm comforter, she was enveloped by
his body. She closed her eyes and snuggled back against
him, enjoying the delicious warmth and tingling sensa-
tions that his nearness evoked.

His breathing was deep, and she felt his chest rise and
fall. She had never felt like this before, so encompassed by
a man, so much a part of his breathing and the rhythmic
beating of his heart. Even her intense love affair with
Gordon had not given her this sense of belonging. Her
present contentment made nonsense of her usual wariness
toward the male sex. It wasn't very often that she admitted to a deep longing for a man who was strong enough to
respect her own individuality. Most of the men she had met
hadn't challenged her either emotionally or intellectually,
and she had put them off after a few dates.

Lying close to Darren, feeling this tingling awareness of
his masculine body, challenged the tale she had been telling herself that her life was full, complete, satisfying. She
knew that she had always come across as a woman who
had no need for a man in her busy, satisfying life, but she
envied women who had an equal partner in life. Even
though the uppermost need since she had met Darren
McNaught had been for physical survival, he had captured her on many bewildering levels. She feared that even
after they were safe and free to pick up their lives again,
the need to be with him would linger. And her customary
comfortable, cozy life-style was at odds with the realization that she might be perfectly willing to traipse off to
Canada with him if he asked her—which was utter nonsense. He wasn't about to let himself care for another
woman after Laura, and even if he did, Linsey doubted
that she had the courage to give up familiar surroundings
and her family for such a drastic change. She sighed and

snuggled back against him like someone trying to store up nourishment for an emotional famine ahead.

The impression that he was still asleep was dispelled by a tightening of his arms around her and a noticeable stirring. "Hmm, nice."

"I thought you were asleep," she said quickly.

"How do you expect a guy to sleep, when you're wiggling that cute little fanny in my lap?"

"I wasn't 'wiggling.'"

"Call it what you like. A wiggling fanny by any other name is just as sweet. Shakespeare."

"He didn't say that," she said with a laugh.

"He should have." Darren's lips lightly skimmed the back of her neck with soft, butterfly kisses.

The sensation was delicious. She turned her head and invited his mouth to find her lips. His body felt delightfully masculine as he kissed her hungrily. She pressed her breasts against his hard chest, and her hands cupped the back of his head.

"Careful, love," he murmured, raising his mouth from hers and searching her face.

"Good morning," she said with a foolish smile. And kissed him again.

Touching her as if she were something wonderful and fragile, he slipped a hand under her jacket. Then he stiffened.

"What happened to your blouse?"

"Beale tore it. He was getting a little carried away, so I fainted."

"You really fainted?"

"No, of course not. I just couldn't think of anything else to do at the moment. Then I found the knife on the floor . . . and you know the rest."

He held her tightly against him. "Don't think about it anymore." He nuzzled the back of her neck. "You're nice in the morning." Possessive feelings stirred as he cuddled her. As wonderful as anything had ever been, she fitted into his arms. So petite, so soft, so wonderfully vibrant. He held her close, wanting to make love to her, but holding back because he knew how vulnerable she was at this moment.

She turned over and slipped her arms around his neck. He knew that the decision was about to be taken out of his hands. She was ten times the woman that Laura had ever been, yet he still wore battle scars from that relationship. An inner voice warned him it could happen again. He kissed her pliable lips with long lingering kisses, and then very firmly set her away from himself.

She smiled, approving of his let's-slow-down-a-bit tactic. She had only loved once before, and the thought of giving her heart away again frightened her a little.

"How about breakfast?" he asked.

"What are you offering?"

"The menu is somewhat limited, but we aim to please," he said solemnly.

"Biscuits and gravy?"

"Sure. Anything your little heart desires." He handed her a half dozen jelly beans. "I saved the green ones for you."

"Thanks," she said dryly and popped them into her mouth. She knew it was the last of the candy and chewed slowly to make them last.

"We're getting out of here. No telling when Jake and Beale will be on our trail again."

"How do we know which way to go?" she asked, her eyes scanning the panorama of mountains, cliffs, and sky.

"We don't. And I'm not sure we have much choice."

His gaze traveled over the high ridge of rocks and cliffs. Clouds seemed to be sitting right on the treetops. A pristine brightness was reflected in sky, cliffs, and clouds. Another outcrop of rocks rose in another geological study in granite, pink sandstone and gray limestone that layered the sheer shoulder of the mountain.

"Climbing in that direction would tax the most experienced mountain climber," he said.

"Only eagles and falcons belong on a cliff like that," she agreed.

A narrow, rock-filled band of land that extended in a northerly direction looked passable. He followed it with his eyes to a forested, black-green mountain that appeared to lie within walking distance.

"What do you think? That way?" he asked, knowing that there was no other choice. He waited for her answer and raised his auburn eyebrows in puzzlement. "Why are you smiling?"

"You're not giving me flat orders any more. How come?"

"I didn't realize that there had been any change. I think you're imagining things."

"Phooey! Admit it. You took me for some dippy dame who needed some man to do all her thinking for her. I had to get myself half-killed to earn your respect. Don't deny it."

He shrugged. "I guess I got badly burned by a self-centered woman who tried to manipulate every breath I drew," he said flatly. "You know the kind. They turn a man inside out for their own selfish ends. I've had enough. From now on my goals come first."

"I see," she said frostily.

"Linsey, this morning—" He touched her arm, but she shrugged off his hand.

"Chalk it up to the altitude."

She strode ahead of him. Great. Just great. Thirty-two years old, and she was ready and willing to hand her heart to a craggy-faced, obstinate redhead who had just made it plain there was no place for a woman in his life. She had always scoffed at lovesick fools, and now she had a suspicion that she was about to become one of them. Because she was angry at herself and at him, she didn't see the danger until she was almost upon it.

She froze in her tracks like someone suddenly encased in ice.

"A bobcat!" she croaked.

The wild animal looked down at her from a overhanging ledge just ahead.

"Don't move," Darren snapped.

The warning was unnecessary. Linsey's feet were rooted to the spot. She couldn't even blink. The brown, black-spotted cat was lying down, his head over the edge of the rock. Just a few more steps would have brought them within springing distance.

Darren and Linsey stood still, waiting for the animal to move. When it didn't, Darren very slowly reached down and picked up a rock.

"What are you going to do with that?"

"Kill him."

"You can't kill him with that," she protested.

"Got any other ideas?"

"Let's get out of here."

"Where? Over the side of this cliff?"

"We can't stand here for ever."

"He'll make a move or lose interest. Stay put."

The bobcat neither moved nor lost interest. They could see sharp teeth in his half-opened mouth.

Darren took a cautious step forward.

"You're crazy!" Linsey cried, resisting the impulse to grab hold of his belt and pull him back. He had warned her not to move, and now he was edging closer to the waiting animal.

"Stay back," he hissed, taking another step forward.

What in heaven's name was he going to do? Attack a vicious bobcat with a rock? Linsey put her fists against her mouth to keep from screaming at him.

With measured steps, Darren moved closer and closer. The animal kept his eyes on him as if hypnotized. It didn't move a muscle.

Linsey couldn't bear to watch, and yet her eyes were riveted on the developing drama. One leap and the animal could have him by the neck with those vicious teeth. She couldn't believe Darren's macho arrogance. He was inviting the animal to attack, challenging him with every step forward.

"Don't go any closer," she pleaded.

He ignored her. To her horror, he reached up and touched the animal's head. Then he leaped up on the ledge beside it.

"It's all right, Linsey. He's harmless."

"Harmless?" She almost choked in disbelief. "Are you sure?" She expected the animal to snarl and charge any second as she, too, cautiously moved forward.

"He won't hurt you." Darren laughed at her furtive approach. "He's dead. See for yourself."

"Dead?" Linsey stared at the head that lay on the edge of the rock. Then she saw that the eyes were glassy and the mouth sagged open so that his teeth could be seen. At a distance the illusion was of a waiting, crouching animal. "How did you ever have the courage to get close enough to find out?"

"There was something about his slack jaw that told me he was either dead or close to it."

"Shot?" She didn't want to get close enough to see for herself.

"Right. Jake must have hit him, and the unlucky fellow made it back here. There's blood all over the place."

Linsey blanched and turned away from the ugly scene. The wanton destruction of the beautiful animal only emphasized the callous attitude to the taking of life that their abductors displayed wherever they went.

"He bled to death," said Darren, turning the animal over.

Linsey's stomach revolted. She stumbled away, shaken by the grim reminder that one of them could have bled to death from Jake's bullet.

Darren caught up with her. "You all right?"

She nodded, her jelly bean breakfast sitting squeamishly on her stomach. "Great." She wasn't about to admit that the sight of a dead animal had become a cue for new terror.

They walked for quite a distance before they stopped to rest. "You were pretty brave back there," she conceded, her stomach having stopped its acrobatics.

"Not really. I just saw something wrong in the way the cat's head lay over that rock."

"Those eyes, staring at us." She shivered. "I couldn't have taken one step forward. Thanks."

"For being ready to hit a dead animal over the head with a rock? You could have done that," he chided. He grinned at her and her heart did a foolish lopsided spin.

They climbed over fallen rocks and through islands of conifers dotting the hillside. When they reached a tiny waterfall that spilled out of a rock, they cupped their hands and drank.

Linsey splashed water onto her face and hair. She had lost the rubber band that held the twist on her head and she tried to smooth down the wiry, cut-off thatch of hair.

"I like the way it sticks up," he said, watching her efforts. "Looks like one of those new spike hairdos."

She knew he was trying to make light of the ugly shearing Beale had given her and was grateful. Darren's sensitivity was one of the things she liked most about him. Of course there were others, including his intelligence, his wonderful sense of humor and—she cut short this line of thinking. "Let's keep moving."

A rock-ribbed gorge kept them confined to an area that bore evidence of numerous landslides. They hiked steadily, stopping only to drink water or to rest briefly before challenging another rocky slope or wooded hillside. It was midafternoon when they finally spied a narrow road that had been cut into the side of yet another forested mountain.

"It looks like someone took a giant razor blade and made a zigzag cut up the mountainside," she said.

"Well, will you look at that?" Darren exclaimed excitedly. "A logging road."

"Do you think someone's working the area?" Linsey imagined good strong loggers waiting to rescue them and take them out of this treacherous wilderness.

He shaded his eyes with his hand and squinted. "Can't tell from this distance. I'm sure it's a logging road, though. I spent a couple of summers logging in the Northwest, and I'm betting that there could be a camp behind any one of those forested knolls."

"And traffic going up and down that road?" she asked hopefully.

"Right." He gave her a broad smile. "Let's pay them a visit, m'love."

The casual endearment foolishly brought a spiral of warmth and a smile to her own lips. She would never forget him standing there, fire in his hair, his brandy-colored eyes sparkling at her, a brush of reddish whiskers on his unshaven face, and exuding virility. He was handsome. Why hadn't she seen it before? Why hadn't she seen a lot of things before?

They had hiked only a short distance when Darren stopped and eyed the sky. "Looks like a storm." He pointed to dark clouds that were massing on the western horizon like a black shroud, and a warning rumble was followed by a spear of lightning cutting through fast-moving thunderheads.

"I hate lightning." She cringed. Wind had already begun to whip through the rocky basin ahead of the storm.

"We'd better find a shelter. That storm's going to hit us in a few minutes."

"How far away is the road?" she asked, reluctant to give up when safety seemed so close.

"A good five miles. Anyway, we don't want to be under those trees when the storm hits. Thunderhead clouds build up intense fields of electricity, and soon lightning bolts will be ripping to earth, snapping and crackling and setting forest fires. We'll have to find a place in the rocks."

"Here?" Linsey suggested.

"It's the best we can do." He motioned her under a projecting crag. They crawled on their stomachs and lay with their cheeks pressed to the ground.

Black and insidious, rolling storm clouds captured mountain canyons, cliffs and wooded hillsides. Invading masses swept into every crevice, gorge and hollow cavern as driving rain and lightning advanced with the force of an army battalion. Deafening cannon booms of thunder and flashes of heavenly artillery bounded from precipice to precipice. A deluge of rain poured out of the blackened sky, obscuring everything in silver sheets of pounding water.

"I hate mountain rainstorms," she grumbled as sharp cracks of lightning bounced off rocks all around them, creating a sizzling like someone frying eggs. Thunder seemed to shake the whole mountainside with deafening claps.

"Sounds worse than it is."

"Are you sure?"

Loosened boulders tumbled from high cliffs, gathering more stones as they fell. Linsey was certain that they were going to be crushed alive, and she might have bolted out into the holocaust if Darren hadn't been with her, chiding her about a little wind and rain.

A thunderbolt struck somewhere above them, and she was positive she could feel electricity tingling in her fingertips as static charges filled the air. She clapped her hands over her ears and shut her eyes. Darren said something, but she couldn't hear him in the thundering deluge.

The mountain was falling apart. Weathered rocks that had clung precariously to high precipices were suddenly washed free by the hammering rain and crashed down like giant bowling balls, smashing everything in their path, gathering more and more stones. Water seeped under the ledge and made a puddle where they lay. Dank smells of wet earth and drenched rocks filled their nostrils.

For nearly fifteen minutes the storm continued its rampage, then, as suddenly as it had come, it moved on, leaving a swath of blue sky trailing behind the departing dark clouds. A smell of powdered rock mingled in Linsey's nostrils with pungent odors of wet earth and pine. Somewhere in the rocks above she heard a bird's indignant trill above the soft patter of decreasing raindrops.

"It's over," said Darren.

"Thank heavens," she breathed. "I hate a goose-drowner rainstorm."

"Goose-drowner?" he chided, laughing.

"That's what Aunt Etta calls them," she said as they crawled out from under the ledge like drowned rodents. The whole earth glistened with a freshness that seemed only to accentuate their dirty clothes and faces.

"Look." Darren pointed to a rainbow.

"Over the logging road," she said excitedly, wiping mud off her face.

"Can't ask for a better omen than that," Darren said with a laugh. "Let's go."

In high spirits, they pushed through rain-drenched branches, slid down wet dirt banks on their bottoms, and made their way through scratchy debris until they reached the road they had seen cut into the side of the mountain.

"Damn," Darren swore.

The moment of victory was hollow. The promise of the rainbow was a mockery. It was a logging road, all right, but there hadn't been any logging traffic on it for a long time.

Linsey stared at the rutted road and the abandoned hillside. Clusters of abandoned, felled trees littered the slopes between remaining lodgepole pines. Tree stumps, blackened and ugly, were as void of bark as the gray logs that lay on the ground in bleached piles. Disappointment brought a sickening ache into her chest. "No chance of running into any loggers, is there?"

Darren surveyed the mountainside that still bore signs of the ravishment that had destroyed the beauty of this wilderness. He shook his head. "No. These slopes haven't been worked for several years. It takes time for wood to dry out like that and turn gray."

"Why did they cut down so many trees and just leave them?"

Darren's eyes sparked with anger. "For the same reasons that irresponsible companies are polluting our skies with acid rain. Profits always outweigh environmental considerations." He straightened his shoulders. "One thing's for sure, there's no sense in following the road any higher."

"But if we go in the other direction, we'll be heading right back the way we've come."

"I know. This road might even connect with the one leading to the chalet."

"Then we can't go that way. By now, Beale and Jake will be looking farther away from the house." Frustration laced her voice. How could she hike down that road, right back into their clutches? "There has to be some other way."

He touched her shoulder in a gentle squeeze. "My love, we can't keep going without food. We've got to get out of these mountains. The only sensible thing to do is head for lower elevations where we can find people."

"People like Beale and Jake! No." She shook her head vehemently. "We've got to keep going until we're far enough away, so they won't be looking for us. We'll find somebody. There has to be somebody who'll help us."

"We aren't going to find people at timberline." His eyes scanned the vista of forested mountains and jagged peaks, then he fixed his gaze on a pinnacle not far from where they stood.

His arm tightened around her with a jerk.

Linsey's eyes flew to his face. "What's the matter with you?" Darren's deep, full laughter was bewildering—and frightening. "Have you taken leave of your senses? What is it?"

"Look!" He pointed.

At first she couldn't see anything but trees and then more trees. Her gaze swept up thickly forested slopes, up to the crest of a snow-covered peak that was etched against the bright blue sky and then back again. She squinted against the glaring brightness of an afternoon sun.

"Right there!"

Her gaze followed his pointing finger until she saw it. A cry of joy burst from her lips. He put his hands around her waist and swung her in a joyous circle. "A ranger's station!"

Laughing, she wobbled dizzily on her feet when he put her down. Food. Telephone. Rescue. These promises vibrated in her head.

They rushed up the road, their spirits rising with every step as the ranger station came nearer and nearer.

They were within a half mile of safety when they heard the engine of a vehicle coming up the road behind them.

Chapter Twelve

Linsey sent Darren a startled look. "Beale? Jake?"

His expression was as startled as her own. "They could have extended their search this far. I was afraid this road might connect with the same one that led to the house."

"Maybe it's someone who will help!" countered Linsey, still the optimist in spite of everything that had happened.

"We can't very well stand here in the middle and wait to see."

She agreed. Someone was driving at a fast speed toward them. Where to run?

The ground dropped away thousands of feet on one side of the road, so they spurted up a steep incline, where the road hugged the mountain in its twisted course up toward the ranger's station.

There was little cover. The logging had thinned out the stand of lodgepole pines so much that finding a hiding place among the sparsely scattered trees was almost impossible. And most of the ground cover had been killed by men and machines, so that the remaining underbrush was sparse and scraggly. As they had been when climbing the cliff wall, they were clearly visible on the steep, barren slope.

From the sound of it, the approaching vehicle was almost around the last curve.

"There!" Darren pointed toward three logs that lay tumbled together in a heap some distance away. They scrambled over the steep ground and threw themselves down on the ground behind the logs, praying that the driver hadn't been looking their way.

Linsey pressed her cheek against the dry, needled deadfall and closed her eyes. How could it be? They had hiked miles over rough terrain, only to reach a road that might lead right down to the chalet. A never-ending nightmare. No matter how hard they tried to get away or how far they hiked, they couldn't seem to evade their pursuers.

The sound of the laboring engine grew louder as the vehicle approached the place where they were hiding. She was prepared to hear the slamming of brakes and a warning blaze of gunfire, telling them that their attempt to hide had been futile, so the message that the vehicle had actually rumbled by without stopping was delayed by her anxious imagination.

"A Jeep Renegade," Darren said, peering over a log, watching it disappear up the road. "A brown one. Only one man driving."

"Not Beale or Jake?"

"Nope."

"We should have stayed in the road and flagged him down," she lamented, sitting up beside him.

Linsey let out the breath she had been holding. Thank heavens, it wasn't their abductors. "Talk about running scared."

He nodded. "If we'd stayed in the road, we could have hopped a ride the rest of the way up to the station."

She groaned and leaned her head against one of the logs.

"What's the matter?"

"Every muscle in my body aches. I don't think I have an ounce of energy left. I wish we'd stayed in the road and not run like scared rabbits."

"And taken a chance on hitching a ride with Beale or Jake?"

She shivered. "No. I'd rather walk."

"The station isn't very far. Once we get there, you can collapse."

"Not before I have a cup of hot tea and food." She sighed in anticipation, and her stomach reacted with hunger pains just at the thought.

He reached over and took pine needles out of her hair. "Makes you look like a porcupine." He grinned. "And you know how they make love."

"Very carefully, I've heard." A wisp of a smile touched her lips.

"I've heard that, too."

She remembered the physical intimacy that had engulfed them that morning. Waking up in his embrace had sent every nerve bud tingling. She lifted her eyes to his face.

"You're some woman, m'love." His warm russet eyes lingered on her dirt-smudged face. "I want you to know that I'd rather get shanghaied with you than any woman I know."

"Thank you. I feel the same about you."

"I'm damn glad it's about over."

His declaration sobered her. Yes, it was about over. A short hike would bring them to the U.S. Forestry facility, and once the authorities had been brought into the affair, Darren would go back to his seminar and take up his life as before. And she would do the same, wouldn't she? Her thoughts balked like a stubborn mule. No, she couldn't go back to her well-ordered, dull life—boring days filled with giving piano lessons and living in an old house that mocked her youth. Having survived days and nights of terror made her want to grab life at its fullest now. She had changed. She was more alive. More confused. More expectant? How could a person change her whole outlook in a matter of a few days? Not a few days, she corrected herself. A lifetime crammed into emotion-packed hours.

"Why so sad?"

"Thinking."

"About what?"

"About being lonely." Her lips trembled.

He pulled her firmly into the circle of his arms. His mouth descended upon hers, and his kiss was filled with a possessive intensity that devastated her senses. Her body responded to his searching mouth and tongue with such a wild flare of desire that she was suddenly frightened of her own feelings. She broke off the kiss, gasping for breath.

"Still lonely?" he quizzed with a teasing smile. "I could try again."

His caresses dispelled the deep-seated emptiness that had been in her life for a long time. She had been fooling herself, believing that the only kind of man she wanted was someone who could reflect her own narrow interests. Darren McNaught was everything she wanted in a man. Intelligent, sensitive, gentle, strong enough to interest her and yet willing to respect her individuality. But he wasn't for her. More precisely, she wasn't for him. "Baby, Don't Get Hooked on Me" was a song he'd been singing to her ever since they'd been thrown into the camper together. She'd be stupid not to heed the warning. She took a deep breath. "We'd better finish off the last half mile to the station. I'm hungry."

"Always thinking about food." he chided. He stroked her cheek gently with one finger. "Linsey..."

"Don't," she said, stopping him. She couldn't bear to listen to any explanations. She knew how he felt about romantic entanglements. He had made that quite clear. There was no room for a woman in his life. Laura, whoever she was, had done a good job on him. He'd never open himself up to anyone else like that again and had told her so. She was glad he had been honest with her from the beginning. It wasn't his fault that despite the warnings, she had fallen in love with him.

Linsey stood up. "Let's go. I want to put this whole thing behind me, too." She avoided looking at his face. She couldn't take any more. She never felt so vulnerable in her whole life.

They went back to the road and hiked the remaining distance in silence. Relief mingled with a deep-seated fatigue had settled upon them. They had been on the move since early morning, and the brassy sun was already disappearing behind distant snow-capped peaks. Thank God, they wouldn't have to sleep out again tonight, hungry and cold, thought Linsey, as she forced herself to put one foot in front of the other.

"The ranger station is obviously maintained year-round," Darren said with relief as they approached it. "Before I saw the Jeep, I had been worried that it might be abandoned. I know that budget problems have closed out a lot of stations across the country."

Linsey echoed his relief. "Thank heavens, this one is still in operation." The log building and a connecting maintenance garage were freshly painted a forest green, and welcomed them with an official U.S. Forestry logo swinging on a signpost at the bottom of a long flight of wooden steps.

Darren slipped his arm around Linsey's waist as they climbed the stairs. "We made it, m'love. A hot bath. Food. Pure luxury." He grinned at her.

"Do you think anyone is going to believe all of this? They might chalk us up as a couple of nuts."

"Can't say that I'd blame them. Who in his right mind would really believe your father planned a treasure hunt that involved a legendary wagon of lost gold?"

"Well, it's true. And as soon as we notify the authorities, we can put the whole thing behind us."

"Are you sure?" His eyes challenged her.

His words hung in the air and she didn't have an answer.

He knocked firmly on the heavy planked door.

They waited in silence.

Linsey tried to brush caked mud from her clothes and gave the cut spikes of hair a swipe. Darren grinned at her feeble efforts. "You look fine."

Almost immediately a uniformed ranger opened the door. A man apparently somewhere in his late thirties, with thinning dark hair and of slender build, he looked surprised to see them. His gaze went over their dirty, bedraggled appearance and he frowned. "Yes? I'm Ranger Harris."

Linsey was appalled to hear herself giggle. Social amenities were so out of place here that they struck her as ludicrous. The idea of making polite introductions and simply explaining why they stood at his front door triggered hysterical laughter. How would the man react if she said, "We're sorry to bother you, but we have been chloroformed, abducted, chased, shot at and nearly murdered like two of our friends, and have climbed cliffs, nearly been drowned in streams and have survived on bread and water and jelly beans, all because my father likes to play treasure hunt and we're following a bunch of nonsensical rhymes to find a lost wagon of gold.'' He would chalk them up for a couple of loonies.

The ranger looked disconcerted. "Can I help you?"

"Yes," said Darren briskly. "I'm Darren McNaught from the EPA, and this is Linsey Deane. We've been through a trying experience and Miss Deane needs to rest. Will you kindly notify the authorities that we have escaped from an abduction and tell them we have information concerning two murders?" His words were controlled, his tone commanding, and left little room for any objections or argument.

Ranger Harris's eyes widened but he stepped back. "Certainly. My word, sounds like you've got some tale to tell."

Darren kept a firm grip on Linsey as they entered the station. "Easy, easy," he soothed. "Don't give way now."

The ranger ushered them down a short hall and into a high-ceiling room blandly furnished as a living room. An office was visible through an open door on one side of the room and a kitchen on the other. The accommodations were compact, utilitarian and colorless, like most traditional government housing, thought Darren.

"You look like you could use some coffee. I think there's some made," the ranger said, as if trying to rise to the occasion by being a good host. His nervousness was evident as he offered a pack of cigarettes, which both Darren and Linsey refused. He took one himself. He obviously was not used to company dropping in unannounced.

Darren said bluntly, "We're in need of food, but first we want to contact the nearest authorities."

"Yes, of course. From what you said—" he blinked at them "—a murder has been committed?"

"One that we know of, and probably two."

The ranger drew deeply on his cigarette. "I don't understand. You say murderers are after you? Why do they want to kill you? What are you doing way up here? Don't you have a car?"

"No, we don't have a car," Darren answered patiently. "We were abducted in a camping trailer."

The ranger's wide-eyed expression almost made Linsey laugh. The poor man was never going to be able to handle all the bizarre details. He looked nervous and ill at ease, glancing from one face to the other.

"We have a long story to tell, Mr. Harris. About that phone call . . . you do have a phone, don't you?"

"I can contact the authorities with no problem. They'll send someone up in quick order."

"Why don't I see about some food?" Linsey said, feeling giddy and light-headed.

"Sure, you rustle up anything you want. I'll make the call." Ranger Harris disappeared into his office.

Darren started after him, but stopped when he saw Linsey wavering on her feet, as if she was about to fall.

Quickly he grabbed her. "Are you all right?"

"I think I'm going to faint." She heard herself say the words, but they seemed to belong to someone else. An insidious weakness made her knees buckle and she lost consciousness.

The next thing she knew, someone was spooning warm soup into her mouth. She gagged as the liquid slid down her throat.

"Swallow!" Darren ordered. He was sitting on the edge of a bed, propping her up with one arm and spooning soup into her mouth with the other hand.

"What happened?"

"You're a woman of your word. You told me you were going to faint...and you did."

"Too many jelly beans," she said with a wan smile.

"I'm glad you waited until there was a nice soft bed within reach."

"I always plan ahead."

He chuckled. "Not always. But you look fantastic in that sleeping outfit."

Then she realized that she was only wearing panties under a long brown shirt decorated with a Forest Service logo.

"Ravishing," he teased.

"You undressed me?"

"I closed my eyes."

"Liar."

He grinned.

"It's all right," she assured him.

"I just washed your hands and face, but if you'd like, I'm great on sponge baths."

"Can I soak in a tub with soapy water up to my chin?"

"I think we can arrange that. I didn't use all the hot water."

She saw then that he was freshly shaven, his hair glistened from a recent shampooing, and he looked very presentable indeed. "The sheriff—?" she asked.

"Will be here first thing in the morning."

She became aware that it was dark outside. Needled branches scraped against the window, and a quickening wind whispered in the eaves of the roof. Maybe it was going to rain again.

"Relax. You've got nothing to worry about. After you finish this soup you can sleep."

"What if they come? What if Beale and Jake find us here?" Her fears would not lie down to rest.

He smoothed the furrows in her forehead with a gentle hand. "How are they going to do that, m'love? Chances are they're a long way from here, and even if they're not, those two baboons aren't stupid enough to try and break their way into a locked government facility. Will you quit worrying and finish this soup? I made it myself."

"Liar. You got it out of a can," she chided, suddenly feeling warm and protected.

"Isn't that where all food comes from?" he asked with feigned innocence.

She laughed. He was a delight, and she was more than willing to accept his pampering.

"I love the way your nose wrinkles up when you laugh." He grinned.

"It does?"

"Didn't anyone ever tell you? You have a very cute nose."

"Cute?"

"Cute, as in attractive—and kissable." As if to prove his point, he leaned over and kissed the tip of it.

She felt a warm rush of buoyancy at his touch. His light brown eyes were flecked with soft golden glints as they met hers; she had never realized how many shades of color were in them. He was still something of a stranger to her, even after all they'd been through. She knew that when he smiled, a dimplelike crease in one cheek softened the firm, bold lines and planes of his facial structure. A thick shock of dark red hair fell in unkempt waves around his face, accenting his strong male profile.

"Remember me?" he asked after enduring her scrutiny for a while. "I must look pretty terrible to make you frown like that."

"No, I was thinking how different you look to me from the time we first met."

"Different? How?" He raised an eyebrow in mock indignation. "I thought I made good first impressions, as a rule."

"You were sarcastic and very judgmental. Under different circumstances I wouldn't have accepted your help at all. I thought you were a chauvinistic, arrogant male."

He laughed. "And now?"

Now? She was afraid to express her feelings, afraid to lay herself open to rejection. How could she confess that she had fallen in love with him? He would smile and be very tender and very kind, and very firm about his reluctance to get involved in another relationship.

"You're still trying to make up your mind?" He grinned at her hesitation. "I would love to try a little persuasion, but sometimes retreat is the better part of valor. When this is all over..." His voice trailed away.

"When this is all over," she echoed with a catch in her throat. "It will be all over."

She wanted him to deny it, but he didn't.

"Yes. And I don't want there to be any regrets." He sighed and stood up. "See you in the morning, m'love."

IN SPITE OF bone-deep weariness, Linsey slept only fitfully. Turning and thrashing about in the narrow bed, she groaned as overworked muscles demanded their toll of aches and pains. Toward morning she slipped into a more restful slumber and began to dream pleasantly.

Floating in slow motion, she found herself back at Aunt Etta's house. Her father was there, looking down at her from the tree house that he was building in the old cottonwood. Linsey couldn't hear what he was saying, but he was smiling and laughing down at her. Her sisters, Kate and Abigail, were in the dream too, little girls having a tea party under the old tree. Linsey recognized some of their favorite dolls, and the china tea set Aunt Etta had given them for Christmas one year. Her sisters motioned to Linsey to join them, but she didn't. In her dream she just stood there looking at her father perched high in the tree. A tire hung empty from one of the high branches on a rope, and suddenly Linsey saw herself swinging in it. As she swung high enough to reach her father, she awoke with a jolt.

She sat up. The pleasant dream lingered for a split second, then faded. Only one thought remained. Her heartbeat quickened. Tree. Family Tree. *Pass along the family tree!* Her excitement was like the explosion of a firecracker. She remembered! Her father had often referred to the aged cottonwood as their family tree, because through the years they had enjoyed so many activities in and under its branches. This knowledge had been trying to surface ever since she'd read the words, but she had stubbornly kept thinking in terms of genealogy.

The insight plagued her as she watched the shadows of night disappear and the gray light of dawn ease into the room. When she heard someone moving about in the station, she leaped out of bed, quickly showered with wonderfully hot water in a nearby bathroom and shampooed her hair. As she did so, she tried to fit this new meaning of "family tree" into every possible context—but came up with nothing. Her enthusiasm began to fade. The clue still didn't make sense. Pass along the cottonwood tree. Along the tree? Up the tree? Down the tree? Over? Under? Somewhere around the tree? Had her father left another clue there?

When she returned from the bathroom, Linsey found that a plaid flannel shirt and pair of bib overalls had been laid on a chair by the bed. Had Darren left them for her? They appeared to be a man's size, were fashionably big on her and wonderfully clean. She rolled up the pant legs a couple of turns into a thick cuff around her ankles and shortened the shoulder straps. The outfit was less than glamorous, but at that moment she was too eager to tell Darren about the clue to worry about her appearance.

She nodded to Ranger Harris in his office and went into the kitchen. Darren smothered a smile when he saw her, but not too successfully. "Well, good morning. What have we here? A girl? A boy? Let me guess. Under those big pockets and baggy legs there must be a clue of sorts."

"Wouldn't you like to know?" she teased back. Sitting down at the round table, she reached for a coffee mug.

"Not exactly the kind of thing to make a man's heart go pitty-pat first thing in the morning."

"Good." She smiled sweetly and held out her cup for Darren to fill from a pot sitting near his elbow. He wore a patched red shirt and jeans that had one knee out. The red shirt should have warred with his copper-tinted hair but it didn't. And the ragged jeans should have detracted from his masculinity, but they didn't either. Just another example of men being able to look sexy in anything, she thought as she scowled at him. "What's for breakfast? You'd better say bacon and eggs and mean it. My stomach is in no mood for jokes. I want the real thing."

"Yes, ma'am. I can see that a good night's sleep has sweetened your temperament—"

"But defogged my brain!" she said excitedly. "Guess what? I had a dream."

"About me," he said, grinning as he handed her a generous portion of scrambled eggs and crisp bacon.

"No. Be serious."

"I am serious." He put down the plate in front of her. "I had a dream about you."

Her heart fluttered. "Romantic?" she pried with feminine curiosity.

"Well, you might say that." He took a sip of coffee, while his eyes sparkled at her over the rim of the cup.

"You're not going to tell me, are you?"

"Nope. I don't kiss—or anything else—and tell."

She laughed. What an infuriating man he was. She tossed her head. "Well, I'll tell you mine, because I think it gave me the answer to 'Pass the family tree.'"

That sobered him. He set down his cup. "Really?"

She deliberately took several slow bites of her scrambled eggs, delighting in the impatient expression that accompanied every forkful.

"Linsey!" he warned.

She chuckled. "All right." She told him as succinctly as she could about her dream. "When I woke up, I knew that my father was referring to the old cottonwood tree beside Aunt Etta's house. That's what he called our family tree. I should have remembered it earlier."

"How can you pass along a family tree?" Darren looked puzzled.

"I've had trouble with that, too. He didn't say pass up...or down...or under...or in. If the next clue is there, I surely don't know where to look for it," Linsey confessed.

"How can you be sure it's *that* tree he's referring to?"

"We don't have any big trees in the yard at home. We had to cut them down about five years ago. It must be Aunt Etta's cottonwood tree, but—" She broke off as Ranger Harris came in.

He looked apologetic, as if he didn't want to interrupt their breakfast. "I talked to the authorities again this morning, folks. Somebody should be on his way up real soon."

"I don't even know where we are exactly," Linsey confessed.

The ranger walked over to a relief map of Colorado that was tacked on the kitchen wall. "Right here." His finger touched a spot on the map. "And Crystal Lakes is here."

The distance from Aunt Etta's house didn't look far on the map, but in emotional terms it encompassed a lifetime. Thank God for the ranger station, she thought. "We really appreciate your hospitality, Mr. Harris. Breakfast was marvelous."

"Glad for the company. The work crew won't arrive for a couple more weeks. Did I hear you saying something about cottonwoods? There's a parcel of them down in the valley, but none at this higher elevation," he volunteered, as if wanting to be helpful. "Well, if you'll excuse me, I've got some reports to do. Plenty of books and magazines around, if you care to look at them." He smiled and left the room.

"How much did you tell him?" whispered Linsey.

"Nothing about the gold. We don't want the news of your father's discovery passed around. If word gets out, there'll be another gold rush in these old hills. We've got to solve your father's clues before anyone else does." Darren reached over and took both her hands. "You can solve it. I know you can."

"What do you think I've been trying to do in between being chased, drowned, assaulted and a few other things?"

"I'd hate to see your family lose out on the gold, after all you've been through. Fire up those brain cells. If you're on the right track about the tree, it'll make sense. You just have to figure out how it fits in."

"Oh, is that all?" she inquired sarcastically.

"I'll get out of your way so I won't distract you." He got up from the table.

"You don't distract me in the least."

He paused behind her chair. "Sure?" He kissed the nape of her neck.

Warmth spread away from his touch and made a liar of her.

"Go," she ordered. "How long do you think it will be before the sheriff or someone gets here?"

"Ranger Harris said about noon."

"I'll clean up the kitchen while I'm thinking."

"Don't go outside," he warned, glancing at the back door.

A shiver of apprehension ran up her spine. "You don't think—?"

"I don't think anything," he reassured her. "But we're not taking any chances. Until the law gets here, we're staying locked inside this building."

Suddenly the bright morning paled, as if a shroud had been cast over the sun. They weren't safe yet; that was what Darren was telling her. He was worried that a false sense of security might make her do something foolish.

"I'll be in the next room," he said as if he'd seen fear flickering in her eyes.

She was glad to have something to occupy her hands as she cleaned off the table and let her mind concentrate again on the phrase, *Pass along the family tree*. Like a dog worrying a bone, tossing it here and tugging at it from every direction, she tried to focus on the words in every possible way. Nothing.

She washed the dishes, poured hot bacon grease into a lard jar, and was just putting the skillet into the wash water when her eyes were drawn to the map tacked to the wall. She dried her hands and walked over to it, staring at it for a long time, letting her eyes scan the green sections denoting mountains, the black lines showing highways and passes and the dots designating towns. She was familiar with a good portion of the Rocky Mountains and their high mountain passes. Loveland Pass, Monarch Pass and—! Something—a flash of inspiration?—snapped in her mind. *Cottonwood Pass!*

"Darren!" she shrieked.

He sped into the room with Ranger Harris at his heels, obviously alarmed at her cry.

"I've got it. I've got it! 'Pass along the family tree' is the clue for Cottonwood Pass." She stabbed at the map with one finger. "Don't you see? My father was telling us that the gold is somewhere on it. We have property in that area, but this map isn't detailed enough to show it." Then her eyes widened as the rest of the clue suddenly made sense. "Crystal Mine! My father bought an old gold mine. Could that be it? 'Raise a glass to history'—'glass' could be a synonym for crystal. But I don't know exactly where the mine is."

"Maybe we can find a map that will pinpoint the location," said Darren. He turned to the ranger. "Do you have another Colorado map that might show more details?"

"There's a bunch of maps in the office. I guess we could look through them and see if there's one that might help you."

"Good." Darren sent Linsey a broad smile and made a victory sign as he followed the ranger. "We appreciate your help, Ranger Harris," she heard Darren say as she stood there, continuing to stare at the map.

She laughed. She'd done it! Cottonwood Pass. Crystal Mine. There was no doubt in her mind that they would find that the mountain scene in the photograph matched the one around the mine. Her father would have been proud of her.

Pass along the family tree and raise a glass to history. It all made sense. Laughing, she turned back to the counter and in her excitement knocked over the canister of coffee with her elbow, spilling the contents all over the floor. Drat! She'd have to sweep up the mess, or they'd be crunching coffee all over the station.

In search of a broom, Linsey opened a nearby closet— and her hand froze on the handle.

Crammed into the small space was the body of a man wearing a U.S. Ranger's uniform. Blood was caked around a bullet hole in his forehead, and he was very dead.

Chapter Thirteen

The horror of the sight plunged Linsey into shock. She shut the door of the broom closet and thought for a moment that she might faint. Her breathing grew short. She hugged herself, arms held tightly across her chest. Her thoughts whirled. Appalling questions exploded in her brain.

She heard Darren and the ranger laughing and talking in the next room, and the sound of their companionable chatter chilled her. She knew that the real ranger lay murdered with a bullet in his head. Who was Ranger Harris? And who, for that matter, was Darren McNaught? The questions were like electric shocks to her system.

"Darren?" She whispered his name as her thoughts plunged down a nettled path filled with the suspicions that were tearing at her. Could he have been in on this from the beginning—a lookout posted above the house to make certain nothing went wrong with the abduction? Had she run right into his arms without realizing it? Everything that had happened to them could have been orchestrated by someone as smart as he was to bring her to this very moment when she had handed them the location of the gold bullion.

No, it couldn't be. She wouldn't believe it. But even as she denied the horrible suspicion, Darren's deep voice floated into the kitchen—like that of a stranger it seemed to her now. "I'm betting she's figured it out," he said.

There was such triumph in his voice that her sickening suspicions sent new terror rocketing through her. Looking back, she saw that he could have cleverly manipulated her every step of the way. A fortune in gold would have been worth the trail of brutal murder that had followed her. She had been stupid to trust anyone. She had given Darren and the impostor ranger the solution to the puzzle, and now her own life might be forfeited, just like that of the innocent ranger who had been shot in the head.

With horror she realized that the ranger station had never offered any real sanctuary. How cleverly the trap had been laid. The man claiming to be Harris had probably arrived at the station just ahead of them, killed the real ranger, and then, like the wolf in *Red Riding Hood*, had been in position to welcome them when they knocked on the door. Linsey knew now that he had never phoned the authorities. Playing the congenial host, he had simply been waiting for her to give him the information he needed to find the treasure.

Confusion and bewilderment assaulted her senses, but two things were clear: she needed time to sort out lies from truths, and at the moment, there was more danger inside than out.

"Let's see what she has to say," she heard Darren say from the living room.

The men were coming back into the kitchen. It would be impossible for her to pretend that everything was normal. One look at her ashen face, and her shock would be obvious. They would know she had found the body.

Rushing across the kitchen, Linsey fumbled with the lock, jerked open the back door, and fled onto a narrow deck that spanned the back of the building.

"Linsey!" Darren shouted. "Don't go out there."

The commanding sound of his voice almost stopped her. She had come to rely upon the deep, reassuring tones. Her reaction only made the moment more horrible, but the knowledge that a dead man lay slumped in the closet overrode any inclination she might have had to obey Darren. Now she was driven only by a primeval instinct for self-preservation. Determinedly she shut out Darren's voice and scrambled down the steep flight of stairs.

"For the Lord's sake, Linsey!" Darren ran out of the house after her.

"Don't let her get away!" shouted the other man. All trace of the shy, friendly Bill Harris was gone. "Come back, Linsey!"

"Wait!" Darren ordered.

She ignored both of them. Flying hair whipped around her face, and cold air rammed her breath back down her throat, but she continued to run away from the station.

Darren took the steps two at a time in a reckless fashion. "Linsey! Stop, damn it!" In his haste, he lost his footing on the last step and went down on one knee, blocking the path of the other man who was right behind him.

"She's getting away." Fury was clearly audible in the man's voice. "Get her."

His anger only fueled her determination. She raced away like a hare escaping two foxes. Dominated by one overriding urgency, all rational thought fled. She had to get away.

Linsey might have had a chance on open ground, but the station was perched high on the crest of a promontory, with a rim of steep cliffs on every side of the building except the front. Desperately she skirted the edge of a sheer drop and frantically looked for a way down. The sides of the cliff were nearly perpendicular, worn smooth by wind and years of heavy snows and harsh rains. She wavered. The urgency of the situation threatened to drive her over the edge, even though she knew that trying to descend that plunging cliff would be pure suicide.

"Don't, Linsey, don't," shouted Darren.

She spun around like an animal caught in a chute—and lost her balance. She screamed. Her hands flailed and found only empty air.

The next instant he had her.

"Let me go!" she cried, striking out at him.

"Linsey, darling. It's me, Darren." He pinned her hands to her sides and held her firmly in his grasp. "What on earth is the matter with you?"

"I know everything! You took me for a fool. All this time you were after the gold yourself." She kicked at him.

"Linsey! Stop it! Are you out of your mind?"

"Bring her back inside," ordered the other man.

"Take the gold. Let me go!"

"I don't want your damn gold!" Darren snapped. Every line and plane in his face was rigid with anger.

"I heard you talking," she said, glaring back at him. "You and him!"

"She's hysterical," the impostor said calmly. "Better get her back inside."

Ignoring her pleas, Darren picked her up as if she were simply a child throwing a tantrum, and carried her back into the house. The "ranger" shut the outside door firmly behind them.

Darren set Linsey on her feet in the kitchen. "Now, what is this all about?" he demanded. "You could have been killed out there. I thought you were going over that cliff.''

Linsey backed up against the counter, staring at both men.

"Linsey, darling, what's happened?" Darren reached out his hands to her, but she moved away. "What's gotten into you? Why are you frightened of me?"

Her anguished eyes flew to the dark-haired man standing behind Darren. She tried to find her voice, but couldn't. Her gaze moved and became fixed on the broom closet.

"What is it, Linsey?" Darren demanded. "What are you trying to tell me?"

For a moment she closed her eyes against the memory of the slumped body with blood clotted around the bullet hole in its forehead.

"Apparently the little lady has figured out a few things," the other man said smoothly, apparently deciding to answer Darren's question.

Sudden rage brought back her voice. "You killed him."

"Killed who?" snapped Darren.

Slowly, purposefully, the murderer drew out a revolver. "I think she means Ranger Bill Harris." His eyes were cold and menacing. The apologetic, ingratiating forest ranger who had seemed so friendly was gone. A stranger stood there, leveling a gun at Darren's stomach.

"What the—?" Darren exclaimed.

The bewilderment in his voice injected a spurt of joy into Linsey's trembling body. There was no pretense in Darren's utter amazement, and the man's threatening finger upon the revolver was proof enough for Linsey that he and Darren were not conspirators. She'd made a horrible mistake.

"I'm sorry," she said in a strangled voice. "I was looking for a broom...and I found a dead body. I lost my head. I should have kept up the pretense until I warned you."

"That would have been nice," Darren agreed dryly, obviously both furious and disappointed that she had turned on him like that. "And you thought I had something to do with it?"

"I couldn't think straight," she offered lamely. She knew now that her unreasoning suspicion had put them both in danger and kept Darren from getting the upper hand.

The man's smile was thin, but tinged with amusement. "Too bad. I was hoping to keep up the pretense a little while longer. Easier for everyone."

"Who in the hell are you?" demanded Darren.

"I don't suppose it matters, but my name is Linquist. I hired Beale and Jake to do a little job for me. Those stupid idiots bungled it. They let you get out of the camper and had to chase you all over the place."

"You're the boss Beale and Jake kept talking about," Linsey gasped. "The one who owns the chalet."

"And the third man in the garage when you jumped us," Darren added grimly.

Now Linsey remembered. "We didn't recognize you in the uniform. We expected a forest ranger, and that's who we saw when you opened the door."

"You were quite gullible," Linquist agreed. "Beale and Jake told me you had gotten away, and I figured you must still be somewhere in the area. I ordered Beale and Jake to spread out along the other road, and I headed in this direction."

"How'd you know we would come here?" asked Linsey, still shocked that they had not seen through the impersonation.

"I saw you two running for cover when I came up the road. I knew you would show up here in a few minutes, so I killed Harris, changed clothes, and waited for you when you knocked on the door." Linquist grunted in satisfaction. "No substitute for brains."

"You never did call the authorities or my family, did you?" Linsey accused him.

"No, of course not. You made it very easy, trusting me the way you did. My men will be here shortly." He smiled coldly with obvious satisfaction.

Darren stiffened. Linsey knew he was thinking about jumping the gun.

"Don't do it!" Linquist warned. "You're expendable, McNaught. I'd blow your guts out now if I hadn't seen the eyes you two have for each other. Might need to use you to persuade your sweetie to cooperate a little more."

"You have what you want...the location of the gold. Take it," Linsey offered, trying to bargain. "It's in the Crystal Mine. I know it is."

"Maybe...and maybe not." Linquist's dark eyes glinted. "I intend to check it out. Beale and Jake will keep you two company. They'll be glad to see you again. Beale doesn't like unfinished business, and he's pretty riled up about all of this. You should have heard him when I told him you'd be here waiting for him, Miss Linsey. He was quite explicit, and just a touch crude...but then you've had a taste of his persuasiveness."

"No!" She backed up against the counter. The threat brought back the memory of Beale's threats—and his knife. Again she lost control. Grabbing up the jar of hot bacon grease from the counter, she flung it at Linquist.

The gunman cried out in surprise and pain as the hot grease splattered his face and hands.

Darren lunged forward. The two men grappled. The gun went off. The fighters fell to the floor in a heap. Blood began to flow to the tile floor.

Linsey screamed. She couldn't tell if it was Darren or Linquist who had been hit. Crashing into the table legs, they sent dishes flying and chairs scattering.

Linsey grabbed up the skillet and was trying to take a swing at Linquist's head when the struggle suddenly ceased. Linquist's body went limp, gave a jerk and then was still. Blood poured out of a wound in his side. Darren pushed the dead man aside and got to his feet.

Linsey pressed herself against Darren's chest, and he gently stroked her hair. "It's all right, love."

"I'm sorry...I never meant to doubt you. I added things up all wrong."

"Damn, who would have thought we could be taken in so smoothly? I feel like an idiot. I never saw him make the telephone calls. We'll have to—"

The sound of a motorcycle gunning up the road cut off the rest of the sentence.

Chapter Fourteen

Through the kitchen window they saw Jake's motorcycle sending up a cloud of dust behind it as it came into view, far below the station. The abductors' truck followed a short distance behind.

"What'll we do?" Linsey tightened control on her emotions. She wasn't going to let fright drive her into another disastrous panic.

"The gun." Darren grabbed Linquist's bloody revolver from the floor. "Five bullets left."

"Maybe there's another gun in the station?" She wouldn't have thought it possible to change so much in such a few short days. Now she felt no hesitation about using a weapon. "There might be another one around somewhere."

"Not that I've seen. Linquist probably hid any that were here—and we don't have time to hunt for one. Five bullets won't hold them off very long. And once they're inside the station—"

"They'll get in, one way or another, now that they know Linquist is here," she said, avoiding looking down at his crumpled body.

Darren searched her face. "Do you want to make a run for it?"

"I . . . I don't know."

"I think we'd be better off in a sniper situation where I might make every bullet count, but if you want to fight it out here, we'll stay."

She took a deep gulp of air. "Let's run!"

"Good girl!"

They could hear Jake's motorcycle and the truck gunning up the last incline in front of the station before they reached the bottom of the back staircase.

Linsey's earlier flight had shown them that sheer cliffs shut off the station in every direction but the front. If they didn't want to be trapped on the narrow precipice, they had only one choice.

"This way!" Darren motioned around the side of the maintenance building. "In here." He opened a side door into the long, garage-like building.

"Why?" she protested, scooting inside. It seemed the height of folly to leave the protection of the station for a garage.

Darren pointed to the two government vehicles that were parked inside.

"Check for keys," he ordered, his face grim, the gun held ready in his hand.

Linsey ran over to a brown Scout and jerked open the door. Her eyes fastened on the ignition, and hope died. Empty.

"None here, either," Darren reported, looking in through the windows of a two-ton truck. "Linquist probably hid them. He'd make certain that we stayed in the trap."

"We can't hide here. They'll find us in a minute. Can you hot-wire one of the cars?" she asked hopefully.

"I've never done it. No time to practice now."

"I'll go back inside and look for keys."

"Linquist would have hid them, I'm telling you. He wasn't taking any chances on us getting away."

Darren's mind sorted alternatives in feverish succession. No time to go back into the station and search for keys. No time to try to hot-wire one of the vehicles. One thing for certain, they couldn't stay penned up in the garage.

Once Beale and Jake found Linquist dead, they'd be after them with ruthless efficiency. "Better to take our chances out in the open," he said aloud. "Agreed?"

"Agreed." The thought of cowering here and waiting for the gunmen to find them was worse torture than trying to escape.

He grabbed her hand and eased out of the side door ahead of her. They were out of sight of the approaching vehicles, but could still hear their pursuers mounting the last incline.

They skirted the back of the long building on the side farthest from the house. "We'll wait until they're inside the station—then we'll make a run for it down the road," he said.

Linsey nodded. She was glad that he had a weapon. Everything had happened so quickly since she opened the broom closet door that the scenes played back in her mind like one of those old jerky movies. How cleverly Linquist had lulled them into accepting his false identity. She was angry with herself for being so easily duped. All the time they had been waiting for the authorities to arrive, Linquist had been expecting his muscle men.

"Here they come," Darren cautioned.

"Linquist's playmates," Linsey said dryly. "I wonder if he really would have shared the gold with them?"

"Not a chance."

Linsey could imagine the fury in Beale's eyes when he saw Linquist dead in a pool of his own blood. The memory of the dead ranger's glassy eyes staring up would be one that would live with her for a long time, too.

Jake's motorcycle roared into the clearing in front of the station. The engine coughed and died. Almost at the same moment, Beale's truck sent gravel rock spitting from under its wheels as it braked to a stop.

They heard Beale shout something at Jake as the truck door slammed. The pounding of the men's steps vibrated on the boards as they hurried up the long staircase.

Darren peered around the corner. The instant that the two men disappeared through the front door, he grabbed Linsey's hand. "Run."

They bounded away from the side of the building and into the open, but had only taken a few steps when Darren suddenly stopped short. He pointed to the motorcycle. Linsey couldn't believe that her prayer had been answered, after all.

Jake had left his keys in the motorcycle.

"Get on!" Darren ordered. He shoved the gun into his belt, leaped on the motorcycle and kicked up the stand.

Linsey scrambled onto the rider's seat behind him. She knew it would take Beale and Jake only a couple of minutes to find Linquist's body in the kitchen.

Darren turned the key in the ignition with a prayerful breath. It had been years since he'd had a cycle of his own, and his small dirt bike had been nothing like this powerful machine. He prayed he could control it. He pumped gas into the carburetor, frantically grinding the starter.

"Hurry," Linsey urged, knowing as she spoke he was doing the best that he could.

"Start . . . start . . . damn you!" Darren swore.

"Thank God!" Linsey breathed when the engine caught with a roar.

"Hold on!" Darren yelled as he sent the motorcycle careening in a tight circle away from the station.

A shout went up. Linsey jerked her head around and saw Beale and Jake rushing out the station door—with their weapons drawn.

Darren gunned the motor. Bullets sprayed the ground all around them.

"The swine!" Darren exclaimed.

Linsey hugged his waist tightly, trying not to think about the inviting target her exposed back made for the firing guns.

The continuing spray of bullets kept Darren's foot slammed down on the gas pedal. The acceleration was too great for the rutted road surface. The motorcycle weaved dangerously, so that their legs almost scraped on the hard ground. Its tires skidded on loose rock and sent the cycle jolting from one side of the narrow road to the other.

Darren fought to control the speeding machine, which was jerking and pulling like a frenzied beast, trying to tug the handlebars out of his white-knuckled fists.

The motorcycle continued to careen crazily, and Linsey cried out, certain that Darren had been hit. They were going to spill at any minute or go over the side, where the earth dropped away thousands of feet to the rocky ravine below.

She closed her eyes, expecting momentarily to go spinning out into thin air over the side of the cliff. For a breathless second, the machine ran along the edge of the precipice, only inches from the plunging hillside. Linsey buried her face in Darren's back. She couldn't look. They were going over.

Miraculously Darren gained control of the motorcycle, and it veered back into the center of the road, but victory was short-lived. The first hairpin curve came upon them. Still he took it with squealing brakes and skidding tires and somehow managed to keep from tipping the machine into a deadly spill.

Immediately the next curve was upon them. The only blessing was that they were now out of the range of gun-fire.

Linsey held on as the motorcycle took a whole series of hairpin curves at terrifying speed. Darren seemed to be handling the machine more easily now. She darted a look back. Beale's truck was racing down the switchback road above them, only a couple of curves behind.

"They're coming!" she yelled. "Hurry...hurry!"

"We can't go any faster," Darren shouted, knowing that increasing his speed would bring instant disaster. His amateur driving would kill them both. Somehow they had to slow down the truck. How? His mind worked feverishly.

Linsey flung back another look. "They're gaining!"

Darren took the next curve at full speed, then braked to a squealing stop.

"Wh—?" she gasped.

"Get off."

Linsey leaped off the motorcycle, and he let it fall into the middle of the road.

She thought he'd lost his mind. They had three or four minutes at most before their pursuers came roaring around the curve. There was no place to run or hide. If they tried, they'd be picked off by bullets as easily as if they were clay birds.

Darren ran to the edge of the steep incline, where a pile of gray logs had been abandoned.

"What are we going to do?" she cried, following him.

"Pick up the other end of this log," he ordered. "We'll put it across the road."

She didn't argue, though the action seemed senseless. What good would one log do? It made a pathetic barrier, she thought, when they had laid it across the narrow road, it was not even big enough to stop a bumper car.

Darren grabbed her hand and they raced back to the inside of the road. He knelt and took aim with Linquist's revolver.

They waited—one, two, maybe three seconds—the truck squealed around the blind corner into view.

Like a scene in a kaleidoscope, the events came to Linsey in disjointed pieces. Beale was at the wheel. Jake had his rifle out the passenger window, his expression wild and eager as his straggly blond hair blew back from his face. He was ready for the kill.

Beale must have seen the log the instant the truck came around the curve, because he jerked the steering wheel and slammed on the brakes.

Darren fired the gun twice and hit a front tire.

The truck careened out of control. The blown tire hit the log with a force that tipped up the vehicle onto two wheels.

Jake's rifle went off in the air as he was thrown back against Beale in the cab. The truck keeled over onto one side, for a precarious moment resting half off the road. Then, almost in slow motion, it went over the edge and disappeared.

Linsey covered her ears as the sounds of metal, rock and torn trees vibrated loudly, then faded away into the stillness. She sank to the ground. They had been on the run so long that she couldn't believe it was over.

Darren gathered her close, sitting on the ground beside her. "You don't have to be afraid anymore, my love.

Linquist and his bullies got what their greedy hearts deserved.''

"Maybe they weren't killed."

"If you'll feel better, I'll make sure."

She watched him walk over to the edge of the road.

"Be careful!" she screamed, fearing that the spot where he was standing would give way and he would disappear before her eyes.

He stood there for a long time, looking over the side.

"They're dead? Both of them?" she asked in a breathless voice when he came back.

"The truck is crushed and on fire. No one got out," he said grimly.

"We're safe!" His daring plan had worked.

"I knew we couldn't outrun them on that damn motorcycle." He sat down beside her once more. "I never want to live those last few minutes again." His heart was racing, and he felt a cold sweat bead his brow. "Darling, we don't have to run anymore." He tipped up her chin, and looked into her eyes. "It's all over," he said huskily. "Well, maybe not *all*. I'm in love," he said simply.

Gently she touched his cheek with her hand. "Don't look so sad. It may not be fatal."

"I think we have some important things to straighten out between us."

Her waiting lips curved softly as he pulled her against him; his mouth melted against hers in a hungry kiss. A dazed euphoria spread through her. He loved her! All the terror and fright faded away in the light of this wonderful realization. She knew now how empty her life had been. The fight for survival had brought out strengths she'd never been aware of before. And she had been changed by the deep love she felt for this man who had repeatedly sacrificed himself for her. She clung to Darren, feeling the hard sinews of his chest as she pressed against him, wanting him with an intensity that almost frightened her.

They were both breathless when he set her away. She saw deep concern building in his eyes—and the sadness in his smile.

"I'm not ready for this," he said.

"Why do you say that? Is it just me, or a commitment to someone?"

"You're probably going to be a very wealthy young lady, m'love. A millionaire. You'll be buying grand pianos for every room and hiring your own orchestra for every gala occasion."

"Don't be an idiot. We're not sure there really is any gold. And even if there is, what does it matter, if we love each other?" A chill chased away the warm euphoria his kisses had evoked. Suddenly she couldn't imagine getting through the rest of her life without him. "What is it you're trying to say?"

"Simply that you deserve to enjoy any wealth that comes your way, my wonderful, courageous, beautiful Linsey. Darling, I've never known anyone as brave as you've been through such a trial as this. And the truth is, I can't be the kind of husband you deserve." His grin was wan. "I tried to change myself for a woman once before . . . and failed."

"Who's talking change? I like you just the way you are—stubborn, opinionated, and completely off base when it comes to understanding what a woman really wants."

"We've been through hell. Neither of us is thinking very straight right now. I think that—" He stopped, hearing the sound of a vehicle on the road.

"Who's coming?"

"I don't know." He stood up and shaded his eyes.

She peered down the road, and when the truck came into view gave a startled gasp, jerked away from him and started running toward it.

For a moment he didn't know why she was laughing and waving her hands like a crazy woman. Then he recognized Hank's green pickup. "Well, I'll be—! That old goat!"

"Hank! Hank!" Linsey cried.

He stopped the truck and threw open the passenger door.

"Well, by cracky!" he cackled. "I've been up and down every road for miles around. And here ye be. I found some motorcycle tracks on one of the roads not far from here. Followed them to a house set back in a box canyon. The gate was open, but nobody was around. I was about to head back home, when I came upon this logging road. I 'membered the ranger's station and I was thinkin' you might have made it up there."

Linsey sprang up and gave him a hug that almost knocked the pipe from his mouth. She laughed and wiped her eyes, which were filling up with joyful tears. "You're not dead!"

"Dead? Why would ya be thinking that?" Hank asked, as if insulted.

"We thought they shot you on the road that night." Darren grinned. "We should have known better."

"Them varmints tried hard enough. I ran out of bullets. Before they knew it, the old fox just faded away into the bushes." He chuckled. "One minute I was there. The next minute gone. They didn't know which direction to look for me."

"Are we glad to see you," Darren said, sliding into the pickup's front seat beside Linsey.

Hank turned the truck at the first wide spot. "Now tell me what's been happening with you two."

Darren told him as succinctly as possible what had happened since they left him.

"So them guys never got their hands on the gold, after all?"

"No." Linsey took a deep breath. "But I think I know where it is." She told Hank about Cottonwood Pass and how she had figured out her father's clue. "I'm betting the gold is in the old Crystal Mine."

Hank slapped his knee. "Well, I be jiggered. My old buddy must have had himself a ball planning all of this. Maybe we'd better go by that old mine and take a peek."

"Let's alert the authorities first," said Darren.

"I don't think that's a good idea. Won't Linsey have trouble keeping other fortune hunters from trying to get their hands on it, once the word gets out?" Hank argued. "Seems like she ought to put some guards around the place right away—if the gold's really there."

Linsey didn't say anything for a moment. Then she took a deep breath. "Maybe Hank's right. I want to know if there really is any gold. This whole thing might have been a game. My father could have been planning something quite innocent that got out of control. I need to know."

"Are you sure you feel up to it?" Darren asked.

"I'm sure." Her gaze locked with his. "If there's no gold, you may have to come up with a different excuse for avoiding me."

"You wouldn't want to move to Canada?"

"Try me," she challenged.

Chapter Fifteen

"There she be, Cottonwood Pass. Got its name from all them cottonwood trees strung along the base of the pass," said Hank. "About twelve miles to the top. This here road is a bear in the wintertime. Why I 'member one time—"

Darren tightened the arm he had around Linsey's shoulders and they exchanged amused glances. Hank was off on another one of his story-telling binges.

She sighed contentedly. No one was chasing them. Darren was still with her—for a few more hours, at least.

The truck rapidly climbed, and cottonwood trees with their shiny green leaves soon gave way to pines and spruces massed together like a swatch of green carpet spread over the steep slopes. The road twisted and turned, mounting steadily as the earth fell away. Far below a tiny stream flowed along the bottom like a silver ribbon.

"My ears are popping," Linsey said, yawning at the high altitude.

"Don't know how them miners ever made it up and down this old mountain in their wagons," Hank mused. "I've heard tell that in the wintertime they just chained the wagon wheels in place and slid down like a heavily loaded sleigh." He took a satisfied draw on his pipe. "No wonder one of them gold wagons never made it out of here."

"You really believe the legend, Hank?" asked Linsey.

The idea of a real treasure hunt had been unbelievable from the very beginning, and deep down she was convinced that somehow they all had been taken in by a preposterous joke. Legends were fun to talk about, but she still couldn't accept the idea that the lost Confederate wagon was for real.

"Yep, sure do. You should have seen your pa on that last hunting trip of ours. As excited as a cowboy riding after a steer. He was up to something, for sure. It stuck out all over him."

"He didn't tell you what he was planning, Hank?" asked Darren. "Nothing about gold—or a family treasure hunt?"

"Nope. Just gave me that card. Told me to keep it. I didn't know what it was all about until you two showed up. When Carrie brought out that hunk of gold, I could have fallen off a log. Made my eyes pop out, it did." He cackled, clearly amused. "Imagine my old buddy Ronald finding the lost wagon."

"I still can't believe a grown man would discover such a fortune and not tell anyone about it," Darren argued.

"Ronald Deane was one of a kind. He loved to spring surprises on people."

"Well, he certainly topped himself this time," said Darren dryly.

Linsey couldn't dispute that. Now that the danger was over, she tried to look at the situation dispassionately and went over everything in her head again. The photos, the clues, the letter written to Douglas Brady.

"Did my father really take those pictures and write that letter—or was it all a clever hoax?" she wondered aloud.

"Linquist thought they were real enough," Darren reminded her. "He hired Beale and Jake to get the clues from Douglas Brady and kidnap you to translate them."

"And there was that there gold bar your pa left with Carrie," added Hank.

"But something's wrong," she insisted. "I can't put my finger on it. Something to do with that gold bar. A remark Beale made." She searched her mind for the evasive memory, but came up empty.

"What kind of remark?" asked Darren.

"I'm not sure. Something that Beale said." She sighed, wishing she could draw out of her subconscious the knowledge that kept tugging at her.

"Relax," Darren advised, seeing her worried frown. "It'll probably come back when you're not trying so hard."

"I suppose so." She shrugged. "Nothing important, I guess. At the moment I'm full of doubts about everything. I'm not sure any more that 'family tree' refers to Aunt Etta's cottonwood. Maybe I was right in the first place that it has something to do with family genealogy."

"I guess we'll soon know. If you're wrong, then you'll have to come at the clue a different way," Darren said in a practical tone. He gave her a reassuring squeeze. "You seemed pretty sure this morning," he reminded her.

She nodded. "I was sure then…but now…" Her voice trailed off. The conviction that she had successfully decoded her father's clue had disintegrated like crumbling clay, leaving her with a strong suspicion that she had leaped to the wrong conclusion entirely. "There could be a dozen hidden meanings in the rhyme, none of them relating to this mountain pass."

"I 'member your pa talking about an abandoned gold mine," Hank offered.

"Yes, but I can't remember him making any big deal about it," countered Linsey. "After his death, Abigail suggested that we put the Cottonwood Pass property up for sale. We did, but nobody had wanted to buy it. It's too far from any ski area, and there are plenty of old gold mines all over Colorado for sale. As far as I know the Crystal Mine has been boarded up for years."

Hank chewed his pipe. "Don't you go to worryin', honey. We'll be there directly and find out for ourselves what old Ron was trying to tell us."

"I'm surprised Linsey's father didn't confide in you," said Darren, puzzled.

"We didn't talk much when we was out hunting, except to tell a few tales now and again." He chuckled. "I suspected that Ron made up most of his stories. He had some imagination, all right."

"Maybe more than was good for him," agreed Darren dryly. He swore silently at Ronald Deane for creating the bizarre situation that had nearly cost Linsey her life. This whole treasure hunt could be as phony as most legends about lost treasures. Then he chided himself for wishing that they wouldn't find anything. Linsey deserved to have a white baby grand piano in every room if that was what she wanted. She'd look beautiful in sapphires and diamonds, wearing all the latest Parisian fashions. Not as beautiful as she did when he'd undressed her and put her to bed, he thought with a secret smile. Lord, how he loved her!

"We're almost to the top," said Hank. "You still got that picture, Linsey, honey?"

"No." She groaned. "It's in my jacket...back at the station."

"No matter," Hank said cheerfully. "I suspect we can see the mine tailings when we get close. I reckon you don't know exactly where the mine is?"

She shook her head. "I've never seen the property. I just remember my father talking about buying land with a mine on Cottonwood Pass. But there wasn't anything distinctive about that picture, anyway. It looked like a thousand mountain scenes you could see anywhere."

"We're at the top," said Darren, pointing to a wooden sign hanging on a post.

Hank pulled off the road into a wide spot designated for parking. They got out of the truck and walked over to a rock wall bordering the lookout. They surveyed the dramatic panorama of high cliffs, peaks rising above the timberline, and the silver stream far below. Three pairs of eyes scanned steep, craggy mountainsides in every direction, searching for a scar or break in the landscape.

"Don't see nothing that looks like a mine," said Hank.

"You can usually see tumbled rocks that form a steep mound of tailings near the mouth," Linsey said. Heaven knows, she had seen hundreds of them in every mountain canyon in Colorado, but the one she desperately hoped to find was nowhere in sight.

A bank of cold air swept over her and she shivered.

"Come on." Darren pulled her back to the truck. "No sense standing out here."

"It has to be here somewhere," she said with a stubborn lift to her chin.

"Reckon it won't hurt none to go down the other side of the pass and have ourselves a look around," agreed Hank.

"Okay, but if we don't find it then, we head back," Darren insisted. "Enough is enough."

"We'll find it," Hank promised.

Linsey and Darren peered out of the truck windows, craning their necks to look in every direction, searching for a black hole and a telltale mound of rocks spilling away from it. They knew that any mine buildings would be long gone, destroyed by years of harsh weather.

Hank drove slowly, and in a few minutes they reached the bottom of the pass. He braked to a stop. "We must have missed it."

"Are you sure the mine is near the top?" asked Darren.

Linsey searched her mind. The more she thought about it, the less sure she was. When Abigail had talked about selling the property, Linsey had had the impression that it was near the top of the pass, but her interest in the matter had been slight. "I just don't know."

Hank turned the pickup once more. "Won't hurt to give another look-see as we go back."

Linsey stared at the passing hillside, trying to draw on her memory of the photo as they started back up. They had gone about a mile when she cried, "Wait!"

"What is it? What do you see?" asked Darren.

"There." She pointed to a dry gulch. "Doesn't that look like it might have been a road at one time?"

Hank cackled. "Sure 'nough."

"It doesn't look like a road to me," said Darren, giving the barren rock bed a skeptical look.

"Them old miners used bedrock whenever they could," Hank explained. "It was a good foundation for their heavy wagons." He cackled again and clamped down on his pipe. "This could be it."

With a shift of gears, he turned off the road and drove along the rocky gulch. Huge boulders on both sides nearly scraped the truck before the passage widened and they came through a band of pine trees.

Linsey gasped.

"What is it?" Hank slammed on the brakes.

She pointed straight ahead. "The mountain scene! The one that was in the picture. The same rocky slope and drift of tall pines threaded with aspen trees. That's it!"

"Yahoo!" Hank shouted.

Darren hugged Linsey, laughing with her. "Some smart lady! That's all I have to say. I'd have never found it in a million years."

"My father must have stood with his camera in about this very spot." She laughed with joy.

"Still no sign of a mine, though," said Darren, looking around.

She sobered as she scanned the mountain without seeing anything that looked like an abandoned mine.

"Looks like this old road twists around the belly of the mountain," said Hank. He shifted gears and the truck traveled forward.

Linsey grasped Darren's hand in a deathly grip. Her heartbeat had quickened. Her breathing was uneven. The suspense of waiting was almost unbearable as the truck mounted the bedrock road, curving around the base of the hill.

Hank uttered another victorious, "Yahoo. There she be!" he shouted, pointing to a crevice in the mountain.

"No wonder we hadn't been able to see the mine from the road," said Darren, peering upward. "Unless you knew where to turn off, you'd never find it."

Linsey gave a thankful sigh. They could have gone up and down the pass dozens of times without seeing the deteriorating rock road. She looked up at the mine. "It doesn't look like much."

High up, the black hole was almost completely obscured. Only telltale tailings, which had spilled down the front of the mountain, revealed where prospectors a hundred years ago had worked it. Nature and time had re-captured the mountainside, and the road had been washed out before it reached the mine. A bedrock passage remained, but it was not wide enough for a car.

Hank parked the truck on an open spot below the mine. "We'll have to hike the rest of the way." He took a shovel and crowbar out of the back of the truck. "Reckon we'll be needing these and a couple of flashlights."

Linsey's heart was still pounding, and her mouth had gone dry. They had found the mine, but maybe it had nothing to do with the lost wagon. How ironic it would be if she and Darren had run the gauntlet of every conceivable danger only to miss all the clues and end up at a deserted, empty mine that hadn't even been on her father's mind when he dreamed up the treasure hunt.

They trudged up a narrow path, which was all that was left of the wagon road. "I wonder how many men, mules, and heavily loaded wagons were lost navigating this treacherous slope?" Linsey mused.

Darren took her arm and watched her thoughtful gaze sweep upward to the mouth of the mine. "Seeing ghosts?"

She looked a little sheepish. "I guess I'm a little superstitious about bad-luck legends and curses. Maybe this old mountain wants to keep her treasure . . . if there is one."

"Men bring their own bad luck," he said flatly. "And don't get your hopes up, m'love. This doesn't look too promising to me. No sign that anyone's been around here for a very long time. We may have found ourselves a dusty old mine and that's all."

"You mean I might not be a millionaire?" she chided. "My, my, what excuse would you have for being a coward?" She laughed at his shocked look. "Oh, not when it comes to life and limb. I'll grant that you're just about the most courageous man any woman could want. But you're scared to death to take a chance on loving someone again. You've been hurt, and that's turned you into a coward. And you're a snob when it comes to money."

"Please, such kind and gentle compliments wound me to the core." He grinned at her lovely, flashing eyes.

"It's true." She jutted out her chin pugnaciously. "If you were the one who might inherit the same kind of wealth, there'd be no question about me sensibly accepting it. Correct me if I'm wrong." She slipped her arm through his. "If I didn't have a dime to my name, you might drag me off to the wilds of Canada with you."

"You'd go?"

His utter amazement made her laugh. "I'd go. Barefoot and pregnant and tied to the kitchen sink. I love you, you fool."

"What about my uneducated tastes in music and food?"

"I'll take care of that—if you'll teach me dirty dancing."

He stopped and took her into his arms. "You're too good to be real." Hungrily his kiss probed the sweetness of her lips. His hands slid down her back in bold desire, pressing her to himself.

She parted her lips, welcoming the deep questing of his tongue. Deep within, latent desire stirred and she knew that she had found the man who could teach her body about love.

Hank had lumbered ahead of them, his shoulders in their usual slump but a wiry eagerness in his steps. "Come on, you two!" he shouted at them. "This ain't no time for sparkin'."

Linsey and Darren laughed at his impatience and took time for another kiss before they caught up with him.

Even up close, the entrance to the mine was nearly indistinguishable from the rest of the rocky slope. Boards that had been hammered over the mouth had collected dirt and rock through years of wind, snow and blowing dust. Hardy grasses and weeds had taken root in the piled-up dirt.

"It's no use." Linsey felt like a fool. "This is the wrong place."

"I ain't so sure," said Hank. "Looks to me like these rocks might have been moved recently. See, they don't quite fit the ground markings."

Linsey and Darren squatted beside him, looking at indentations in the dirt, which only someone like Hank, who was used to tracking, would have noticed. The rocks had changed positions!

"They're stacked differently," Darren agreed. "I think we may have found your treasure, after all, m'love."

Linsey wanted to deny ownership of anything they found. Darren would never believe that she would gladly give up everything to keep him in her life. He would never let her make any sacrifices for him. *Please, don't be there*, she found herself praying.

The three of them lifted rocks and tossed them to one side. If her father had found the missing Confederate wagon in the mine, he had done a good job of hiding his presence here, thought Linsey. But there was no reason to jump to the conclusion that he had moved the rocks, she cautioned herself. A rock slide or winter ice could have done it. Mountains were not static but in a constant state of change. Besides, it had been over a hundred years since this mine had been worked and abandoned. Probably nothing about this hillside was the same as it had been when prospectors labored here.

"There, that should do it," said Hank, when they had made an opening wide enough for them to squeeze through. He took a flashlight out of his back pocket and went in first, Linsey next, and Darren last.

They followed the two circles of flashlight that darted ahead into the musty darkness. Sunlight had obviously never penetrated into the dark caverns, and the stale air held a dank chill that prickled the skin. They couldn't see very far ahead, because the passage twisted and turned. Dirt walls rose on every side. Linsey hated being underground. It was like being buried in a crypt, she thought with a shiver.

"Easy," said Darren, keeping a firm, guiding hand on her arm as they followed Hank.

"Those timbers look rotted. Ready to collapse," she muttered.

As if to verify her words, a rock tumbled from above and landed at her feet. The walls oozed water, and a greenish patina coated them.

They walked along the dank, poorly timbered tunnel without finding any evidence that the mine was anything but a crude hole in the side of the mountain. A strong sulfuric odor from the yellowish walls mingled with a penetrating aroma of wet earth.

When Hank's circle of light flashed across a tumbled mass of boards, his triumphant cry, accompanied by the habitual slap on his leg, echoed through the underground chambers. "Yahoo!"

The remains of a wagon were identifiable, even though the old boards had decayed, the metal had rusted and its spoked wheels had fallen off. The wagon bed had sunk into the ground and was covered with dirt.

"What do you think?" Linsey croaked. She couldn't see any gold.

"It's an old wagon, all right," said Darren, moving his flashlight over the heap.

A mound of decaying cloth and dirt had obviously been disturbed on one side. A shredded piece of cloth that might once have been canvas fell away at Hank's eager touch.

Linsey watched with a myriad of conflicting emotions.

"It's gold, all right. Feel the weight of that baby." Hank handed a dusty bar to Darren and picked up another one, cackling like a kid in a toy store.

Darren scratched at the dirty surface. Dull gold showed under the mark. He held it out for Linsey to see.

She swallowed hard. The sunken wagon bed was loaded with gold bullion, just as the legend had promised.

"I guess the treasure hunt is over," Darren said, watching the play of emotions upon her face.

"Your pa found the lost wagon, all right," Hank chortled. "How much do you think it's worth?"

Darren thought for a moment. "I remember some Canadian gold miners discussing the weights one time. I would guess that each of these bars weighs about five pounds, which is one-fifth of an ingot, the usual melted form for gold. Probably on today's market, this much gold would be worth about five million."

"You're rich, Linsey. Holy Jehoshaphat! You can buy everything you want."

"Not everything," she said, unable to look at Darren. Her newly found wealth might just have destroyed the only chance she had of real happiness.

How differently her father had visualized this moment, she thought with a thrust of pain. Ronald Deane had planned for his daughters, his newly acknowledged son, and Carrie, his sweetheart, to be here with him when they had followed all the clues to a successful conclusion. What a bittersweet moment the discovery had turned out to be! The sight of the gold bar in Hank's hand brought back the memory of Carrie's sweet face when she'd unwrapped the tea towel and showed them the gold bar. Linsey felt sick.

"We ought to make sure how much is here, before other people get to messing around," said Hank.

"Probably a good idea," Darren agreed. "I wonder how the Confederate wagon got here in the first place."

"Them critters what stole it stashed it in here after they made off with it during the Civil War."

"Why didn't they come back for it?"

"Probably got themselves killed," Hank said bluntly. "Linsey honey, there's a lantern in the back of my truck. Would you get it? We're going to need more light."

She nodded, grateful for an excuse to get out of the oppressive atmosphere of the tunnel. The talk of murder and killings made her spirits as leaden as the rock walls around her.

Linsey quickly retraced her steps. When she stepped through the opening and into the sunlight, she blinked at the sudden brightness. For a moment she just stood there and drew in deep breaths of air, sorting out conflicting emotions. *Damn the gold!* She wished they'd never found it! She kicked angrily at a stone and sent it sailing over the edge of the high cliff into the ravine far below.

As she walked down the steep path to Hank's truck, her thoughts swirled about like a devil's wind. She knew Darren's stiff-necked pride would never let her give the money away, nor would he be willing to overlook her share of five million dollars.

When she reached Hank's truck, she looked into the back for the lantern. The pickup was loaded with everything from tools to a pair of old tires, but she couldn't find a lantern. Thinking that it might be in a long toolbox mounted along one side, she lifted the lid—and stopped breathing.

A jolt like an electric shock went through her. She immediately recognized the object that lay there. The knowledge exploded in her head, even as she sought to deny her own vision. It couldn't be! With trembling hands she reached into the toolbox and took out a bar of gold, wrapped in Carrie's striped tea towel.

Chapter Sixteen

How had Hank got ahold of Carrie's gold bar? The answer came like a kick in the stomach. Beale and Jake had not killed Carrie. Linsey began to tremble all over. The remark of Beale's that she had been trying to recall surfaced. Now she remembered. When she had accused Beale of taking the gold and killing Carrie, he had looked surprised and said, "You must have me mixed up with someone else. I ain't got no bar of gold." At the time she had been too emotionally distraught to believe him. Now she knew. Beale had been telling the truth. Hank had said that their abductors had come to Carrie's house—but no one else had seen them. That night, when she and Darren had rushed down the steps from their bedroom, Hank had been pacing the porch with his shotgun. They'd believed him without question when he said the men had gotten away. But he had lied.

Linsey stared at the gold as if it were a crystal ball, flashing the horrible truth in front of her eyes. Hank had shot Carrie and taken the gold bar. How cleverly the good old boy with his homespun ways had manipulated them, pretending he knew nothing about her father's discovery. Hank had probably tried to solve the riddle her father left with him, and when she and Darren showed up at his door with additional clues, he had played along. What fools they'd been, trusting him without question. He'd never called the sheriff from Carrie's house. And when he found them today, he was the one who'd suggested that they check out the last clue before notifying the authorities. And she had led him right to the wagon of gold.

Darren! Linsey's heart jerked to a stop. He was in the mine with a murderer and didn't know it. Where was Linquist's gun? Did Darren still have it?

Linsey jerked open the cab door. Her heart sank. The gun was on the floor of the truck. Darren was unarmed. She picked up the revolver. Her mind raced. One bullet had killed Linquist; Darren had fired two shots at the truck's tire. There were three bullets left.

She raced back up the narrow path. "Darren! Darren!" she called out.

Hank emerged from the mine just as she approached the opening. In his hand he had a crowbar, stained with blood. The expression on his face was as fierce and diabolical as any she had ever seen.

She shrieked and raised the gun, firing wildly as he threw the crowbar and struck her in the knee. She pulled the trigger twice and saw amazement written in his face. Then he was gone. True to his nickname, the Fox had darted to one side and disappeared into the midst of tumbled boulders and trees.

Pain forked like hot lightning in her knee when she tried to put weight on the wounded leg. Her kneecap felt as if it had been pushed out of place, and jagged pain like hot fire radiated clear up into her thigh. Sweat beaded on her brow, and she clamped her teeth tightly against a searing jolt of pain every time she moved. Holding the empty gun in front of her, she dragged herself grimacing with pain, toward the mouth of the mine. She expected Hank to jump her at any moment, but when she saw a splatter of blood at the entrance, she knew that her last wild shot had hit him.

"Darren!" she shouted frantically, limping into the mine tunnel. The blood on Hank's crowbar showed that he had attacked Darren. She screamed again. "Darren! Darren!" His name echoed in the mine tunnel and faded away. Darkness stretched in front of her, and the farther she went from the opening, the more disoriented she became. Had she taken the wrong turn? She knew she could easily get lost in the underground caverns.

The pain in her knee was like a hammer, the knee itself threatening to buckle at every step. Tears were flowing when she nearly stumbled over the wagon.

"Darren!" she cried once more. Her eyes searched the shadowy darkness. What had Hank done with him? Killed him? Thrown his body down a shaft?

"Darren!"

A feeble groan answered her, from some distance away.

"Darren? Where are you?" Heading in the direction of the sound, she hobbled farther into the mine shaft, nearly fainting from the pain in her knee that was now flaring like burning phosphorus.

"Here."

She stumbled forward with a cry of relief. "Thank God! I thought Hank had killed you."

Darren sat on the ground with blood pouring out of a wound in his head. He used his sleeve to wipe his face. "The old boy went crazy. Hit me with a crowbar. I got away from him. Ran down this way and then fell from dizziness."

She let herself fall to the ground beside him. "He killed Carrie," she said, sobbing. "And took the gold."

"What? Oh, my God!" Anguish cracked his voice.

"I found her gold bar in his truck." Linsey cried out in pain as she tried to move her leg.

"What happened to your leg?"

"Hank threw the crowbar at me. Dislocated my knee-cap, I think. But I shot him."

"You shot Hank?" he echoed in utter amazement.

"I knew he had attacked you. The crowbar was dripping blood. I don't know how badly I wounded him. He ran off. I saw a little blood, so I'm sure I hit him." Her voice trembled. "I thought Hank really cared about my father and our family. What made him turn into a murderer?"

"He probably got used to killing in the war. When he saw a chance to get five million dollars, the rest came easy."

"All along he kept insisting that we follow up the next clue. How stupid we were."

"Yes. We believed everything he told us," Darren said grimly.

"What are we going to do now?" If only her leg didn't hurt so much, she might be able to think.

"We can't stay here," Darren said flatly.

"But what if he's outside, waiting for us?"

"Give me the gun."

"There aren't any bullets left in it."

"He doesn't know that. Can you walk?"

She nodded, but doubted she could take another step without her leg giving way. Her knee was swelling and felt like a ripe grapefruit.

"Lean on me," he ordered, helping her up.

She bit back cries of pain; it seemed to take forever for them to reach the mine's opening.

"Stay here," Darren told her. "I'll have a look outside."

"Be careful." She resisted the temptation to cling to him. He looked like a battle-worn soldier. His vibrant red hair was matted with blood, his face scratched and bleeding.

"If something happens—head for the truck. Promise?" He stroked her cheek.

"Don't let anything happen," she said in a trembling voice.

"Promise me you'll get out of here as fast as you can, m'love?"

"I refuse to promise anything."

"What am I going to do with you?" he asked softly, in exasperation.

"You could marry me," she said boldly. "Even if I'm filthy rich."

Her face was dirty, her hair stuck up on top like porcupine quills, and the baggy overalls hung on her, giving her the air of a ragamuffin.

"You're beautiful," he said huskily.

"Don't change the subject. I'll get rid of the money by supporting important environmental issues and the like. You'd approve of that, wouldn't you? And the rest we can put in trust funds for all our redheaded children. How about it?" she asked shamelessly.

"Linsey..." He choked on her name. How could he think about the future, when they might never leave here alive? He had lost confidence in his ability to keep her safe. Any minute Hank could kill them both. He cupped her face between his hands, as if storing up a precious memory. "I love you." He kissed her tenderly. Then he turned and slipped out of the mine.

Don't go! she screamed silently. If she'd had two good legs, she would have darted after him and dogged him as closely as his shadow. As it was, she hobbled into the mine opening and fought an urge to call after him to wait for her.

She watched him take a few steps away from the mine. He held the empty gun menacingly in one hand as he looked around. Tilting his battered head in a listening fashion, he waited.

Linsey couldn't hear anything, but her heart was thumping like an unbalanced washing machine. Where was Hank? How badly wounded was he? Had the Fox fled? She couldn't see the truck from where she huddled in the mouth of the mine. Maybe he'd driven away.

Darren turned, paused, took a few steps forward.

Linsey screamed. Too late!

Hank came flying down at him from above the mine in a vicious tackle. Both men went down.

Linsey lurched forward. Her knee gave way with shattering pain. She crumpled to the ground. Crying out, she tried to walk, but her leg wouldn't hold her.

The men rolled along the narrow cliff, first one on top, then the other. Darren tried to hit his attacker with the gun, but Hank knocked the revolver out of his hand and it went flying over the edge of the precipice. Linsey heard it tumbling into the ravine far below.

The two men punched and pounded, kicked and rolled, beating each other in the face, hitting with clenched fists, smashing lips and eyes and grabbing at the other's throat. Darren's head had begun to bleed again, and blood was now running into his eyes, effectively blinding him.

"Watch out!" Linsey cried.

Hank gave Darren a murderous blow on the jaw. Darren lashed out and fixed his hand on Hank's throat. They rolled dangerously near the edge of a treacherous drop. Like two mad dogs, the fighters tore at each other, each using every ounce of strength to try to subdue the other.

Hank's wiry body showed no signs of Linsey's bullet. If she had hit him, the wound must have been slight, she thought in despair. Hank was obviously in good, hard physical condition, and Darren's bleeding head gave the wily Fox the advantage. Both men had suffered harsh blows that should have ended the struggle. They rose, fell, rolled in the dirt and pounded the earth with their bodies.

A rumbling of the ground under them gave a warning. Inches from where they struggled, dirt and rocks began to slide away from the edge of the cliff. With a roar, the earth began to fall in ever-widening chunks.

"Get back! Get back!" Linsey screamed.

Darren and Hank grabbed at the falling bank, but it crumbled under their clutching fingers. A cloud of dust rose, and the rumble of dirt and rocks was accompanied by human cries as the men disappeared from sight.

Linsey tried to drag herself down to where they had fallen, but excruciating pain made her tumble into a heap a few feet from the mine.

"Darren." Now she was sobbing hysterically. "Darren ...Darren."

Repeatedly she tried to move her twisted leg. Pain and grief lashed at her like forked whips. She dug her fingers into the dirt in spasms of anguish. Pounding the earth in a frenzy of anger, she rolled over—and the kneecap snapped back into position. For a moment the pain was so intense that she screamed herself into oblivion.

When she opened her eyes again, her leg felt numb and the fiery pain had gone. She was still sprawling on the ground, but her head was cushioned by something warm and firm. She looked up.

Darren's russet eyes, fringed by auburn lashes, crinkled into smile lines. His face was covered with blood and dirt, but his grin was the same as ever. "Hi."

"You're dead." Her mind refused to function. "Am I dead, too?"

He chuckled. "No, we're both very much alive, thank God."

"But I saw you fall." She suppressed a rising joy, as if not daring to believe in such a miracle.

"I was able to grab onto a hardy juniper that had strong roots. It took all my strength to inch my way up to the top again, but I did it. Hank wasn't so lucky. His greed cost him his life."

Tears dribbled down her cheeks. Darren was alive. Safe.

"I came up to get you and found you passed out. What happened?"

"My knee. I tried to walk…and couldn't. I blacked out, I guess."

Darren gingerly rolled up her baggy pant leg. "Looks pretty swollen."

"Yes, but it popped back into place. It doesn't hurt the way it did before."

"Maybe not." Gently he wiped away her tears with his thumb. "But I think you're going to need some tender loving care for a while."

"Know where I can get some?" She smiled wanly.

"Why don't we check into a fancy resort for a few days, and I'll see what I can do in that department?"

"Is this a proposal or a proposition?" she queried solemnly, a smile hovering at the corners of her lips.

"Let's call it a honeymoon rehearsal."

"Like in wedding bells, you-carry-me-over-the-threshold, and we-live-happily-ever-after kind of dress rehearsal?"

"No, an undressed rehearsal. After all, we might not even recognize each other after a hot bath. We should see how we feel about each other after eating a few good meals and sleeping in a soft, sweet-smelling bed.''

"It's a good idea," she said solemnly, "but it won't work." Her eyes were smiling as she wiggled invitingly against him. "Whoever heard of anyone getting sleep on a honeymoon?"

DOUGLAS BRADY hung up the phone in Aunt Etta's kitchen. "Who was that?" asked Kate, coming in from the garage.

"Linsey." He laughed excitedly. "She told me quite a tale, and it's all coming back to me now. I'm beginning to remember everything...why I came here...and what those muggers took off me. Wow, you'll never believe the exciting adventure your sister's had!"

"Linsey? Are you sure it was Linsey you spoke to?" Kate set down the groceries. "An exciting adventure?" She gave a merry laugh. "Nothing exciting ever happens to Linsey."

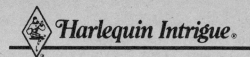

Harlequin Intrigue ®

High adventure and romance—
with three sisters on a search . . .

Now that you have met the Deane sisters and have shared with Linsey her hunt for the long-lost gold, don't miss their further adventures.

Join Kate on the mad chase for the lost gold in #122 *Hide and Seek* by Cassie Miles (September 1989). Then follow Abigail in #124 *Charades* by Jasmine Cresswell (October 1989) as she hunts for those behind the threat to the Deane family fortune and dodges a stalking murderer.

Available where Harlequin books are sold.

DEA1-1

SWEEPSTAKES RULES & REGULATIONS

NO PURCHASE NECESSARY TO ENTER OR RECEIVE A PRIZE

1. To enter and join the Reader Service, check off the "YES" box on your Sweepstakes Entry Form and return to Harlequin Reader Service. If you do not wish to join the Reader Service but wish to enter the Sweepstakes only, check off the "NO" box on your Sweepstakes Entry Form. Incomplete and/or inaccurate entries are ineligible for that section or sections(s) of prizes. Not responsible for mutilated or unreadable entries or inadvertent printing errors Mechanically reproduced entries are null and void. Be sure to also qualify for the Bonus Sweepstakes. See rule #3 on how to enter

2. Either way, your unique Sweepstakes number will be compared against the list of winning numbers generated at random by the computer. In the event that all prizes are not claimed, random drawings will be held from all entries received from all presentations to award all unclaimed prizes. All cash prizes are payable in U.S. funds. This is in addition to any free, surprise or mystery gifts that might be offered. The following prizes are offered: *Grand Prize (1) $1,000,000 Annuity; First Prize (1) $35,000; Second Prize (1) $10,000; Third Prize (3) $5,000; Fourth Prize (10) $1,000; Fifth Prize (25) $500; Sixth Prize (5,000) $5.

   * This Sweepstakes contains a Grand Prize offering of a $1,000,000 annuity. Winner may elect to receive $25,000 a year for 40 years without interest; totalling $1,000,000 or $350,000 in one cash payment. Entrants may cancel Reader Service at any time without cost or obligation to buy.

3. Extra Bonus Prize: This presentation offers two extra bonus prizes valued at $30,000 each to be awarded in a random drawing from all entries received. To qualify, scratch off the silver on your Lucky Keys. If the registration numbers match, you are eligible for the prize offering.

4. Versions of this Sweepstakes with different graphics will be offered in other mailings or at retail outlets by Torstar Corp. and its affiliates. This promotion is being conducted under the supervision of Marden-Kane, Inc., an independent judging organization. By entering this Sweepstakes, each entrant accepts and agrees to be bound by these rules and the decisions of the judges, which shall be final and binding. Odds of winning in the random drawing are dependent upon the total number of entries received. Taxes, if any, are the sole responsibility of the winners. Prizes are nontransferable. All entries must be received by March 31, 1990. The drawing will take place on or about April 30, 1990 at the offices of Marden-Kane, Inc., Lake Success, N.Y.

5. This offer is open to residents of the U.S., United Kingdom and Canada, 18 years or older, except employees of Torstar Corp. its affiliates, subsidiaries, Marden-Kane and all other agencies and persons connected with conducting this Sweepstakes. All Federal, State and local laws apply. Void wherever prohibited or restricted by law.

6. Winners will be notified by mail and may be required to execute an affidavit of eligibility and release, which must be returned within 14 days after notification. Canadian winners will be required to answer a skill-testing question. Winners consent to the use of their name, photograph and/or likeness for advertising and publicity in conjunction with this or similar promotions, without additional compensation.

7. For a list of our most current major prize winners, send a stamped, self-addressed envelope to: Winners List, c/o Marden-Kane, Inc., P.O. Box 701, Sayreville, N.J. 08871

If Sweepstakes entry form is missing, please print your name and address on a 3" × 5" piece of plain paper and send to:

In the U.S.	In Canada
Sweepstakes Entry	Sweepstakes Entry
901 Fuhrmann Blvd.	P.O. Box 609
P.O. Box 1867	Fort Erie, Ontario
Buffalo, NY 14269-1867	L2A 5X3

LTY-H89
© 1988 Harlequin Enterprises Ltd